The Marriage Pact

The Marriage Pact

M. J. Pullen

THOMAS DUNNE BOOKS
St. Martin's Press
New York

THOMAS DUNNE BOOKS.
An imprint of St. Martin's Press.

www.thomasdunnebooks.com
www.stmartins.com

Library of Congress Cataloging-in-Publication Data

Pullen, M. J. (Manda J.)
     The marriage pact : a novel / M. J. Pullen.
        pg. cm.
     ISBN 978-1-250-07093-7 (hardcover)
     ISBN 978-1-4668-8189-1 (e-book)
   1. Single women—Fiction.   2. Middle-aged women—Fiction.
3. Man-woman relationships—Fiction.   4. Love stories.   I. Title.
     PS3616.U465 M37   2015
     813'.6—dc23

                                                        2015029772

Our books may be purchased in bulk for promotional, educational, or business use. Please contact your local bookseller or the Macmillan Corporate and Premium Sales Department at (800) 221-7945, extension 5442, or by e-mail at MacmillanSpecialMarkets@macmillan.com.

First Edition: November 2015

10 9 8 7 6 5 4 3 2 1

For my family, with love

Let men tremble to win the hand of woman, unless they win along with it the utmost passion of her heart!

—NATHANIEL HAWTHORNE, *The Scarlet Letter*

The Marriage Pact

1

Austin, Texas—April 2011

M arci Thompson marked the occasion of her thirtieth birthday by leaving her 480-square-foot apartment early and going to the dentist. Dr. Kim, the only dentist in Austin who had 7:00 A.M. appointments at the last minute, sang an off-key "Happy Birthday" while he poked and prodded in her mouth with bitter-tasting latex gloves. It was a pathetic start to a new decade.

Even though her dentist father was four states away in Georgia, and even though she was thirty years old today, she still could not disappoint him by missing the traditional birthday deadline for her annual appointment. Since she had put it off until last minute, the cleaning meant missing her own private tradition of hot coffee and birthday pancakes with gobs of blueberry syrup. She longed to be at a window booth at Kerbey Lane Café instead of at a sterile office with a mouth full of instruments. But this was the only thing her dad still asked of his adult daughters, and Marci preferred it by far to her mother's frequent hints about grandchildren.

She escaped Dr. Kim's office and ran to catch the 8:13 bus. When she unearthed her phone from the mess in her purse, there were three messages waiting. Her sister, Nicole, who lived in Washington, D.C., with her fiancé, Ravi, wished Marci a happy birthday and announced that she'd just e-mailed pictures of several wedding cakes on which she wanted Marci's prompt and honest opinion. Nicole, in contrast to her older sister, always had her dental appointment done and report submitted a month in advance.

In the second message, her mother sang, a little better than Dr. Kim. In the background, her dad chimed in and yelled that he'd be calling later to ask about her teeth. "Oh, Arthur!" her mother scolded. "She's turning thirty today. I think she can handle taking care of her own teeth!" Then, in a quiet undertone, she murmured into the phone, "Please do get your checkup, sweetheart. You know how your father is about it . . ."

The final message was the soft drawl of her best friend, Suzanne, who still lived in Atlanta but called from a hotel room in Chicago, where she was helping to put on a large party for one of her corporate clients. "Enjoy your big three-oh, darling! Love you much!" The message was genuine, but the tone artificially perky. Marci knew Suzanne was not a morning person but sometimes pretended for the sake of her profession. And birthdays.

Marci hung up the phone and stared out the bus window. She felt loved and lonely at the same time. The messages were all three sweet and thoughtful, and all long-distance. With one possible exception, they were the most personal birthday wishes she would receive all day. She was so lost in this reflection that she almost missed the stop for her temp job.

The lobby of the high-rise that housed TDL & S Advertising (named for its founders Teague, Dodgen, Lane & Stanton) was decorated in a style that could only be described as "cowboy formal." Deeply polished mahogany walls and exquisite marble floors were accented with cowhide rugs, leather furniture, and wrought iron shaped into Texas's signature five-pointed stars. Between the elevators, native wildflowers were gathered in a crystal vase shaped like a boot.

Marci could not resist the temptation to examine her distorted reflection in the polished brass doors as she waited for them to open. Her frizzy brown curls were their usual untamed mess, hazel eyes oddly gold looking in the imperfect light. Not skinny to begin with, she had put on at least ten pounds since January, and her black polyester pencil skirt strained across her ass, which she hoped looked broader in the reflection than in real life.

Behind her, she heard the confident clack of tiny heels as Candice from human resources strode toward the elevator in a flowing pastel skirt and peasant blouse, with a wispy tan scarf that did not match, but mysteriously worked.

"Hi, Marci. How's it going?"

"Great, thanks." Marci tried to sound chipper. Candice, who had been her first contact at TDL & S when she came from the temp agency, still signed her timesheets. So in a certain light Candice was technically a sort of supervisor, though Marci rarely saw her.

"Wonderful," Candice said. "Victoria tells me you're quite an asset over there in accounting."

"Thanks, I'm . . ." She looked for words that were both positive and truthful. "I'm glad to be useful."

With a perfunctory smile, Candice returned her gaze to the shiny doors. Marci fidgeted with her knit blouse, trying to stretch it down to cover more of the bulge around her waistline without exposing too much of her ample, lightly freckled cleavage.

As they stood side by side in the warped brass reflection, Marci tried to refrain from comparing herself to the tiny human resources manager. She refused to notice, for example, that the girl was five years younger and looked more polished and put-together than Marci did on her best day. Kind of sickeningly petite and adorable, too. And there was no point in observing that, at twenty-five, Candice had an actual, grown-up job with an office and a nameplate on her desk. Or musing that she probably had a boyfriend who would acknowledge their relationship on Facebook. Not that Marci was comparing.

She'd heard on a talk show recently that when women made comparisons between themselves, it undermined their self-esteem and feminist solidarity or something. She didn't want to undermine her self-esteem and her sisterly relationships on her birthday, for heaven's sake. So she waited, not wondering about Candice's online relationship status or envying her tiny waist at all.

They had just entered the elevator when Candice reached out to keep the doors from closing. "Hurry up, Doug!" she called.

Marci felt a tremor of excitement run through her. The insecurities that had been piling up just seconds before were erased entirely as a familiar brown loafer stepped onto the carpeted elevator floor. Doug was wearing pressed khaki chinos, a blue chambray shirt with the sleeves rolled up, and sunglasses on top of his head. He smelled amazing.

"Hey, Candice, what's up?" he said, smiling at the HR manager, and then tossed Marci a quick wink and said, "Good morning, Megan." She nodded and suppressed a shy grin, her cheeks burning. Originally a mistake, "Megan" had become their little inside joke. Sometimes people corrected him when he said it at the office, but today Candice did not seem to notice.

"Are you coming to the happy hour today?" Candice asked him.

"Not sure yet," Doug said. "Somebody has to keep this place running."

"You should come; it's going to be fun," she implored. Then Candice seemed to remember that they were not alone in the elevator, because she hurriedly added to Marci, "Of course, you're welcome to come, too. It's five thirty at Maudie's."

Marci thanked Candice and the elevator doors opened. In a flash, the chambray shirt was on its way to the corner office near the production area ("the creatives," they were called), while Marci and Candice disembarked toward the administrative end of the office. A long day of filing and data entry awaited, and she felt disappointed that she and Doug hadn't been able to exchange anything but glances.

At noon, she stalled with a stack of files in the copy room to avoid an invitation to lunch with the rest of the accounting department. She liked her coworkers, despite the oppressive dullness of the work. Her supervisor, Victoria, was the kind of woman who in her late thirties seemed married to her career and religious about her daily routines. But as long as Marci did her work carefully and on time, she was a reasonable boss and always cordial.

Two other chatty women in the department kept a running tab on all the office gossip, never expressing any interest in Marci herself. Finally, there was Jeremy. Hired just a year earlier, he was around her age and bent over backward to include Marci in all department lunches and conversations. She was never sure whether his efforts were just friendly or if there was more to it. Whatever the case, it was her birthday and she didn't want to make small talk over salads today.

When Marci heard Victoria's and Jeremy's voices drift safely toward the elevators, she finished her copies and returned to her desk to wait. She had not been able to talk to Doug privately in a couple of days. But about once every two weeks, they managed to get away together during the lunch hour, almost always for the short drive back to her place, and she now realized she not only hoped this would happen today, she'd counted on it.

Marci shuffled the files a few times, sorted her in-box unnecessarily, and straightened the supplies in her desk. She tried to do some data entry but found she could not concentrate and kept having to go back and erase the invoice numbers she had put in the system and start over. All the while, she kept glancing over her cubicle, hoping to see Doug's smile emerge any second.

By 12:40, she was restless and hungry. Cell phone reception was notoriously bad in this part of the building, but she decided to check her e-mail anyway. She glanced around the department to make sure she was alone. Personal e-mail was strongly discouraged at the advertising firm and absolutely forbidden by the temp agency, so she rarely risked it. Even though she had only ever checked it briefly while on a break, she was plagued by fear of being called to a meeting with some IT person, who would have a stack of documentation of her errant ways.

She had thirty-two new messages. At least half were automated e-mails from online retailers wishing her a happy birthday with 10 percent off and free shipping. Along with the note from Nicole, there were a few e-cards from friends, which she decided to open later. A couple of notifications from writing discussion lists of which she was a member but never made time to read. A forwarded chain e-mail from Suzanne's grandmother, alerting her that her UPS delivery driver might be a member of Al Qaeda. A sale on her favorite jeans at the plus-size outlet store. Happy birthday from her chiropractor.

As she neared the bottom of the highlighted portion of her inbox, she saw the first new message had been sent at 12:01 A.M. from Jake Stillwell, one of her best friends from college. Nothing was in the subject line, but she saw there was an attachment. After a split second's hesitation, curiosity beat out the scary IT guy. She clicked to open it, read the two short sentences Jake had included, and sat back while the image loaded on the screen. *No. It couldn't be. Had he really kept it?*

The consternation must still have been visible on her face a few moments later, when Doug's head appeared around the side of her cubicle, because he stopped his momentum to ask, "Everything okay?" despite his obvious hurry. Startled, she lunged forward and clicked the windows closed, even though Doug certainly would not care that she was checking her e-mail from the office.

"It's fine. I'm . . . fine," she said.

"Okay, good. Listen, babe," he began, and Marci looked around wide-eyed to make sure no one was around to hear the familiar term. He laughed at her panic, as usual. "I already checked—we're alone, kiddo."

Kiddo.

"I just came by to say I can't go to lunch today. There's a meeting at Motorola this afternoon—a big project we might be doing for them. I have to be there. Frank's been really riding my ass about bringing in new clients lately . . . Hey, are you sure you're okay?" He looked genuinely concerned.

"Yes, I'm fine," she said, pasting on a smile. "Just a weird e-mail from home."

"Oh."

Marci remained silent. She couldn't really explain it to Doug.

"Anyway, sweetheart, I'm sorry that I can't go to lunch with you on your birthday. I promise I will make it up to you tonight. Cathy's, um . . ." He hesitated, flustered, and then finished in a rush. Usually he avoided saying his wife's name to Marci. "Well, I'm free for a while tonight."

Without warning, he leaned down and kissed her. He had

never so much as touched her hand in the office before, and her body tingled with the danger and excitement in response. Afterward, he kept his face close to hers. She smelled his clean skin and resisted the temptation to put her palm flat against the crisp white undershirt beneath the blue chambray.

His voice in her ear was husky. "I really *did* want to take you to lunch." His tone suggested eating lunch had probably *not* been on the agenda. Her heart pounded and she looked around wildly, expecting to see someone come around the corner at any second and find them in this pose, for which there was no feasible professional explanation. "I'll find you later." She closed her eyes, inhaling his scent. When she opened them, he was gone.

Two seconds later, Jeremy appeared at her desk. He tossed a small styrofoam box on her keyboard. "Where were you? We went to Guero's."

His obvious disappointment that she had missed lunch was flattering. She smiled at him. "I got caught here, making copies."

"Well, here you go. Happy birthday."

"Oh, how did you . . . ?"

"I overheard you mention it on the phone yesterday. Sorry if that was eavesdropping. I'm not a creep—I promise." His tone was eager and solicitous, as always. Marci opened the box and found a rich-looking chocolate layer cake with some sort of raspberry sauce drizzled over the top. "I know how much you love chocolate," he said proudly.

Jeremy reminded Marci of a golden retriever who had just dropped a treasured chew toy at her feet and wanted a pat on the head. She thanked him for the cake and gave him a quick hug. She really was grateful, because Victoria had just come back to the office with the rest of the team, and Marci's stomach growled menacingly.

The afternoon passed at a snail's pace. Marci couldn't tell

whether Doug was back in the office or still out at Motorola. She wished someone on the production side of the office would ask for her help with filing. Not only did those days put her in a position to interact with Doug, but also that side of the office had a wall of windows with a spectacular view of Town Lake.

More than that, those days brought her into the midst of the writers and designers, who did the work she was desperate to do herself. Nine months earlier, *that* had been her initial reason for taking this assignment; the staffing agency had insisted it would be a great way to get her foot in the door as a copywriter. She had jumped at the chance, even though it paid two dollars per hour less than any other temp job. The more often she could show her face on the production side, the more likely they would be to think of her for entry-level opportunities.

But no such luck today. None of the other departments had requested her help, so she plodded along entering invoices into the accounts receivable database. Her mind drifted to Doug frequently, and her excitement that he would be free tonight. She wondered what was pulling Cathy away.

Since the unexpected start of their relationship five months earlier, Marci had tried hard to block thoughts of Cathy from her mind. Primarily because they made her feel like a horrible person, somewhere between pond scum and dog feces. But lately a kind of morbid curiosity had begun to overtake her when she and Doug were together. Perhaps it was a self-preservation instinct, but she couldn't help questioning whether Cathy really believed the explanations for Doug's frequent absences and whether his excuses were really as believable as he seemed to think. Maybe it was also because she had seen Cathy in person now.

Knowing the spouses would attend, she had carefully avoided the company Christmas party back in December. But a few weeks ago, Marci had been asked to fill in for one of the secretaries in the fancy wooden cubicles in the more public part of the office, just a few offices away from Doug and the rest of the vice presidents. She liked working for Elena and Tracy, the account managers, and it was nice to be able to see the office running, people going back and forth all the time, discussing creative choices and arguing about visual impact.

Cathy had walked into the office around midday, laden with bags and packages, in fashionable skin-tight jeans tucked into knee-high boots and a long thin sweater. She had a perfect body, perfect hair—slick-straight light brown with blond highlights—and a lovely tan face accented with subtle pearl earrings. On seeing her, Tracy had practically run to help with the packages. "Hi, Cathy. What a nice surprise! Doug didn't tell us you were coming by today."

At the name, Marci had frozen in the act of pushing back her chair to offer to help with the packages. Tracy had escorted Cathy halfway to Doug's office before Marci could get to her shocked feet. "Oh, he didn't know, sweetie," she heard Cathy saying to Tracy. "I was down at the League and needed a place to stash some of these auction items for the Valentine's Gala. We just don't have any more room in our garage."

Marci cringed at the mention of "our garage" and immediately pictured Doug in faded jeans and a sweatshirt, working on an old car surrounded by boxes and, apparently, decorations and auction items for the Junior League of Austin's annual gala. Her stomach churned, and she felt light-headed. She sat down, and before she knew it, Cathy was gone again.

"I don't know why everyone says she's such a *bitch*," Tracy said to Elena a few minutes later, with the final word whispered so softly Marci could only assume that was the word used. They were in Tracy's office a few feet away. "I think she's nice."

"Well, she *can* be," Elena said carefully. Marci mindlessly typed a memo while she strained to listen. "She's just a typical Junior League trophy wife."

"What do you mean? I have friends in the Junior League and they actually do a lot of good charity work." Tracy sounded defensive. Tracy was the youngest account manager, and Marci knew she idolized Doug. Clearly, her admiration extended to Cathy.

"Yeah, I know. I probably shouldn't say anything," Elena conceded. A brief silence ensued, and for a second Marci thought the conversation was over. But then Elena continued, softly, "I've just always had the impression that she was kind of . . . well, kind of hard on Doug. Like when they started the company after college, Victoria told me she was always pressuring Doug to quit and go work for her dad in Beaumont instead. Then when the company started getting successful, she suddenly changed her tune and started broadcasting to everyone who would listen that her husband was Doug Stanton. And she made him buy this huge expensive house off Thirty-fifth, even though he really wanted to keep his mom's ranch . . ."

This last part Marci knew to be at least somewhat true, because Doug had mentioned it. Elena's voice got even lower then, and despite straining hard to hear, Marci could only make out the tail end. ". . . Doug really wants kids. He'd be a great dad."

"I'm just saying"—Tracy was talking now—"you can't tell what a marriage is really like from the outside, and she has always seemed like a nice person to me."

"Yes, that's true," Elena replied with a sigh. "You never know."

The conversation had ended there, and Marci had never

mentioned any of it to Doug. Since that day, however, her musings about his marriage had increased tenfold. In their stolen moments alone together, she found herself asking more and more often about Doug's life, trying to understand his feelings and, maybe, venerate her own behavior. It was as though she was perhaps hoping to hear something terrible enough about Cathy that it would justify what she and Doug were doing. Maybe she just wanted fuel for her own fantasy of what a domestic life with Doug would be like: to imagine herself breezing into his office for lunch or folding his laundry on Saturdays. Deep down, though, she knew she would never have the garage and the old car and weekend mornings. Because they weren't rightfully hers.

Marci always felt on guard, even in the privacy of her tiny apartment—obsessing about whether Doug's car was parked far enough away, his alibi watertight, contingency stories ready if someone discovered he was not where he said he would be. Marci also created excuses for dodging her own friends. In the past few months, she had pretended to be taking a pottery class, going to church (she couldn't imagine what special place in hell awaited her for that one), and, once, to avoid a blind date, stricken with walking pneumonia.

In the long, lonely stretches away from Doug, it all sounded perfectly absurd to her. She knew, for instance, what Suzanne or her mom would say if they knew. It was not just that she was helping violate the sanctity of marriage (Mom), but that she was allowing herself to be exploited and putting her life on hold for a man who could not—*would not*—do the same for her (Suzanne).

In her mind, she had ended it a thousand times. She would spend hours rehearsing three versions of the parting speech:

RATIONAL:

Doug, I can't do this anymore. Neither of us intended for this to happen, but it has to stop. I love you [Should she say that?], but I can't be responsible for breaking up a marriage, however unhappy it might be. I deserve better than this. I need someone who is free to make a life with me, and you are not. I know in my heart that part of you still loves Cathy, and I think you should return to her and really invest in your marriage.

MAGNANIMOUS AND MELODRAMATIC:

Listen, Doug. This has been wonderful. It really has. But it's wrong and it's been wrong from the start. It's tearing me apart. I am not an adulteress. I deserve to be more than "the other woman." I can't live with myself for another day this way, and I can't let you do it, either. Go back to your wife, your home, the life that you chose all those years ago. I will treasure our time together and you have my word that I will never tell anyone about us.

JEALOUS AND GENERALLY PISSED OFF:

Doug, your little weekend getaway with your wife gave me time to get clarity and realize that I am better than this situation, and better than you. If you loved me, you would no longer be married. If you loved your wife, you would not be with me. You act like this is torture for you, but really you're just a typical cheating sleazebag who wants to have his cake and eat it, too. I want you out of my life forever. If you try to speak to me again, I will call Cathy and tell her everything. Get out.

This last version was the most emotionally satisfying, of course. She would march into work armed with these words, confident, resolute, and ready to take back her life.

Until she saw him. She'd find a sticky note on her keyboard: "It was awful. I missed you." Or he would pick her up at lunch, and they would drive to the top of Mount Bonnell and look over the Texas hill country and talk. She would feebly threaten to end it, crying pathetically and remembering none of her kickass speeches.

Occasionally he shared his agonizing feelings about his marriage. He'd been with Cathy since high school and genuinely loved her. She was everything he had ever wanted. Their families were close, and she knew things about him that even he had forgotten. But their relationship had changed over the years, and he now described their interactions as distant, even businesslike. But one thing was clear: he was totally unprepared to leave his wife.

Doug often talked with sadness about the day that Marci would end things for real, the day she would realize, fully and finally, that he was wasting her time. He joked with a touch of pain in his voice about the guy she would ultimately end up with: "He'll be funny, obviously," he would say, tapping her nose lightly, "like you. And he'll be good-looking, I'm sure, and probably an all-around great guy. Smarter, better than me."

She would squirm, rejecting his self-deprecation. "Doug, stop, let's not talk about it."

But he never wanted to stop. He needed to suffer. "You know it's true. You deserve better than me. But in my eyes, no one will ever deserve you."

No matter how often he said them, these words were a knife to her heart. She was the other woman; she was putting someone's marriage in danger. Who was to say what she deserved?

By the time her thirtieth birthday rolled around, Marci knew the ball was in her court. Tortured as he might be, Doug seemed willing to continue their relationship indefinitely. It would be her responsibility to someday choose the high road and make a better life for herself. She sometimes wondered whether she would ever find the strength to do that. Her relationship with Doug was the only one she'd had in two years, and more intense on every level than anything before it. How could she walk away from that for some tepid date with Jeremy or to be fixed up with someone's single friend?

She had explored Internet dating, but it was difficult to be fully present in the small talk and getting to know you, when she knew Doug had arranged to be at her place for several hours the next weekend. It was unfair that Doug expected her to be the one to cut the strings, especially when she couldn't help noticing that he made an extra effort to be present in her life when she mentioned having a date.

So they limped along in a relationship netherworld—not together, not apart, each day full of the twin possibilities of limitless passion or good-bye forever. With stacks of invoices and mindless tasks in front of her each day, Marci had entirely too much time to contemplate both ends of the spectrum. Today was no different, except for the fact that she was officially no longer wasting her late twenties in a hopeless relationship.

Thirty had arrived, and a new decade was waiting. And there was an e-mail from Jake.

2

At 5:15, she was dawdling nervously at her desk when an e-mail popped up from the internal server: *"Go to the happy hour. I'll meet you there in forty-five minutes."*

An hour and a half later, she was sucking down the last of her second margarita, which had been surprisingly strong. She sat on the cool patio of Maudie's Mexican restaurant with Jeremy, of course; Cristina, the new receptionist who clearly had a crush on him; Elena, Candice, and a couple of guys from the design department. Several others, especially those with kids, had come and gone already. The liquor was now flowing and the talk was turning to office gossip. When Doug appeared, Elena and Candice both expressed surprise.

The executive team members were all married and usually exhausted, so while they liked to pretend they were just typical workers like everyone else, it was rare for them to actually attend social functions with the staff. By way of explanation, Doug kissed Candice and Elena both lightly on the cheek and said, "Cathy's in Beaumont with some girlfriends tonight, so I thought I'd come see whether you two were plotting to take over the company." They both blushed noticeably.

"Hi, Marci," he said directly to her and let his gaze linger momentarily. She felt her cheeks burn a bit, too.

"You remembered my name," she said. Everyone had been drinking, and no one seemed to notice.

He grinned and turned to the rest of the table. "What's up, Jeremy, Dave, Chuck? And hi there. You must be Cristina. I'm Doug. I'm sorry I haven't had a chance to introduce myself. Welcome to the team." He grasped the new receptionist's hand, a friendly gesture with just a touch of flirtation. Cristina turned pink, too.

At one point, this type of flirty behavior had bothered Marci and made her wonder whether Doug was really telling the truth about never having strayed from his marriage before her. But over time she had concluded that this kind of thing was what made him a great salesman and probably kept the company in business. When you were with Doug, he made you feel like the world revolved around you, and that's exactly what clients want to feel.

It also meant he could get away with winking or teasing her in public, and if anyone noticed, most people would dismiss it. She had to admit, too, looking at three beautiful professional women who had turned to jelly beneath his smiling gaze, she was pretty proud that Doug would be in *her* arms a few hours later. And no one knew.

By 7:30, Elena, Candice, Dave, and Chuck had all excused themselves and headed home. Marci slurped down the last of one more margarita, buzzing with alcohol and excitement. She couldn't wait to get away from the restaurant. If Cathy was in Beaumont for the evening, it meant Doug could spend the night. It had happened only twice before because it was so risky and hard to arrange, but waking cradled in his bare arms had been an unforgettable sensation, sustaining her through weeks of contrived situations and covert messages.

Jeremy, however, had ordered another beer, and kept steering the conversation toward topics that could take all night to discuss. Meanwhile, Cristina was hanging on his every word, but by all appearances she would've had better luck with the waiter, who had finally just brought them a check in exasperation. Doug and Marci could not leave at the same time, and Jeremy seemed in no hurry. So they were stuck with forced conversation and tortilla chip crumbs. Marci snickered as she realized it was literally a Mexican restaurant standoff.

"This could go on for years," Doug muttered in Marci's ear while Jeremy asked the waiter whether he could split the check among the four of them. "Don't bother; I'll get it," he said louder to Jeremy, handing a credit card to the waiter.

"Doug, there's no need," Jeremy started. Was it Marci's imagination, or did he seem resentful? Could he sense that something was going on with her and Doug? *Silly, paranoid . . .* she thought. Hoped.

"No, really," Doug interrupted, "it's my pleasure. Not often I get to spring for drinks for some of our best support staff."

"Oh, thanks! That is so sweet," Christina purred. Marci giggled. She wasn't sure why.

"It really is sweet, actually. You guys are a bunch of lushes," Doug commented as he looked at the lengthy bill. He stood abruptly. "Now, does everyone have a ride home? You guys have been drinking all afternoon, at least according to my credit card."

"I'm fine to drive," Jeremy said matter-of-factly. "And Marci, you're on my way home. I'll drop you off." Marci cringed. *He had to be kidding.*

"Great," Doug said, and Marci was slightly wounded by his enthusiasm. "Cristina?"

Cristina seemed disappointed. "I can actually walk from here," she said grudgingly. "I just live two blocks down."

"Oh, Jeremy, you should walk her home!" Marci threw in, perhaps too quickly.

Before anyone could debate further, Doug took charge again. "Well, as long as no one's driving drunk . . . I have to get going, but thanks for inviting me. It's nice to find out what's really going on in my own company once in a while. Cristina, if you don't want to walk, I'll be happy to drop you. Jeremy, do NOT let her drive." He pointed at Marci, and she frowned at him.

The new receptionist seemed to have sobered up enough to realize that she could only hurt her chances with Jeremy by hanging around, so she grabbed her purse and followed Doug out the patio gate toward the darkening parking lot. Marci fumed in her chair as Jeremy swallowed the last of his beer. *Why is Doug walking out on me? And taking Cristina home? On my birthday!*

She stood without speaking and stumbled to Jeremy's silver pickup. The truck was familiar enough from the times they had been out to lunch together, and once when he'd taken her to a movie. As he opened the door for her now, she saw these moments in a new light. The slight inkling about Jeremy's feelings for her that she'd chosen to ignore was beginning to tighten around her.

Ugh. The last thing she needed tonight was to have to let a friend down easy while her boyfriend—if you could call him that—was driving the hot new receptionist home in his BMW. She stared out the window, hoping to avoid Jeremy's eye.

They were at her building in less than ten minutes. To her surprise, when he pulled up, Jeremy made no move to take off his seat belt or shut off the car. "You okay? Got your keys?" he asked sincerely. She nodded. "Don't need me to come in, do you?" She couldn't tell whether he was hopeful, resigned, or just worn out.

"No, thanks," she said, and then added quickly, "I really do appreciate the ride, Jeremy." He smiled wanly and she swiveled to get out of the truck. As she did, he grabbed her hand.

She tried not to appear annoyed. *Why can't some guys take a hint?*

"Jeremy . . ."

"Marci, be careful, okay?"

"What? I'm fine; it's just up those stairs."

"That's not what I mean, Marci. Just, please, be careful. I . . . I don't want to see you get hurt." He was looking at her uncritically, with genuine concern in his eyes.

The realization of what Jeremy meant, what he knew or had guessed, stopped her cold. No one knew about Doug and her. Not even Suzanne, who had been her best friend since sixth grade. For five months she had been holding on to a secret so precious and so well guarded, she was even hiding it from parts of herself. And now this guy, whom she knew only casually, had figured it out. And he didn't hate her. He didn't call her a slut or a home wrecker. He was just concerned about her.

For a moment, it was all she could do to hold it together.

She took a breath and patted his hand. "Thanks, sweetie. I'm fine. I'll see you tomorrow, okay?" Her voice sounded far more casual than she felt, but Jeremy nodded and put the truck in gear.

She was in her apartment for less than five minutes before the knock at the door.

"I thought he would never leave," Doug said, and held Marci's head in both hands, kissing her hard. His smile faded as he pulled back to look at her. "Have you been crying?"

"No." She hesitated. "Well, a little. Nothing serious; just weepy from the margaritas, I guess."

Anger swept over Doug's handsome features. "Did that little twerp try something with you in the truck? I will *so* fire him."

The reference to everyone's working relationship pulled her back to the precariousness of the situation; she felt protective of both Doug and Jeremy. She had to fix this. "No, nothing like that. I guess I am just . . . homesick. And a little drunk."

"Oh, right—you said you got an e-mail from home?"

"Yeah, from my college friend Jake. It's a long story."

"I like long stories," he said softly. He had taken her hands in his and was leading her to the tiny couch. For a split second she imagined trying to explain Jake to Doug, their college friendship—with benefits—and the e-mail she'd received earlier that was surely, *surely,* a joke. An affectionate memento of many shared drunken nights, and one silly promise . . . Jake was kidding. He had to be.

Marci tried to focus instead on the man in front of her. It had taken them hours to get away from work and colleagues; their meeting in the elevator with Candice seemed like far more than just twelve hours ago. She would not let herself be distracted from him, not now. She gently kissed the fingers interlaced with hers and looked into his ice-blue eyes. "Can you really stay?"

"Did I say I could stay?" he said, and her heart sank. A smile crept to the corners of his mouth, and he cradled her jaw with his palm. "Oh, I guess so. It *is* your birthday. How old are you, anyway? Twenty-seven?"

"You know I'm thirty."

"Wow. A milestone. At least we get to be in the same decade for a few months. And no big party?"

"Nope. This is it."

"Wow, that's pathetic. Spending the big three-oh with some old guy from your office."

"Shut up," she pleaded. Even though he was teasing, she didn't like being reminded of their age difference or their work situation. *Too much reality.*

He shook his head. "Rude, rude. Young people today have no manners."

She hit him in the head with one of the couch cushions. His blue eyes were sparkling and playful. "Oh, that's it. Guess your birthday present is staying in the car."

She brandished the cushion at him again, but it tumbled to the floor as he grabbed both wrists and brought them down by her sides. Keeping her hands pinned, he leaned forward and kissed her hard, the same as he'd done hours earlier in the stolen moment in her cubicle. He sat back for a moment, looked at her intently, and made a soft growling noise—like a puppy with a rawhide bone—as he moved forward to kiss her again.

The next kiss was far softer, lingering. She wanted to reach for him, but her arms were still immobilized in his surprisingly strong grip. He kissed her chin next, nudging it up with his nose and lips as he turned his attention to her exposed throat. He remained there for what felt like a long time, and between the margaritas, the inability to move her arms, and his stubbly chin rubbing against her throat as he kissed her mercilessly, she began to lose herself. The ceiling above her shimmered and she yielded to gravity until her head came to rest on the rough fabric of the worn couch.

She was not sure when precisely her arms had been freed; only that she was able to shimmy out of her knit blouse. She hungrily reached beneath his shirt to feel the soft, white undershirt she had longed to touch hours ago—and the heat of him beneath it. He did not allow her to enjoy this tactile luxury for long, though, for soon he had pulled away from her and sunk to his knees on the dingy white carpet. She felt his firm grip on her thighs, his warm breath against her skin, her fingers clutching his thick blond curls. Soon all thought left her, and she melted into bliss and oblivion beneath his touch.

An hour or so later, they lay in silence on a pallet of cushions and throws, listening to the cicadas swelling outside and the screech of the band rehearsal next door. Being able to lie here curled in his bare arms was positively heavenly. She was almost afraid to break the spell with words. "You're really not leaving?" she whispered.

"Well, maybe for a minute," he whispered back. "Got to get stuff from the car."

"Not yet," she whined, tightening her grip on the arms wrapped around her. "Not yet."

But he kissed her bare shoulder and extracted himself. "I'll be two minutes. And you must promise not to move an inch, or the punishment will be severe."

He pulled on his khakis and the blue shirt, slipping on his loafers as he neared the door. He looked deliciously disheveled and strangely vulnerable as he headed out into the night. She tried not to notice that he paused to find his cell phone on the bookshelf before exiting.

Marci lay there for a while, battling a drowsy sleep that kept threatening to overtake her. After some time, she heard Doug's footsteps outside and his voice on the phone through the thin wall. He was clearly talking to Cathy in Beaumont, his tone familiar and casual. Of course with Cathy out of town, he would have to check in with her at some point. Obviously he was using the trip to the car as an opportunity to do that preemptively, so she would neither interrupt his evening with Marci nor call an unanswered phone later.

Cathy was apparently telling him some sort of story about her evening, because there were long stretches of silence punctuated by, "uh-huh" and "really?" and "What did she say to that?" Whether it was genuine or simply to avoid suspicion, he sounded interested in what she was saying and did not rush her off the phone. Marci wondered whom they were talking about. Cathy's mother? A friend? They had been together for twenty-three years, so there must be very few people Cathy knew that Doug did not, and vice versa.

Bitter jealousy swept over Marci like an icy wind. Doug could not understand that this, exactly this, was what made her feel the worst in their relationship. Of course, it was bad enough knowing that he slept in the same bed with Cathy every night and awoke to her each morning. She could not bear to think—much less ask—whether he was still intimate with his wife, though his descriptions of his marriage always led her to believe he was not, or at least not very often.

But conversations like the one he was having now, familiar, with a shared history and the sound of friendship that had become second nature—these were what she envied and resented most. Doug would never meet Marci's family, never know Jake or Suzanne or any of her other friends. The people important to her could never even know he existed. Given the nature of their relationship, the stolen moments and limited hours . . . would he ever just sit and listen to her recount a conversation with a friend or complain about a fight with her mom or Nicole? Would Doug ever stand out on a balcony and listen while she talked about her day?

Suddenly, Marci was sharply conscious of her nakedness and the fact that she was still lying on the floor, where he had left her. She got up, went to the bedroom, threw on a ratty T-shirt and sweats. She felt the urge to be busy, but unsure with what, and finally decided to turn on the computer.

Her desktop was in the corner of the tiny living room, under the window where Doug paced back and forth on the narrow landing a few inches away. Marci assured herself that she had not chosen this activity to better overhear his side of the conversation.

Even though she had several more unread birthday messages since this morning, and she knew exactly what it said, Jake's e-mail seemed to draw her to open it again. She forced herself to focus on a new message from her dad, updating her on how his garden was coming along this spring and acknowledging that her mother had already wished her happy birthday on his behalf. She smiled. Dad always found a way to speak for himself.

Outside, she could hear Doug explaining the punk rock band next door. "Yeah, I have the music on kind of loud in the garage—some demo CD Kevin wanted me to listen to."

She opened Jake's e-mail.

To: marci.b.thompson
From: jakedawg03
Date: April 7, 2011 12:01 a.m.
Subject: *[none]*
Message: Happy birthday, Marcella Beatrice Thompson. I'm game if you are.
Attachment: napkin.jpg

As she clicked on the attachment, she knew what she would see. The bar napkin was at least eight years old and obviously had been through some careless treatment since she had signed it herself so long ago. It was discolored, whether from the years or from Jake's scanning it to mail it, she wasn't sure. But it still had the distinctive Globe logo in the corner, a stain from some kind of pink beverage Suzanne must've been drinking, and the contract, smudged but legible in blue ink from a waitress's pen.

I, WE, Jacob Cartwright Stillwell and Marcella Beatrice Thompson, being of sound mind and ^somewhat sober body, swear hereby promise that on April 7, 2011, when we are both 30 years old, if we are not married or seriously involved in a relationship, we will get married to each other.

And there underneath, almost identical to the one on last week's temp agency timesheet, was her signature.

She had forgotten it, their silly agreement, until this morning. Thinking back, Marci remembered Jake would occasionally bring it up jokingly when she went back to Atlanta for the holidays or vacation. But it was never serious.

The door behind her creaked open and she jumped. Doug was looking down at his phone and didn't notice her alarm. "There. It's off for the night. I promise." He tossed it back on the bookshelf with finality and crossed to her.

"Oh, so you have time for me now, do you?" she challenged, swiveling back to face the monitor and quickly closing out the window.

Solicitously, he began rubbing her shoulders. "Oh, come on, don't be that way. Hey, you're not where I left you," he scolded, "and certainly not wearing the lovely nothing from before." He ran his hands forward in one sweeping motion over her shoulders, into her T-shirt and over her breasts. *Does he really think it's going to be this easy?*

"Well, you were gone for a while." She tried to sound merely cold and dismissive, but her words came out bitter, petulant. She removed his hands from her shirt angrily, but did not object when he replaced them on her shoulders.

"Marci, I'm sorry," he said softly. She did not answer, staring at the black keyboard as though the crumb between the G and H keys were the most fascinating thing she'd ever seen. He bent down and swiveled the chair around, getting on her level as though he were comforting a child with a skinned knee. His eyes implored her.

"It's just, when you are talking to Cathy . . ." She saw him flinch at the mention of the name and immediately regretted saying anything. Why could she never just enjoy the time they had? She had an average of twenty-three hours a day to obsess without him; why ruin a rare evening like this one?

His expression was fixed. He waited for her to finish. "Well,

I just don't understand how you can be so casual and normal with her, and then two minutes later, you're . . ."

"I'm what? Groping you?"

"Well, yes. I was going to say 'being affectionate with me' or something nicer like that, but . . . yeah."

He smiled, his lips upturned only slightly. "Always the delicate one. You know you can just say what you really feel with me, right?" *Why on earth am I nodding at him, placated and stupid?* His ability to disarm her was infuriating.

"Listen, babe." He put his hand on her cheek. "I know you think this is easy for me, but it's not. I wish I didn't have to answer that damn phone. Hell, I'd like to throw it in the river. But you know I have to, and you know why."

"I know."

"That, out there"—he gestured toward the landing on the other side of the wall—"that's me doing the right thing by her, at least . . . somewhat. And if I don't do that, then all of this comes crashing down tomorrow, and I have to come move in here with you and the Blues Brothers."

"They're punk."

"Okay, fine, the Punk Brothers."

"They're called Plastic Utensils."

"Fine. Whatever. Look, Marce, I know this is hard for you, but it's hard for me, too. This is uncharted territory for me, and I don't know the best way of handling it. I never, ever planned to cheat on Cathy. I love her; I married her."

"Stop. Please stop." Marci could feel tears coming from nowhere.

"No, wait. You brought this up, okay? You asked me how I can talk to my wife, who I promised my life to, and then touch you. Well, you make me wish my life was still mine to promise. And the answer is either that I'm some lecherous creep with no feelings . . ." He was looking at her pointedly.

She could not speak.

"Or, Marci, it's that I'm just as confused as you are and I'm doing the best I can to not hurt anyone while I figure things out."

"Okay," she said, deeply regretting having said anything, longing for the playfulness to return to his voice.

"It's not okay. Don't you think I know how not okay this is? I am not this guy. I know guys who spend every other week on the road and think nothing of taking a waitress back to their hotel room after saying goodnight to their kids on the phone. That's not me. I've always been proud not to be that guy, always deplored that behavior. And then you . . ." He stumbled; his voice cracked.

"I don't know how to explain this, what's happened between us. I know the right thing to do is walk out that door right now and go work on the car like I told Cathy I was, but I can't. Something happened to me that night in my office, all those months ago, and I just honestly don't know what to do. So I separate the two things: marriage is marriage, and this . . . well, I think we both know that this is turning into love."

Marci looked up at him. They had never allowed themselves to use that word.

"Maybe it's chickenshit to think that I can keep from hurting her and minimize how much I hurt you while I try to figure everything out. I know it's selfish. But I just don't know what else to do. So I take the phone outside and talk to my wife about her sister who has cancer."

"I'm sorry; I didn't know."

"I try to do what a husband should do. And I absolutely *hate* that when she's talking about chemotherapy and radiation and whether we'll be able to have the anniversary party for my in-laws this summer, all I can think about is getting back in here to you."

Tears flowed freely over her cheeks. His eyes were wet, too. "I'm sorry," she said again, meekly.

"Me, too," he said, softening. She reached for him and ran her fingers through his hair. He pulled her close and they embraced in silence. After a minute, he seemed to continue a previous thought. "I think that's why it drives me so crazy to see you with Jeremy."

"What?" *Jeremy?*

"Because anybody with eyes can see that kid's got it bad for you. I get so jealous because I want to drive you home from happy hour; I want to be able to hang out with you at the Christmas party. I want to protect you. But the reality is, I know that he would be so much better for you than me. He could give you more than I can, even if he is a whiney little douchebag."

"He is not!"

Doug rolled his eyes. "Oh, you know he is. You could do better than him, too, but even he would be less likely to hurt you than I am."

His tone was sadness and playfulness and frank appraisal of reality all at once. This odd combination attracted Marci to him even more. She pulled him closer, whispered an apology, and kissed him as sincerely as she ever had.

Too soon, light came streaming through her tiny bedroom window. Marci's head ached from the margaritas and total failure to eat anything substantial the day before. She felt Doug's warm body curled tightly behind her and had the sense that they had been this way most of the night. She debated getting up to take an Advil and drink some water, which would make her workday more tolerable in a few hours, but couldn't bring herself to move.

What felt like ten minutes later, her eyes opened again to

brighter light. She heard footsteps coming from the living room and Doug was lying next to her again, except this time he was fully dressed. His hair was wet and he smelled like steam and some sort of manly body wash or deodorant. She inhaled deeply and started to turn toward him.

He stopped her with a hand on her shoulder. His voice was husky and gentle in her ear. "Don't. You can go back to sleep. It's only seven. I have an early meeting. And I think we both know you aren't going to roll in until around 9:30 today at best."

Gently, he kissed her neck, and she felt something cool around her throat. "The Internet said that the April birthstone is diamonds, but you didn't seem like a diamond kind of girl. Anyway, happy birthday." He hesitated for a second as she turned her head to look at him and added, "You know I love you, don't you?"

She nodded, breathless. She had known, but this was the first time he had said it in those words. She looked up at his freshly shaven face. His eyes were bright, and face pink. He kissed her perfunctorily and pushed himself to standing, winking at her. "Don't get up. You can thank me later if you like it." The front door closed and she could hear him jogging down the stairs outside.

It was absurd to think that any woman would go back to sleep after her secret boyfriend had given her jewelry and run away. Marci wrapped herself in the bedsheet and went to the mirror. Hanging from a thin leather strap around her neck was a roughly shaped pewter heart surrounding a small, shiny oval turquoise. The simple and rustic piece was beautifully understated. Much more Marci's taste than diamonds would've been. He loved her, and he had bought her jewelry. She heard herself make a squealing noise a lot like those she'd heard in her seventh-grade locker room.

Contrary to Doug's teasing prediction, Marci made it into

the office early. Even with the luxury of a long, hot shower and a stop at Kerbey Lane for her belated birthday pancakes, she still managed to check in with Victoria at 8:45. The hangover was painful, and Victoria was in one of her demanding moods, but Marci didn't care. The heart around her neck seemed a talisman against anything unpleasant.

She'd chosen a tailored white blouse and denim miniskirt with her brown cowboy boots because they seemed to fit best with the necklace. She had coaxed her chestnut curls up into a heap that had miraculously left her with wispy ringlets along her jawline—a look that she could never seem to achieve intentionally, even with hours and pints of hairspray. Rarely did Marci feel completely satisfied with her appearance, but today was different. Maybe thirty wasn't going to be so bad.

She made excuses to walk around the office, hoping to catch Doug's eye and let him see how his gift looked on her. But his door was closed all morning, presumably for the meeting he had mentioned. She caught the sound of his voice once or twice as she dawdled in the hallway for no good reason. Finally, she gave up on stalking him and returned to her desk to attempt focusing on work.

Jeremy stopped by her desk around 10:30, and she dreaded what might be coming, but his manner showed none of the tension or concern from the previous evening. Apparently, he had either forgotten their conversation or decided to pretend that it had never happened. Either way was fine with Marci. He complained about the strong margaritas and asked whether she had any pain relievers. As she handed him the bottle from her purse, his eyes came to rest on the heart necklace, but he said nothing. He thanked her for the pills and was gone.

At 11:30, a new e-mail from Doug appeared in her inbox: *"Do you like it?"*

She replied quickly. *"SO much. Thank you."*

"Good."

She waited expectantly and stalled before finally going to lunch, but she did not hear from Doug again until almost 2:00.

Then, another new e-mail. *"Did you look at the back?"*

She couldn't see the back of the pendant without taking the necklace off, so she undid the clasp and held it in the palm of her hand. Tiny letters were etched in the pewter: YOU ARE MORE THAN I DESERVE. LOVE ALWAYS, D. A rush of feeling swelled in her chest as she ran her fingers over the engraving.

"Did it break?" The sudden voice startled her so much she almost dropped the necklace. Marci had not heard Candice appear in her cubicle, but now she leaned against the gray wall, looking directly at Marci's hand, where the inscription seemed to burn.

"Um . . . sorry?" Marci stuttered.

"Your necklace," Candice said, "did you break it? I have those tiny pliers at my desk if you need them."

"Oh," Marci breathed, "no, I don't think it's broken. It just . . . fell. Maybe I didn't have it clasped all the way." She quickly put it back on.

"Pretty," Candice continued, leaning closer, and Marci wondered why she would choose today to notice such things. "Is it a Kim Tate?"

"Thanks. Um, I'm not sure. It was a—a gift."

"Looks like Kim Tate. I just love her stuff. Have you been to that shop down on SoCo yet? The one with the purple walls? I can't think of the name of it, but it's fabulous."

"No, but I've been meaning to check it out," Marci said enthusiastically, feeling ridiculous. She had never so much as laid eyes on the place. Why did she feel the need to lie about that?

"Anyway," Candice said, peeling herself off the wall. "I just wanted to tell you that I'm trying to cut out early today to head to Dallas for the weekend, so if you want me to sign your timesheet, just bring it by before three or so."

"Oh, okay. Thanks for the heads-up."

"Sure." Was it Marci's imagination that Candice's eyes flickered toward the computer screen behind her?

"Okay, then. I'll get it to you in a minute. I'm just finishing something."

When Candice clicked away, Marci turned back to her computer, cheeks burning. The e-mail was still up on the screen. Fear swept over her. *How much had Candice seen? Would she have noticed anything?* Feeling a bit absurd, she stood and went to where Candice had been standing against the wall and looked over at the computer screen. She could see the e-mail window, but did not think it looked particularly suspicious. It took some focusing to make out Doug's name above the standard company signature line, but the text of the question was more easily readable.

"Did you look at the back?" Nervously, she thought, *It could mean anything, right?* The back of an invoice or an expense report, maybe. Surely a casual observer like Candice would not immediately assume the e-mail and the necklace to be related. She probably did not even read the e-mail. Who reads what's on another person's computer screen? Wasn't it natural for eyes to dart to the bright screen whenever anyone had a conversation in a cubicle? She tried to think about her own habits when she visited someone else's desk.

Stop it. Marci scolded herself. *You're like a detective on the world's worst crime show.* She closed the window and forced herself to fill out her timesheet. When Marci arrived, Candice was on the phone but gave Marci a friendly smile as she signed the timesheet and handed it back. As she sat to input invoices for the rest of the afternoon, she vowed that, however this ended, she would never have a secret life again. It was exhausting.

3

The next three weeks were a roller coaster. Cathy was spending much of her time in Beaumont with her sister, who had started chemotherapy and radiation treatments. Doug was therefore back and forth frequently, sometimes taking half days on Friday afternoons and Monday mornings to be there for her over the weekends. Marci felt admiration for his dedication to his wife and her family, tinged with moments of intense jealousy.

On the plus side, Cathy's absence during the week seemed to help Doug settle into his relationship with Marci. At least twice a week they had dinner together in her tiny apartment; about once a week he spent the night, rising before dawn to sneak home and dress before work. It was as close as Marci had been to domesticity in a relationship since her early twenties, when she had attempted to move in with an artist boyfriend in San Francisco, whose incredible mood swings proved completely insufferable after two short months.

Sometimes she and Doug cooked together, squeezing into the four-foot strip of her apartment that barely qualified as a kitchen. He taught her how to make a spicy Texas dry rub for pork loin and ribs; she introduced him to collard greens and buttermilk-fried chicken.

After that particular meal, which also included homemade biscuits and okra with tomatoes, he smacked his full belly appreciatively and said, "Whew! A man could get used to this."

"Sugar," Marci teased, in her best Southern drawl, "you'd better just hush up, or I'll hold you to that!"

His smile faded a little, and then he pulled her onto his lap. "My little Southern belle."

Cathy and his home life were touchy subjects. She let him take the lead on the rare opportunities he mentioned his family and grudgingly became accustomed to his forays outside to talk with his wife. He often used it as an opportunity to make a run to the grocery or liquor store, never failing to bring back something—a dessert or a bottle of wine—for Marci when he returned. An unspoken peace offering and apology for the situation; she learned to accept the little gifts in that spirit as much as she could.

Weekends, Doug spent in Beaumont, but he tried to call when he was in the car alone or away from Cathy for some reason. These opportunities were sporadic, and he had little time to talk when they occurred. She kept her cell phone on her at all times to avoid missing his call.

One Saturday afternoon, Marci nearly broke her neck trying not to miss him. She had been waiting eagerly all day and finally decided that if she was going to keep her date with her former coworker Wanda to paint pottery that evening, she would have to get in the shower. She had just worked shampoo through her hair when "Walk the Line"—her ringtone for Doug—echoed against the tile.

As she fumbled hurriedly for the shower curtain, shampoo dripped in her eye, stinging painfully. Unable to see, she slipped awkwardly over the side of the tub, pulling the shower curtain with her and twisting into a sudden seated position on the toilet. The curtain rod clanged into the tub, and water soaked everything, including the bath mat. Marci made the split-second decision to turn off the water before reaching for the phone, which stopped ringing as soon as she could get to it.

Two minutes later, she listened to the voice mail. "Hey, Marce, it's Doug. I didn't think you had any plans today, but apparently you changed your mind. You're probably out on a date or something. Anyway, I was hoping to talk to you. This is probably the last chance for today. Hope you're having fun. See ya." His sulky tone annoyed her. *A date? Really?*

She spent the next hour wringing out her bath mat and wiping up the floor with every towel she could find. By the time she had carted everything to the laundry room and back, it was time to meet Wanda. Three glasses of wine and one jet-black coffee mug with red polka dots later, she had recovered from the afternoon's frustration. By the time Doug called again the next evening, Marci was able to laugh about her little mishap and to ignore the vague sense that he did not fully believe why she had not answered her phone.

A few times during this period, Doug even brought work "home" to her apartment in the evenings, marking up storyboards on the couch while Marci attempted to hammer out something on her computer that could pass for an original work of writing. Though she found it hard to concentrate on what she was doing, she treasured this companionable parallel activity. It felt so normal, so domestic, so . . . right.

One night he brought home a stack of résumés he was reviewing for the two office intern positions opening next fall. While she sipped her wine and pecked away at the same sentence she had been editing for two weeks, he sat on the floor and placed résumés into various piles, snorting and scoffing as he went. He hated hiring interns, but the other three partners had long ago saddled him with the task, because he complained more than anyone about the competence and abilities of those selected.

"You have to see this one," he said when he was about halfway through the original stack. "This idiot forgot to change my name in the body of his cover letter. Obviously, he sent this out to every open internship in town."

Feeling a bit of guilt, she squeezed next to him on the floor and read:

Mr. Doug Stanton, Hiring Manager
T, D, L & S
400 Cesar Chavez
Suite 1560
Austin, TX

Dear Mr. Walters:
Thank you so much for the opportunity to apply for the internship position your company will be sponsoring in the fall. I am including my résumé so that you can see that I am a hard worker, a great student, and very involved with extracurricular activities at the University of Texas.

My goal is to find a company that will help me break into advertising or marketing through a position in copywriting or editing. Thank you again for your consideration. I look forward to hearing from you.

Sincerely,
Houston Lee Stevens

"I mean, first of all," Doug said when Marci had finished reading, "aside from calling me Mr. Walters for some reason, which part of this says why he wants to work at our company? I mean, take ten minutes to look at our Web site, for God's sake. This is all about him and what he wants. What is he offering us? And WHY would I hire someone for copywriting or editing who didn't even edit his own damn cover letter, which was about as original as a Kleenex? Not that interns get to do that stuff anyway."

"It is a pretty generic letter," Marci admitted, though she remembered her experience of job hunting during and after college and felt just a little sorry for Houston Lee Stevens.

"Yeah, to say the least," he said, still gathering steam. "This is why I hate doing this bullshit. The only thing worse than cover letters are thank-you notes. 'Dear Mr. Stanton, Thank you for the opportunity to meet with you about job X. It was a pleasure meeting you, and I look forward to hearing from you soon . . . blah, blah, blah.' They're all the same."

"I hate writing thank-you notes," Marci said. "My mother insists that we write them for everything. But I never know what to say."

"I mean, I get that it's hard to be creative when you only met someone for an hour, but come on! Remember *something* about our conversation, say *something* about the job, give me something to go on . . ."

Marci remembered the few job interviews she'd had in recent years, and how never once had it occurred to her to send a thank-you note, despite its being drilled into her that a note was expected for every gift and invitation to someone's home. She felt stupid for not realizing it was something you were supposed to do after a job interview. Is that why she never got hired? Or were her cover letters too generic? She was making mental notes for future job searches when Doug moved on to complaining about a note he got from his niece after her high school graduation.

" 'Dear Uncle Doug,' " he was saying in his best impression of a teenage girl, which was pretty awful. " 'Thank you so much for the graduation gift. It was nice of you to think of me during this special time in my life. Love, Annabelle.' She didn't even mention what the gift was! It's as if she had all these notes prewritten and just added people's names at the top. She's lucky I didn't go over there and take the gift back, ungrateful little brat."

"What did you get her?" Marci asked.

He hesitated. "I don't know," he said. After a long pause, he admitted, "I had my secretary send it."

They laughed for a long time.

The last week in April, Doug was over every night until at least nine and spent the night twice. Despite all his recent trips to Beaumont, he seemed the tiniest bit resentful that Marci was taking Friday off and leaving early to head home to Atlanta for Nicole's bridal shower.

"I don't like you being so far away," he whined Thursday evening as they sat on her tiny couch watching TV. He was running his hand in circles on her back beneath her shirt, coaxing her. Her suitcase waited by the door for an early-morning departure to the airport.

"I have to go," she insisted. "It's my sister's bridal shower, and my mom is cohosting with my aunt. Don't you think my absence would be noticed?"

"I guess." He pouted. His hand moved up and began working on her bra clasps. "But what about me? I need you, too."

"You need me? You're going to be in Beaumont all weekend. You won't even know I'm gone."

"I'll know," he said, suddenly serious.

"Shut up," she said, and kissed him. It was a silly conversation, and he knew it. Doug resisted at first, as though there were more he wanted to say, and then relented. He pulled her onto his lap and held her head in both hands as they kissed.

Later that night as they lay curled together in her bed, he whispered, "I want to take a trip with you."

"Mmm-hmm," she murmured, sleepy.

"I want to go to Atlanta and meet your family."

She remained quiet.

After a moment, he went on, even more softly, "I want to be free to be with you."

Her heart pounded, but she forced herself to preserve the illusion of sleep. This was too serious a conversation to start now. She wanted him to be able to take back what he'd just said if he regretted it later. She lay looking at her alarm clock, every muscle tensed, until she heard his breathing become steady and soft. Even after that, it was a long time before she drifted into sleep.

In a state of confusion and sleep deprivation, Marci boarded her 6:55 flight to Atlanta the next morning. She sat huddled in the window seat with her worn leather satchel draped across her body, staring out the window and fiddling with the edge of the *Newsweek* she'd picked up at the book stand. She tried to avoid thinking of Doug. It was too intense to experience directly, like looking at the sun. And yet she could think of nothing else.

He had dropped her off at the airport before going into the office for the morning, refusing to allow her to take a shuttle. As they had navigated the darkness in his sleek black car, he did not reiterate what he had uttered in the middle of the night. He did, however, hold her hand the entire ride. His mood seemed different. Nervous, maybe. Excited.

Whatever it was seemed to be infectious, because Marci fidgeted uncontrollably in the passenger seat as she stared out the window. "Relax," Doug had said at one point, kissing her hand. "You'll make it. We're not that late."

Now she fingered his necklace at her throat and fidgeted in

her seat on the plane. Her back and knees ached with sleeplessness; she wished she were at home in bed instead of gearing up for an intense day with Nicole and her mom. Nicole, normally the sanest member of their family, had been increasingly intense and pushy about the wedding plans now that the event was so close. She had sent Marci at least fifteen e-mails in the past week, confirming and reconfirming details and reasking questions that had been decided months ago. As annoying as it was, Marci was relieved to know her perfect baby sister was human after all.

A chipper lady with a smear of bright orange-red lipstick and too much perfume sat next to her and immediately introduced herself. Marci smiled politely and began rummaging in her pack for her headphones. The last thing she wanted was a conversation with a real estate conventioneer or Baptist missionary. She put on music and tuned out the safety announcements. As the plane taxied, she began to feel sleep overcome her, and her next awareness was a brown layer of smog amid the gray clouds and the pilot announcing the descent into Hartsfield-Jackson Atlanta International Airport.

4

Mom and Nicole both looked like poster children for caffeine overdose as they waved to her from the top of the baggage claim escalator. Until she fell into their joint embrace, Marci didn't realize how much she had been missing her family.

Marci collected her duffel and listened to Nicole chatter nonstop about the wedding plans as they schlepped out to the parking deck and drove to the Flying Biscuit for breakfast. Ravi's mother was still boycotting their nuptials, angry that Ravi had chosen Nicole over the woman from Mumbai she had arranged for him to marry. Much of the rest of Ravi's family had relented, however, including his brother and sister, who also lived in the States, and they were helping Nicole create an Indian-Presbyterian blended ceremony.

Marci pushed eggs and black bean cakes around on her plate as she listened to Nicole. "... the reception hall was damaged in a fire two weeks ago, so of course I'm completely freaking out about that. Plus, it's so hard to find a rental company with enough of the right kind of tents. There are all these different parts of the ceremony, and they require so many tents. But wait until you see the dresses!"

As a concession to Ravi's family, Nicole had decided to

wear a traditional white wedding dress for the ceremony and a custom-made sari for the reception. With Nicole's amazing but expensive tastes, Marci could only imagine what the bill would be for those two items alone.

As though reading her mind, Mom shook her head. "Four thousand dollars for two dresses. I think that was the cost of mine and your dad's whole wedding!" She glanced at Nicole and hastily added, "Worth every penny, of course, honey. It's just a good thing your sister has no wedding plans on the horizon, or we'd have to sell the house!"

Thanks, Mom.

Marci spent the day trailing behind her baby sister through a slew of department stores, alterations shops, and various coordinators' offices. Somehow Nicole had evolved into a self-assured, gorgeous woman in the last several months. She spoke to sales clerks and catering managers with an assertiveness that might have been demanding from someone less radiant, and yet no one seemed to respond to her with anything but an increased desire to make her happy. It reminded Marci of her best friend Suzanne, whose self-assuredness was legendary. Marci watched Nicole with a touch of awe and just the slightest hint of jealousy.

She worked hard to control the urge to check her cell phone every few minutes for something from Doug. She knew it was silly to expect anything—he was at work, and they'd seen each other just hours before—yet she longed to hear from him. Around lunch, she turned the phone off entirely to force herself to be more present for Nicole. *Let him be the one to wait for me this weekend.*

By the end of the day, the tired ache in Marci's knees and back had eclipsed nearly everything else. She was beyond relieved when they piled into their mother's sedan for the last time and steered toward home. Marci's dad and Ravi met them in the driveway. She was so happy to see her dad she could hardly stand it. He gave her a desperately needed hug as she entered the house. The five of them ordered pizza and spent the rest of the evening playing cards and drinking beer.

The next evening, Nicole's local friends had scheduled a combination engagement / bachelor party / shower for her and Ravi. Since Ravi and Nicole lived in D.C., many of Nicole's old Atlanta friends had not met Ravi, so her childhood best friends Ellie and Rachel had combined everything into one huge party at an upscale restaurant/bar in midtown Atlanta. Because Marci's presence was nonnegotiable, Nicole had allowed her to add Suzanne, Jake, and her longtime friend Beth to the invitation list as well.

After nearly two hours of musical banquet chairs, dinner, and seemingly endless weepy toasts from Nicole's sorority sisters, the party broke into smaller groups at the bar. Marci and the other three were finally able to get a small table to themselves to catch up.

They moved from the wine that had been served with dinner to beer and cocktails. They talked about Beth and her kids, Suzanne's big event in Chicago, and Jake's recent move to freelance video production. He had managed to secure an in with the Atlanta Silverbacks soccer team for a couple of their promotional videos and was hoping this would lead to bigger things with the other major sports franchises down the road. He was also shooting footage for a couple of local hip-hop artists, but documentaries and sports were his real loves.

Suzanne related the latest man drama in her life, a conversational staple since college. Suzanne was an acknowledged serial dater; she went through relationships as fast as most women went through bottles of shampoo. Her latest victim was a nice, funny stockbroker named Reggie, whom Marci and Jake had both met. Though she always tried not to get too

invested in Suzanne's love life, Marci had been quietly rooting for Reggie, who was handsome and self-effacing and—
maybe to his detriment—seemed to see through the smart-ass
Southern-girl veneer Suzanne wore as protection.

"What happened to Reggie, anyway?" Jake said when Beth
opened the door by asking about Suzanne's single status. "I
liked that guy."

"Ugh," she said dramatically. "Let's just say it was a hygiene
issue, okay?"

"What? Did he have crabs or something?" Jake probed,
grinning. Marci, who knew the story, snickered.

"Ew! No, nothing like that. Never mind. Let's move on,
okay?"

"No," Beth pleaded. "I never get to hear the gossip! Please
tell."

"All right," Suzanne relented, and Marci knew that she was
only half sorry to have all the attention focused on her. "As
y'all know, Reggie and I had dated for about three months, so
he was staying at my place pretty often by the end, a few times
a week when we were both in town. Anyway, I started noticing
that he didn't seem to wash thoroughly after, um . . ." She hesitated here, looking for the words.

"After *sex*?" Beth asked. A few cocktails before, it probably
would have occurred to Beth that Suzanne would not have
hesitated to discuss intimate details of her love life. Other base
human functions, however, were another story. In high school,
she had once maintained for *weeks* that she had never farted,
holding her ridiculous ground against a persistent onslaught of
teasing from a couple of football players who sat at her table in
chemistry class.

A trace of that childish discomfort appeared now. "No, after
using the bathroom. You know, *number two*." The other three
exchanged smiles at the fact that Suzanne actually whispered

the last two words. "I started noticing that he'd come out of the bathroom really quickly after flushing when he'd been in there a while, and that his hands were usually dry."

"It couldn't be that he dried them, like maybe using the towel?" Jake teased.

"No, I checked," she answered seriously. "I mean, sometimes the towel was damp, but not always."

"Yuck," Beth said sympathetically. "That is pretty gross."

"Yes," Marci said. "But tell them what you did next."

Color rose in Suzanne's face, and she shot Marci the glare before going on. "Well, I didn't want to just dismiss him for no good reason . . ."

"Because that would be *totally* unlike you."

"So I went in one morning and made a tiny mark on the back of the soap container where the level of the soap was. He was over for a whole weekend, and when he left I went back and checked. No change."

"Wait," Jake said. "Wouldn't it be lower from you using it? You do wash your hands, don't you? Or have you given up going to the bathroom altogether?"

"Of course I thought of that," she said resentfully. "I bought a second bottle of soap and kept it under the sink for me to use during the experiment. At the end of the weekend, I told him it wasn't working out."

By this time, Jake and Marci were both in stitches. Beth was some combination of amused, grossed out, and impressed that Suzanne went to such lengths to discover whether her boyfriend washed his hands after pooping. "Did you explain why you ended it?" she asked.

"I said we had different interests."

"Yeah," Marci snorted. "Like how you're interested in not getting some weird bacterial infection and he's interested in shaving thirty seconds off his dump time."

Suzanne held her serious face for as long as she could, and then threw the straw from her drink at Marci before breaking. The laughter of her three best friends washed over Marci like a healing salve, and for the first time in weeks, she felt at home and completely free.

An hour or so after dinner, two minivan taxis arrived outside the restaurant to transport the party to a trendy new place in the Virginia Highlands. "You're coming, right?" Nicole tottered as she approached their table, now sporting a bridal veil hanging from a plastic tiara. Marci was glad Ellie and Rachel had sense enough to reserve hotel rooms and obviously intended to use taxis for their bar hopping. She looked at her table for a verdict; but her own friends' faces indicated a less than strong interest in following along. Suzanne's head gave a nearly imperceptible shake to the side.

"I think we old folks are going to find a quiet place to hang out. Like a nursing home."

"Noo . . ." Nicole pleaded, though Marci was positive their presence would not be missed in the slightest. "You have to come; it's going to be So! Much! Fun!"

Ellie was pulling on Nicole's arm, urging her toward the door and giving Marci a farewell wave. Ravi had obviously already been hustled into the cab by some of the guys in the group.

"Go ahead," Marci said. "Be safe, okay?"

"I love you," Nicole slurred. "You know that? I love my sister! And my sister's friends!" She moved around the table and launched herself at Suzanne and Beth, throwing an arm roughly around each of them. "You guys are, like, my other big sisters!"

"Thanks, Nic," said Jake.

"Oh, Jakie! And my big brother!" She turned to the entire bar behind her. "Everyone, this is my big brother Jake, and I will fight anyone who messes with him. Anyone!!" She balled up her petite fists in what was clearly supposed to be a menac-ing gesture. Even ridiculously drunk, Nicole managed to be adorable.

When no one at the bar seemed interested in challenging Jake's honor in any way, Nicole turned back to the table and became suddenly solemn. "Seriously, Jake, when are you going to make it official and really be my brother?"

Marci laughed uncomfortably and pushed her drunken sis-ter toward Ellie. "Go! Love you."

She could not help hearing, however, that Jake's answer had already floated past her: "As soon as your sister will let me."

As Jake flagged down a server for another round, Beth excused herself. "Ray is going fishing early tomorrow, and the kids are not going to let me sleep in. Marci, it's been amazing to see you." She blew kisses all around and was out the door.

Suzanne, Jake, and Marci made it through two more rounds before finally winding down the evening. By 1:00 A.M., the bar was so thick with people and noise it was difficult to believe it was the same restaurant where they'd sat at the beginning of the evening. Suzanne went to call a cab and wait in line for the restroom while Marci and Jake pushed their way through the crowd to settle up at the bar. He held her hand as they walked.

The young bartender looked completely overwhelmed. They signaled to her and waited while she poured a line of six cosmopolitans, maybe for another bachelorette party. "Hey," Jake said, turning Marci around by her hips and placing his hand beneath her chin. His skin looked ruddy and healthy as always, his thick brown hair rebelling against his attempts to slick it down. He still had a few faint freckles on the bridge of his nose. "Look at me."

She knew where this was going. She supposed she had al-ways known.

"You know I would do anything for you, don't you?"

She nodded. "Jake, I—"

But before she could even formulate the next words in her mind, Jake was kissing her. It was soft and wet and familiar. Nice. He pressed against her, pushing her into the bar a little as they were jostled by the crowd. She allowed herself to push back against him, to kiss him back. She felt familiar warmth spreading through her as the bar and the crowd and even thoughts of Doug receded. For a moment, she wanted to allow herself to be carried away by this kiss.

But he pulled away, looking serious. "So are you going to tell me about it?"

"What?"

"Whatever it is you're hiding from everyone."

Marci could think of nothing to say. His brown eyes gazed at her patiently and waited. She shook her head pathetically.

"Okay," he said sadly. "Listen, Marci, I know that whole thing wasn't really supposed to be serious, you know. The napkin thing? But I do love you, and I think we both know we'd be great together. What could be better than marrying your best friend, right?"

She had swallowed a piece of granite, apparently, the size of an egg. Her lips moved, but no sound would come out. Again, he waited, but not for long. Suzanne appeared from the restroom hallway thirty feet away and began picking her way through the crowd toward them.

"Okay," he said softly, reaching over her to collect the tab from the bartender. "I'm here for you if you want to talk about . . . whatever, okay?"

"Okay," Marci said, more ashamed than ever.

5

By the time she had left the cab, staggered up her parents' impossibly long driveway, stumbled pseudo-quietly up the stairs, brushed her teeth, and fallen into her childhood bed, it was after 3:00 A.M. Her old room still had posters of R.E.M. and Pink Floyd from her high school days, and her stuffed animal collection cushioned her drunken collapse.

Across the hall, Nicole's room was dark and the door open. For a moment, Marci experienced a flash of big-sister worry, until she remembered that Ellie had arranged for their whole group to crash in a hotel room downtown. Marci wondered whether they were all still out, and how Ravi was faring with Nicky's crazy friends. She was trying to imagine poor Ravi doing lemon-drop shots with the sorority sisters when blackness overtook her.

Not until *very* bright and not so early the next morning did Marci even think to check her phone to see whether Doug had called. She woke to this realization and a vicious hangover, scrambling to reach her purse from the bed as her head pounded in her ears and her stomach lurched menacingly.

He had called. Twelve times. *Damn.*

Fighting the urge to vomit, she sighed and held down the voice-mail key on her phone. Four messages. *Great.*

Saturday, 8:02 P.M. "Hey, Marce, it's Doug. It's about seven o'clock here, and I know you were planning to go out tonight so I just made a quick run to the store, hoping to catch up with you. Maybe you're already out? That's right, the time difference. Shit. Well, if you're not out or you can sneak off to the bathroom in the next few minutes, give me a buzz. Hope you're having a great time with your family. Okay, well, hopefully I'll talk to you soon."

Saturday, 8:46 P.M. "Marce, hey, just on my way home and wanted to try you again before I get back to the house. There's some family coming over tonight to play cards and stuff. I'll leave my phone in the car so you can call if you want. Okay, babe? Love you. Be safe."

Saturday 11:36 P.M. "Hey, hey, hey, Marcella"—a loud crash in the background, possibly a trash can being knocked over—shit!" More clanging, mumbling. "Well, bummer—came all the way out to the car, and no message from you. You must be having a damn good time out there. Forgotten all about me, I guess. Heh, heh. All right, girl. Take it easy. Going in for the night. Talk to you tomorrow."

Sunday, 9:32 A.M. "Hey, party girl. Skipped church with the family so I'm here alone for the next hour and a half or so. Hope you had fun last night. Call me."

She ended the call and looked at the clock on her phone. It was 11:15 Georgia time, just past the window he had mentioned in the last message. She debated calling him back anyway, on the chance that his family returned later than expected. But between the coldness in his voice, the pounding in her head, and the fact that her mouth seemed filled with fiberglass insulation, she opted to put the phone back in her purse and go down for breakfast instead. The damage was done, obviously, and a few more hours wouldn't make a difference now.

Downstairs, Nicole slouched over the kitchen table with an ice pack on the back of her neck and a plate of untouched pancakes and bacon in front of her. She seemed to be wearing the same jeans from the night before—with rhinestones down the seams, ridiculous on Sunday morning—and one of Ravi's Georgetown sweatshirts. Ravi and their father were visible through the sliding glass door, sitting with coffee on the back porch and engaged in a conversation lively enough to indicate that Ravi was clearly not as bad off as his betrothed.

"Heavy starch and grease, girls. That's the hangover cure I swear by." Their mother was so bright and perky she could've been sharing the secret for perfect cupcakes on her own cooking show, rather than nursing the hangovers of two wayward adult daughters. "Pancakes, Marce?"

"Please," Marci muttered gratefully. She set her plate across from Nicole's untouched breakfast and headed for the medicine cabinet.

"Must've been some night," Mom continued, smiling.

"Ugh." This sound emanated from somewhere in the vicinity of Nicole.

"Well, you'd better get hydrated and take some Advil, because that shower is happening today come hell or high water. Aunt Theresa hasn't talked about anything else for the last three months."

Three hours later, they pulled up in front of Aunt Theresa's house—a small brick bungalow off Habersham Road in Buckhead, one of the older and more prestigious Atlanta neighborhoods. These affluent streets had modest, older homes like Aunt Theresa's, with ample yards and very old pine trees, mixed in with enormous mansions that covered all but a thin strip of grass.

Inside, Theresa's house reflected her own eclectic style more than the pretense of the neighborhood. The walls were brightly colored, and every room was dotted with collectibles— everything from African tribal masks to a real honest-to-God bear rug from Siberia. Marci's dad often joked that Aunt Theresa had killed the bear herself. In reality, she was a photojournalist, and the souvenirs were from a lifetime of traveling. Growing up, both Marci and Nicole had always thought she hung the moon; she was one of the reasons Nicole had chosen journalism. And perhaps the reason Marci had always . . . well, *wanted* to write, anyway.

Today Theresa's warm little house was enhanced by the sound of happy chatter as about twenty or so of their female relatives and family friends mingled in the various rooms. The three of them walked into the living room, their mother pushing Nicole from behind, whispering, "Big smile, big smile!" They were greeted with a collective gasp and oohs and ahs and "Here's the bride!"

Almost immediately, Marci felt a bony death grip on her arm and caught the smell of menthol cigarettes. *Dammit.* She could go to no family function, it seemed, without their decrepit great-aunt Mildred latching on to her immediately and cornering her for the entire event, demanding to know who she was dating and why she wasn't married with kids already. Ever since her baby sister had gotten engaged first, Marci had been dreading her next meeting with Mildred.

Her mother glanced back apologetically and mouthed "Be nice," as she followed Nicole into the center of the main living room while Mildred held Marci hostage in the foyer. For the next twenty minutes, Marci nodded politely and attempted to watch what was happening at the shower—there was some kind of game going on in which Nicole had a secret word taped to her back and the other guests were trying to get her to guess it. Bursts of giggles were breaking out periodically, which seemed only to invigorate Mildred's diatribe for being interrupted.

"That's what I was just telling the black girl who helps me . . ." she was saying.

Marci cringed, knowing that "the black girl" was actually Odessa, a tolerant woman in her fifties with four adult children of her own. She also knew that Aunt Mildred's own children had all chipped in every month for the last six years to pay Odessa a secret bonus to keep her from quitting, as so many of Mildred's "girls" had before her.

"It used to be young ladies didn't worry about their careers, especially good Southern girls. You served God and your family first and that's the way it was. Nowadays you girls are so selfish." Here she pointed a skeletal finger directly into Marci's face. "You think that your happiness matters before anything else. What about family? Don't you care about anyone but yourself? I hope your sister intends on staying home with the children when the time comes, not gallivanting all over the world like—"

"Like me?" Theresa appeared out of nowhere, smiling. "Don't worry, Aunt Mildred," she trilled, tossing an arm around Marci's shoulders and wheeling her toward the living room, "I can't get these girls to visit me often enough to be a bad influence on them. Shall I get you some tea? We're about to do gifts."

Marci heard Mildred mutter some sort of reluctant assent, but she was too grateful for her freedom to risk looking back and making eye contact again. She quickly made her way to the punch bowl on the other side of the room and engaged in hasty conversation with a second cousin from Valdosta while

Theresa tended to Aunt Mildred. A few minutes later, Marci had just realized she'd left her cell phone in the car and that she had not yet spoken to Doug, when Theresa raised her punch glass for a toast and announced to emphatic applause that it was time to open gifts.

It was amazing how many things the world suddenly thought you needed when you were getting married. Marci knew for a fact that Nicole could barely put together a grilled cheese sandwich, and yet out of countless wrapped boxes she pulled cooking devices and serving trays that looked foreign even to Marci. A deviled egg platter. A crème brûlée torch. Espresso maker. Panini press. Waffle iron. She tried to picture Nicole and Ravi, who both worked at least sixty hours a week and knew the Chinese takeout man on a first-name basis, sitting to an elegant brunch of fresh-squeezed orange juice, cappuccino, and waffles.

Marci, who *did* know her way around the kitchen a little bit, couldn't help feeling a twinge of resentment knowing that most of these items would be returned for store credit or kept in garage storage while Nicole ate frozen waffles and delivery pizza. Next, Nicole opened an oversize Dutch oven, beautiful and expensive, and gushed, "Oh, I can't wait to cook a Thanksgiving bird in here!"

Marci snorted involuntarily, and had to fake a coughing fit when the whole room turned to look at her. Her mother shot her a warning glare, so she took the opportunity to step out the back door, on the pretense of being unable to stop coughing.

While Nicole opened a monogrammed crystal punch bowl, Marci crept around the side of the house and realized that her mom's Buick was in full view of the front window, where the shower was. What excuse could she make for running out to the car? Cough drops? Allergy pills?

Marci, stop. This is ridiculous. You are thirty years old and are allowed to leave a party for five minutes to check your phone. What if you had an important business call or something?

Just to be safe, however, she ducked behind some bushes and skittered in a hunch to the far side of the car as though she were in a shoot-out, flattening herself against the hump in the floorboard to retrieve her purse from the other side. She settled back onto the hidden side of the floor of the car with her feet hanging out the open door while she pulled out her phone. No missed calls—Doug was either completely pissed or had given up on reaching her.

Almost 3:45. She tried to think what time he might be leaving to head back to Austin and decided that if he wasn't already in the car, he certainly would have his phone off or hidden as usual. She dialed the number, trying to think how to explain last night's phone neglect.

"Hello?" Cathy's upbeat voice hit Marci like sharp steel in the chest. Her breath caught in her throat.

"Hello?" Cathy repeated.

"Um—hi, may I speak with"—she searched her brain, panicked—"Nicole, please?"

A pause. Or did Marci imagine it? Cathy's voice was polite, however. "I'm sorry, you have the wrong number."

"Oh, sorry. Um, thanks," Marci stuttered. The call had ended before she'd finished.

Shit, shit, shit. Why had she called him? Why hadn't she checked her phone last night and called when he had told her it was okay? He was going to kill her. What was going on there now? Were they together in the car? An absurd jealousy began to mingle with her panic. *Why would Cathy be answering his cell phone?*

"You, too, huh?" The voice startled her out of her miserable spiral, and she looked up to see Melissa, the cousin from Valdosta, sucking hard on a cigarette near the bushes. "I keep trying to quit, but damn I hate bridal showers."

Marci laughed weakly. "Uh, yeah, me, too," she muttered, and pushed herself back toward the house. Forgetting the clandestine nature of her trip to the car, she walked directly past the window and through the front door in a daze.

Inside, the gift-opening portion of the festivities had finally drawn to a close, and everyone seemed to be giving the bride advice about marriage. Marci hovered in the entryway.

"Try to live near family if you can; it makes things so much easier, especially once you have kids."

"Don't have kids too soon. You need time to enjoy being together."

"But don't wait too long, either; those eggs of yours won't be young forever!"

"Never go to bed angry. Even if you have to fight it out until three in the morning."

"Don't fight about the little things. Don't get mad because he doesn't pick up his socks."

"Girl, you're about to find out what pigs men can be—Dan didn't put his underwear in the hamper for the first ten years of our marriage. I had to quit doing his laundry entirely before he learned that lesson . . ." Giggles and mutters of assent rose from around the room.

"Nicky, just don't lose yourself." Marci looked up at the familiar voice and saw their mother in tears with her hand on Nicole's knee, but also looking up pointedly at Marci as she said it. "Enjoy your husband, but you be sure and live your own life, too."

Ravi had a conference call that evening, so the four Thompsons rode together to have dinner and take Marci back to the

airport. Marci held her cell phone cradled in her hand the en-
tire ride, and stared aimlessly out the window while Nicole and
Mom recounted the details of the shower and the gifts, and
Dad feigned polite interest.

She couldn't seem to stop herself from running through all
the various scenarios from this afternoon. Even though she
knew it didn't matter, the details of why Cathy had answered
Doug's phone, whether he knew she had called, and what, if
anything, had transpired between them—all these things
seemed to matter greatly. And the fact that Doug had not called
her back since it happened three hours ago was particularly
worrisome. She imagined a horrible fight in which Cathy
threw his phone out the car window. And worse.

Lost in this reverie, it took a moment for her to realize that
Nicole was now talking directly to her: ". . . I don't know how
you put up with it. I am so sorry she cornered you like that.
You missed the games! What a creepy old bat."

"Nicole Elizabeth Thompson!" Their mother actually reached
back and smacked Nicole on the knee from the passenger seat.
"You will not talk about your great-aunt that way! She has lived
a long time, and she deserves your respect. Didn't she give you
that wonderful little bowl?"

"It was an ashtray, Mom. What am I going to do with an
ashtray? It's 2011."

"Well, at any rate. She is a dear old woman—"

Their father snorted in the driver's seat.

"Arthur!"

"What? She's a bitter old witch, and you know it. Ease up."

Nicole laughed and stomped her feet in triumph, and even
Marci couldn't help smiling.

"I can't believe you would say that!" Their mother was outraged with their father, one of her very favorite emotional
states.

"Elaine," he said slowly, "maybe if you explained why she's such a nasty old crone, the girls would have a little sympathy for her."

"I don't know what you're—"

He looked at her pointedly over the glasses he used for driving.

"Oh, come on, Arthur. That's a silly rumor . . ."

"What rumor?" Nicole asked, leaning forward.

"You have to admit it makes sense, don't you?" he said, looking back at the highway.

"Whether it makes sense or not, I am not going to spend Marci's last hour in Atlanta gossiping about a poor old lady who has no one left to be kind to her, Arthur. Anyway, I think all that mess with Dottie has been blown way out of proportion."

"What mess?" Nicole and Marci said in unison.

Their mother had folded her arms in what they all knew was an irrevocable refusal to speak further and was now staring out the window at the trees and billboards along I-285.

"Your mother's Aunt Mildred," their father began, and an exasperated sigh floated out from the passenger seat, "is very . . . er, opinionated, as you may have noticed. Especially about the subject of marriage. Well, before she married Herbert, who you two never knew—"

"Marci met him. She was two. The year before he died."

"Okay, well, yes. Anyway, before she married Herbert and had their two sons—"

"Your Uncle Ron and Uncle Mike," their mother put in, as though this might be interesting enough to distract from the delicious gossip both girls could sense was coming.

"—she actually got married sort of late for her time. She was in her late twenties when she and Herbert finally tied the knot. Before that, she was a teacher."

"First woman in our family to go to college!" Mom piped up.

"Yes, a sharp lady, Mildred is. Anyway, during college and while she was teaching, Aunt Mildred had . . . a friend."

"A *roommate*, Arthur," Mom corrected. "Which was not uncommon at the time."

"Sure, sure." Dad went on. "Anyway, many folks in the family, including your grandmother when she was alive, believed that Mildred and Dottie were more than just friends, if you know what I mean."

They did. Marci and Nicole looked at each other, dumbstruck. Picturing mean, stony Mildred with a husband and raising kids was difficult enough. A forbidden lesbian lover was just too much to bear. They grinned gleefully at each other.

"They lived together for more than seven years and were more or less inseparable. The story goes, your great-grandfather—maybe he was catching on, I don't know—anyway, he threatened to cut Mildred off entirely if she didn't get married in a year or something like that. He was a wealthy man, and I think family meant a lot to Mildred. Well, we all know how the story ends." He looked at his wife again, all playfulness gone from his voice, and put a hand on her knee. "Personally, I can't imagine having to make a choice like that."

She seemed to soften at this. "How do you know this story anyway? I never told you."

"Well, your mother hinted at it once or twice, but I got the full story from your Uncle Alvin one Christmas. Too much eggnog, I guess. I think he always felt ashamed that he never stood up for Mildred . . . just watched her marry Herbert and hoped she'd be happy. Obviously, she never really was."

Their mother seemed unable to argue with this last statement. She put her hand on his and squeezed it affectionately. Marci felt like an intruder on a private moment.

Wow. Marci wondered what Dottie was like, and what had become of her after Mildred had ended things. Did she go on to her own loveless union, or escape to another relationship in a more liberal climate than the Old South? Or perhaps her broken heart was too much to bear, and she became a spinster librarian with eleven cats and a collection of porcelain dolls. *How awful,* Marci thought. *No wonder Aunt Mildred resents all the choices I have available.*

Half an hour later, as she dragged her wobbly college suitcase through the terminal, checking her phone every two minutes, hoping to see a call from Doug, she couldn't help wondering what she was really doing with all the choices she had.

By the time he called, it was nearly midnight. She had unpacked fretfully, with the windows open to let in the calming night air and the sound of Plastic Utensils rehearsing, which made her feel less lonely. She had stalled for a while, cleaning, knowing that she would be unable to sleep until she heard from him. By the time the phone vibrated on her nightstand, she had been lying in bed staring up at the ceiling for about twenty minutes.

"Hey," he whispered.

"Hey," she echoed.

"Sorry it took me so long to call back—it was kind of a long afternoon." She held her breath, but he didn't offer details. "How was your trip?"

"It was fine. Doug, I am so sorry I called your phone today; what happened? I've been so worried. Are you okay?"

He chuckled mildly. "Yeah, using your sister's name was pretty good thinking, I guess."

"She told you?"

"I was right next to her. We ended up driving back together because her brother needed her car . . . it's a long story. I accidentally dropped my phone in the center console without thinking, and she answered it. Anyway, I haven't been able to shake her all afternoon, which is why I'm just now calling you back. I knew it was you, of course. None of my other mistresses are ballsy enough to call my phone in the middle of the day."

She said nothing. She knew he was joking, but she couldn't make herself laugh.

"Oh, come on. I'm kidding. You should be glad I'm handling it so well, shouldn't you?"

"Do you think she suspects something?"

"She might suspect that there's someone named Nicole with a number similar to mine, if that's what you mean."

"How did she seem? I mean, after the call?"

"I don't know. Normal, I guess."

"But she wouldn't let you out of her sight? Don't you think that means something? Where is she now? Where are you now?"

"Marci, calm down. How about 'Hi, Doug. I love you and I missed you so much while I was partying all night in Atlanta.' I tried to call *you* a couple of times, as you may have noticed."

"I'm sorry," she muttered. And waited.

"All right, all right, you need to know? My wife did not seem in any way unnerved, confused, or angry about the wrong-number call to my cell phone. She seemed very much as if she had just received a call for the wrong number. She said nothing else about it, though I think in the future it might be good if we avoid that happening again, okay?

"We were together all afternoon because her brother is borrowing her car in Beaumont for a couple of days and she had set up dinner for us when we got back tonight with some friends of ours and forgotten to tell me about it. After dinner, the four of us came back to our house and played cards until late, which is why I couldn't get away to call you. They are really good friends, and it would've seemed weird for me to back out of the card game. She is now sound asleep upstairs, and I am outside in my car on the phone with you at midnight, and pretending to look for some work papers I need to go over by the morning. So, Nancy Drew, does it sound like I have filled in all the holes to your satisfaction?"

She was embarrassed to admit it, but it actually did help to hear all the details. Cathy had apparently not figured everything out from the phone call. Marci felt silly for how worried she had been.

They talked for only a few minutes, and she gave him the basics of her trip, leaving out the details about Jake and the kiss at the bar, of course. These were two different worlds. Doug needed to go back inside, and when they hung up the phone, she fell straight into an exhausted sleep.

6

Cathy decided to stay in Austin for the next few weeks, since her brother was helping out in Beaumont. Work was crazy for Doug, too, so his availability to be with or even talk to Marci diminished substantially. They exchanged brief, thinly coded e-mails at work and talked on the phone very late at night while he sat outside in his car. Once he even fell asleep in the driver's seat, telling Marci later that he had awakened to the sound of the garbage truck and had to pretend he'd just gone out to get the morning paper. His overall mood was rather dark, and the stress seemed to be wearing on him and his patience with Marci.

Their relationship had returned to the status of the early days—stolen moments here and there. But while those brief encounters had been thrilling early on, they were now a sad contrast to the semidomestic bliss they had been enjoying before Marci's trip to Atlanta. Loneliness pressed in on her when she prepared meals for herself in the tiny kitchen. Memories of cooking with Doug created emptiness, where before him there had been only simple solitude.

The second Tuesday after her return, Doug managed to come by her place for about an hour after work. She spent all of Monday evening cleaning her apartment and ran out to buy his favorite beer. But her preparations mattered little. As soon as he walked in the door, he ravished her like a hungry animal. He kissed her forcefully, not with the gentle affection she had come to enjoy most of the time, but as though he had been in the desert for weeks and she was a first jug of water.

The sex was furious. As soon as she had fumbled the door locked—somewhat challenging with Doug's tongue taking over her whole mouth—he reached under her lightweight skirt and tore down the tiny, cute panties she'd obsessed over picking out the night before. He pushed her, a little roughly, toward the wall and boosted her against it almost effortlessly. She wrapped her legs around him instinctively to hold herself up, and it took him just seconds to lift her skirt around her waist and to push himself into her. She wondered insanely how long he could hold her up this way, feeling distracted and self-conscious about her weight, but it was over quickly after all the time they'd spent apart. "I missed you," he said with a small grin as he lowered her to the floor, sweating.

She went to the kitchen and opened two of the beers. He sat at her tiny kitchen table and pulled her onto his lap when she tried to walk past. "I really, really missed you," he said hungrily into the back of her neck as she took a swig from her bottle. "You smell amazing. God, I love you so much." She still felt a thrill to hear him say it.

Marci tried to think what she wanted to talk about with their limited time—their conversations had been so cropped lately, and his patience so short, that it seemed important to get today *right* while they were together. "I've written something new," she offered. It was one way that her evenings alone were actually paying off.

"Mmm . . . really? What is it?" he said into the back of her head, running his hands over her shoulders in a half-massaging, half-smoothing motion. The feeling was so intense that she was having trouble remembering exactly what it was that she had written.

"Well, it's kind of an essay, I guess . . ." she started, unsure how to describe what she'd written. A satirical look at the life of a temp, it pieced together funny and demeaning stories from her assignments over the years. She had no idea if it was publishable and, if it was, who would want read it. She had half-hoped Doug would be impressed by it and give her some direction about what to do next, but she was also pretty nervous to put it in front of his critical eye. "It's based on some of my work experiences from the last few years."

"Mmm-hmm. Great." But he wasn't listening to her words. He stood, keeping an arm around her shoulders, and moved both beers to the counter. Gently but insistently, he pressed her upper body to the table and pushed her legs apart. He started slowly, using his hand to massage her as he moved into her again. But soon he grabbed both her hips and pounded with an intensity that was both thrilling and a little bit painful. He made none of his usual effort to keep quiet because of her thin walls, but moaned loudly and even bellowed her name a couple of times. This recklessness was so unlike him, and yet it was everything she'd wished for during all the times when he was so careful and quiet. No one had ever called out her name that way.

By the time they had finished the second time, he had only ten minutes left before he had to go, which he used to take a shower. As she sat on the couch waiting for him, she thought she heard him whistling the theme to *The A-Team*.

When he plopped down next to her, he looked invigorated, ready to take on the world. "Thanks, babe, it was wonderful," he said, brushing her cheek. She smiled back thinly. "I've got to get back for that meeting. I'm sorry we didn't have much time to talk. I'd like to read that essay, though. Soon. Okay?"

Once the door had closed behind him, she stayed in the

same spot on the couch for a long time, staring at his half-full beer bottle.

The following Saturday, she came in from walking around the trail at Town Lake to find a message from Jake on her machine. "Hey, Marce. I was just thinking, I don't have plans for Memorial Day weekend, and I haven't been out to see you in a while. Maybe it's time for another tequila tour of Austin? Give me a call, okay?"

Two years before, Jake, Suzanne, and their college friend Rebecca had made the trip out to Austin for the South by Southwest festival. Marci had managed to take half a week off from the temp assignment she'd been working at the time, and the four of them had spent four days and nights boozing and listening to music in just about every bar, warehouse, and alleyway in the city. She smiled at the recollection.

What Jake was suggesting now was something different. Not a road trip and casual reunion of friends, but just the two of them and a long weekend alone together. She thought of the kiss they'd shared at the bar a couple of weeks ago and her heart began to beat faster. Could he really have feelings for her after all these years?

She'd never told Doug about that kiss, and she'd never told Jake about Doug at all. Jake was one of her best friends, and keeping the secret from him was even more painful than keeping it from Suzanne. At least Suzanne's heart was not at risk. Jake's heart . . . she couldn't think about it. She saved the message for later and headed for the shower.

Another exhausting week followed. Work had become crazy for everyone at the company, and the recent stress Doug had been exhibiting seemed to have infected the entire office. Even Victoria snapped at Marci for asking too many questions about an assignment, which was out of character for the always-together accounting manager. Meanwhile, Marci's normally empty desk became crowded with an overflowing in-box and a slew of instructional Post-it notes from the seven people for whom she was working on minor projects.

Marci was grateful to be busy and distracted. Doug had little time during the day to e-mail her, and their late-night conversations were somewhat perfunctory. He seemed to realize his inattentiveness, however, and did actually manage to sneak out one day and send flowers to her apartment, with a note that read simply, "I love you always.—D." She wanted desperately to bring them into the office but decided that even without the card it was too dangerous.

The good news was that Cathy would be going out with girlfriends on Friday night, so Doug could at least make it over for dinner. Marci planned to learn from her mistake the previous week and keep her expectations as low as possible. She did not clean the apartment, nor did she buy special beer or plan an extravagant meal. *If* it worked out, *if* he showed up in time for dinner, they would order pizza and he could buy whatever he wanted to drink on his way over.

She tried to keep her evenings full in the meantime, talking with her mom, Nicole, Suzanne, and Beth for at least an hour each at some point during the week. She mustered the courage to call Jake and explain that Memorial Day weekend just wasn't a great time for her. She didn't offer any further explanation, because all the ones she'd thought of sounded lame when she rehearsed them, and he didn't ask.

In fact, Jake seemed neither hurt nor terribly disappointed by the rejection of his plan. Marci had definitely been imagining his feelings for her, she decided. They were friends. They lived a thousand miles apart. Sure, they joked about getting married, shared the occasional drunken kiss, and of course there was the one time in college . . . But that was just what it was, and nothing more. There were probably hundreds of little promises like theirs written on cocktail napkins across the country, and people pulled them out to laugh at their immaturity in the old days. They didn't follow through on them.

When Friday afternoon rolled around, she put all her papers into neat piles, shut down her computer, faxed her timesheet to the temp agency at 4:55, and headed quickly out the door. Despite her attempts to control her excitement, she bounded up the apartment stairs like a kid finally home for the summer. In her pocket she still had the folded sticky note Doug had left on her desk while she was in the restroom: "6:30."

She helped herself to a glass of white wine from the fridge and turned on the TV to help the hour pass more quickly while she waited for him. The knock on the door came at 6:29, and she forced herself not to bounce to the door to greet him but walk, like an actual grown-up person who had received visitors before.

Their reunion was passionate, but without the roughness and rush of last time. They shared a glass of wine on the couch and argued playfully about what kind of pizza to order. Doug rubbed her thigh under her skirt affectionately but did not push beyond that. With uncharacteristic disclosure, Doug explained that Cathy and seven of her girlfriends had gone all the way up to Round Rock to try a new restaurant and were going to a movie afterward. He had until at least eleven.

After the pizza, they made love quietly—conventionally— in her bed, in the dark, under the covers. She had almost fallen asleep when he began to talk about taking a trip with her, and it took her brain a moment to realize that he really was saying it. ". . . she goes on a girls' trip to South Padre Island every June, for at least four or five days, and I was thinking maybe you and I could go somewhere during that same time. Somewhere quiet, like maybe in the West . . ."

"You mean go on a trip together?" Marci said, astonished. "Wouldn't that be dangerous? How would we pay for everything without it showing up on your credit card bill? What if—"

"I have a plan," he said conclusively. "I just need to know if you want to go."

Could it be real? Full days and nights together? No work, no e-mail, no rushing out at dawn? "Of course I want to, Doug, but—"

"Good. Then it's settled." He wrapped his arms more tightly around her. After a moment, he added very softly, "I'm thinking of leaving her."

"What?" Her heart pounded so hard she could almost see the sheet over her bare breast moving with it.

"I'm thinking of leaving her."

"So this trip is . . . running away?"

"No, of course not. I guess it would be kind of a dry run. Just to make sure you can really stand being around me twenty-four/seven."

Her head was spinning. This was everything she wanted, and yet—"So this is like an *audition*?"

"No, Marci, no. Come on, that's not what I meant."

"What did you mean, then?" She got out of bed, grabbed her robe off the bathroom door, and flipped on the light. Doug was sitting up against her pillows, looking at her incredulously.

"I thought you'd be happy—I was just saying it would be nice to have a trip together."

"So if you're leaving your wife, why don't you just leave her, and then we'll plan a trip? Why do we still have to sneak away while she's on South Padre?" Marci's anger was incomprehensible, even to her own ears. She should have been happy he wanted to plan a trip; she should have been happy he wanted to be with her. Why did it matter that the two things could be happening in tandem? Yet she couldn't hold back. She glared at him, her eyes demanding a response.

He surrendered entirely, for the first time since she'd known him. "You're right," he said, looking down at his hands folded in his lap. "I haven't thought it all through yet, and I shouldn't have said anything until I had.

"It's just, these last few weeks have been hell, Marci. My marriage is getting more miserable by the day, and not being able to see you, to touch you, it's been . . ." He trailed off.

"I know," she said.

When he looked up, she saw that his eyes were glistening. "Marci, I am so sorry. I need to think more about all of this, and then we should talk about it and decide everything together. It just felt so good to be lying here with you again; I guess I got carried away. Please sit down, and let's just pretend this didn't happen, okay?"

Now it was her turn to cry. She sank to the foot of the bed, and he leaned forward to brush her hair out of her face. So many emotions churned inside her; she couldn't seem to label any of them. "Okay," she managed, "okay."

The clock next to her bed now read 10:20, and she knew he needed to get moving. He followed her gaze to the nightstand and said, "I don't want to leave."

"But you have to."

"Maybe I won't," he said defiantly, almost serious. "That would be one way to bring all of this to a head real quickly."

"No," she said. "Not like this."

He sighed, kissed her on the cheek, and rolled off the edge

of the bed. She stared at the worn hardwood planks beneath her feet while he showered and dressed, and it seemed like only seconds later that he was standing in front of her, holding his keys. "I wish I didn't have to go," he said.

"I know."

"I love you. Don't freak out, okay? We don't have to decide anything right now."

"Okay."

"Marci?"

"I'm fine, Doug. It's fine."

She walked him to the door, where he kissed first her lips, and then her forehead. "I'll find a way to call you early tomorrow. And whatever happens," he whispered, "we're going to be great."

7

For the rest of her life, when she heard the phrase "on pins and needles," Marci would think of the days that followed. Contrary to his assurance, Doug did not call Saturday. This did not greatly concern her until around 8:00 P.M., because she did not know what his definition of "early" might be. Even then, she was more annoyed with herself that she'd spent the whole day attached to her phone for no reason. By midnight, she was angry and ready for a fight. By 2:00 Sunday morning, she began to feel panicky. Missing their goodnight call was exceptional, even on a weekend.

She did not sleep well, and was up and dressed by 7:00 Sunday morning. She forced herself to leave the apartment, sticking her phone and apartment key into the pocket of her third-day jeans and wandering out into the clear, quiet morning. She walked a couple of blocks south from her apartment to Lake Austin Boulevard, where the mist rose off the river and Deep Eddy pool. She jutted along a dirt path to the river and followed the tree-lined walking trail for a while, her jeans and sandals looking out of place among all the running shoes and spandex.

After a couple of miles, the trail opened up again to the city. She fished in her jeans pocket and found a ten-dollar bill, so she turned north on Lamar and walked a few blocks to a coffee shop for a caramel latte and croissant. She walked and ate, gazing in the windows of record and book stores, novelty gift shops, hipster clothing boutiques, and folksy furniture stores—none of which were yet open for business. Everywhere she saw the slogan of the local, independent businesses, "Keep Austin Weird." *My life has certainly been weird since I moved here.*

She trudged north, with no real plan. Her mind drifted back to Doug as she walked, their conversation Friday night and his failure to call yesterday. Maybe Cathy's sister had made a turn for the worse and they'd had to rush back to Beaumont. Or maybe he'd been upset by her hesitation and was now pouting to prove how much she needed him.

She *did* need him. Even now, his absence was palpable and painful. So why was the idea of his being free to be with her so terrifying?

She left Lamar, heading east, twisting and turning until she was on Twelfth Street, following it toward the looming, regal capitol building. By the time she got to the capitol lawns, a few tourists were already out taking pictures of the dome against the bright blue sky. She ditched her empty coffee cup in one of the public trash barrels and turned south again on Brazos Street.

Saint Mary Cathedral was a block in front of her. The Gothic white stone and enormous circular window were beautiful in the morning light. She had seen many photographs of the cathedral reflected in the glass windows of an office building across the street, a symbolic juxtaposition of modernity and tradition, which many people seemed to think typified Austin. But this was the first time she remembered noticing it head-on. The doors were open beneath the beautiful Gothic arch, and people filed in for the 9:30 Mass. On a whim, she crossed the street and joined the parishioners going inside.

Marci sat in the farthest corner of the back pew, whose only other occupant was a homeless man muttering to himself several feet away. She was not Catholic and wondered how her Presbyterian parents might feel if they could see her right now. But the soft, monotone Latin of the priest felt comforting to her, even though she had no idea what the words meant. She wondered whether someone might approach her—in her parents' church at home, visitors were always singled out and accosted as soon as they'd found a seat. But no one did.

She watched as the parishioners kneeled, sat, and stood in some dance they all seemed to know by heart. She saw children coaxed into participating or occupied with coloring books and Cheerios, depending on their age. Young couples held hands. A few rows in front of her, a man wearing a gold wedding ring absentmindedly rubbed his wife's back. Women leaned over the pews to greet one another in whispers and silent laughter. She felt like a child standing on the edge of a birthday party to which she had not been invited.

This was the heart of her longing, and the heart of her fear. This was the one thing she did not have in her life in Austin. *This* was what Marci envied about Doug and Cathy's life together. They went to church sometimes, but it was more than that. It was late-night card games with long-established friends. It was the connection of their families and their second-nature devotion to those families. It was the rings they wore that told the world they were a unit, together.

She knew, of course, that Doug could—did—take that ring off. Marriages ended sometimes and people chose new partners, as he was now suggesting. But he could not know how small she felt, here in this room. How what they had built in her tiny apartment over the last few months felt insignificant in the context of an entire community. She wondered whether he really knew what he would be giving up—the card games, the couples' dinners, working on old cars with his brother-in-law.

If he left his wife, they would be starting over with nothing, no one. Would his family support him after he ditched his childhood sweetheart, who had celebrated the last twenty-three Christmases and Easters with them, for some tart at the office they knew nothing about? Would Marci's family and friends accept with open arms the older man who had obviously taken advantage of a vulnerable subordinate, and of course could not be trusted to be faithful?

Could they stay in Austin, where his friends would all understandably align with Cathy after she'd been so wronged? Move to Atlanta, where he would have to sell out his partnership in the firm he'd founded and start over working for someone else? She tried to imagine Doug joining her for a night out with Suzanne and Jake, or even Beth and Rebecca. What would everyone talk about?

When Holy Communion started, she stood and quietly slipped out of the church. She breathed the fresh air deeply and tried to calm her spiraling thoughts. *It was so unfair.* Why hadn't she met Doug before he was married? She tried not to answer herself that she was in middle school when he got married. Why couldn't she be crazy in love with Jeremy, who was available, or Jake, who might even want to marry her? But if Doug *could* be available . . .

Didn't it sometimes work out this way? So many of her parents' friends were on their second marriages and seemed as happy as clams. Surely at some point her family would understand and learn to trust him. And they could move somewhere new at first, like Colorado. Marci had always wanted to live in Denver.

They could escape all the history and start fresh. Maybe on a ranch. They could have horses. Farm goats. Make cheese.

Marci felt dizzy. Maybe she shouldn't try to think about everything all at once. She was suddenly aware that her legs ached from walking all morning and she was still probably an hour from home on foot. She rummaged in her jeans pockets to find a few dollars for the bus and her phone to call Suzanne. It was time for someone else to drive for a while.

Doug did not call for the rest of that day. Nor was he at work Monday or Tuesday. She had the horrible thought that he was in a car accident on the way home from her place, but logic told her that she would've heard something about it at the office. She kept thinking up excuses to access the file cabinets on the creative side of the office, verifying that his office was still dark and the door closed, but could get no information about why he was out. Was there a business trip he'd forgotten to mention to her? But then why hadn't he called?

During one of these forays across the office, she thought she noticed Tracy and Elena whispering and glancing in the direction of Doug's office, but she could not make out what they were saying. When she turned to try to see Elena's mouth moving, they noticed her and she had to quickly ask, "Have you seen the McDougal invoices file?"

"That wouldn't be in those cabinets, would it?" Tracy replied. "It would be in Victoria's area, right?"

"Um, yes, normally," Marci stuttered. "It's . . . just that we can't find it, so I thought it might have been misfiled here. Thanks anyway." She hurried back to her cubicle.

On Wednesday morning, her fears about his physical safety, at least, were laid to rest. As she got off the elevator, running late, Doug walked past her with one of the other partners, talking intently about a client account. They ignored her, which she told herself was normal, but she was saddened nonetheless by the coldness of it. No looking back to wink at her over his shoulder, no teasing reference to her as "Megan."

She tried to focus on her work and to remember their conversation Friday night. He was thinking of leaving his wife to be with her, for heaven's sake. This odd behavior couldn't be about *her*. Marci had given him no reason to be angry with her, so that couldn't have been the problem. Unless you counted being a little taken aback by his whole proposition, but who wouldn't be? Surely he didn't blame her for that?

There had to be some other explanation. Maybe he was preparing to leave Cathy and wanted to be on his best behavior in the meantime. She thought about all the TV shows she had seen where couples got divorced and where the spouse who had committed infidelity always got nailed in court. If he were getting ready to leave Cathy, they would have to be extracareful not to be found out. Maybe the seriousness of his new mind-set also had him being more cautious. If that was the case, Marci was glad. She always thought he had been a little reckless . . .

She decided to focus on the positive possibilities. Despite her hesitance over the weekend, she now realized that she would give just about anything to sit and talk with Doug again, and have him push her hair back from her face. That had to mean something.

When no one was looking, she went to a couple of Denver real estate Web sites just for fun and searched for ranches for sale. It was a silly exercise, she knew, but it was calming to look at the pictures of wide open spaces and mountain views. She pictured herself standing on a rough-hewn porch at sunrise with a cup of coffee, looking off into the majestic distance, and Doug quietly coming up behind her and wrapping her in his arms. In this fantasy, they shared an enormous workspace where he ran an advertising consultancy and she wrote all day, her hair held up by a pencil . . .

Just after 2:30, her heart skipped a beat when she looked up and saw Doug walking through their department. He nodded at her and then at Jeremy in one smooth motion, courteous but professional. He looked exhausted. His golden hair was a disheveled mess, and there were dark circles under his eyes. He passed them and went into Victoria's office and closed the door. She saw Jeremy glance at her before turning back to his work.

He emerged a half hour later, and she hoped he would stop by her desk, but Victoria walked with him down the hall. Victoria, at least, did not seem to sense that anything was amiss. She was chatting animatedly about a band she had seen that weekend.

Just before the end of the day, an e-mail from Doug popped up in Marci's inbox. *"Are you available to stay late this afternoon?"*

Relief washed over her. *Finally.* She noticed that he'd been careful to make the e-mail sound appropriate from a vice president to a temporary office worker. Maybe he was learning something about discretion.

She typed back hurriedly. *"Sure! Whatever you need, Mr. Stanton."* She hoped the veiled flirtation of her response would at least make him smile. She'd never seen him look so worn down.

The response came a few minutes later. *"Great—just stop by my office when everyone over there is done for the day."* She knew this meant to wait until the office was deserted so that they could be alone. Her memory drifted back to their first out-of-control kiss, which had taken place in that office more than six months before. If she had only known.

Part of her wanted to refuse to stay late to talk to him. Why would she have nothing better to do but wait for it to be convenient for him? Why shouldn't he suffer in the same uncertainty she'd been living with for days? She knew she should want to hurt him as much as he had hurt her. But all her anger, frustration, and fear from the last few days had evaporated, pushed aside by the excitement of being in the same room with him, talking to him, having her curiosity satisfied. Maybe today they would start devising a plan for moving forward. She warned herself that he might need to cool things off for a bit while he settled things with Cathy. She prepared herself to be supportive and understanding.

Then it occurred to her—*he has already told Cathy he's leaving*. It explained everything: the tired face, the lack of communication with Marci for all that time, the absence from work. She could only imagine the hell he must have been through. They probably had a big fight; poor Cathy must have been devastated. Doug was a good man: he would've stayed with her, comforting her, trying to help her understand. Maybe one of them had been packing.

The end of business seemed to come in slow motion. Jeremy dawdled at his desk, finishing reports for the next day. Victoria came back upstairs twice after forgetting first her keys and then her workout shoes. Marci kept trying to look as if she were packing up so she wouldn't get in trouble for trying to milk extra hours on the clock. The custodian stopped to chat about his new granddaughter and showed her a picture. The baby was adorable, but to Marci at that moment she could've been a pet rock for all she cared. Still, she smiled and oohed and aahed and congratulated him.

When everyone was finally gone and the office dark, Marci made her way to Doug's office. He was facing away from the door when she walked in, so she sat in a chair and waited as he typed. She heard a shuffling noise down the hall and asked softly, "Would you like me to close the door?"

He did not turn around, but gave a terse "No." Then he seemed to consider for a moment and added less coldly, "No, that's okay. I'll be just a second."

The excitement of being alone in a room with him began to leak out of her, and her knees trembled. *Jesus, what was going on?* His typing was quick and purposeful. A few clicks of the mouse, and he swiveled around. He looked awful.

"I need to apologize," he said abruptly, "for the other night. I got carried away, and in the end it is going to cause both of us more pain. So, I'm sorry."

She could not process this. What was he talking about, *more pain*? She looked around nervously at the source of the shuffling sound a few offices away. He followed her gaze but said nothing else. He was waiting.

"I'm . . . I'm not sure what to say," she said. It was true. A lump in her throat threatened to choke off her air supply.

He looked at her directly with his tired eyes and took a deep breath. Very softly, he said, "I have to end it. You and me. It has to end."

Marci could not breathe. "What?" she managed. Against her will, a whimpering sort of sob convulsed out of her throat.

This time he looked up at the door. She tried to choke down the sobs, which only made it worse.

"Take notes," he muttered, and handed her a legal pad from the desk. She stared at it in disbelief, thinking this must be some kind of cruel, horrible joke.

A couple of seconds later, Doug said to the doorway over her head, "Hi, Frank. Taking off?"

"Yeah. What are you doing here so late, Stanton?"

"Just going over some last-minute numbers before the

meeting tomorrow. And getting some help with that thing for Victoria." He gestured toward Marci vaguely.

Frank Dodgen, the *D* in TDL & S, had never formally met Marci before, though he had smiled politely at her as she passed in the hall, and she had done some work for him through his secretary. She felt him shift behind her, probably to acknowledge her presence, but she could not turn around with tears running down her cheeks.

Doug interrupted quickly, "Are you headed to the bar?" The partners, Marci knew, had a standing night out once a month in the back of the Ginger Man.

"Yeah," Frank answered.

"Do me a favor—pick up some good cigars this time, would ya? None of those nasty things you brought last time . . ."

They debated for a moment the merits of various cigars, and Frank's apparent failure to buy those that the rest of the group found acceptable. This gave Marci time to wipe her eyes as covertly as possible and to take a couple of deep breaths while pretending to look diligently down at the notepad.

". . . Well, I guess I need to ask the wife for a bigger cigar budget from now on. I'm sure that will go over great." Frank chuckled warmly and turned to Marci to include her in this little joke at his wife's expense. She managed to look up at him and fake a smile.

"Well, goodnight. And, Marci"—she was shocked that Frank Dodgen knew her name—"don't let this asshole keep you here too late, okay? We can't afford too much overtime this month."

"Shut up, Frank. I'll see you in thirty." Doug began rattling off some random instructions to her, which she absurdly wrote down, while both listened for the sound of the elevator and Frank leaving for the night.

Then she looked up at him, appealing with her eyes for him

to return to sanity and say anything that made sense. Anything at all.

They stared at each other for a moment, and then his cold expression softened a bit. "Look, Marci, I really am sorry to do it like this. You"—he paused, considering—"you deserve better than this. But then, that's what I've always told you."

Her fingers rose automatically to the necklace at her throat. Doug's gaze followed her movement, and he flinched slightly before continuing.

"I guess the best thing to do is just tell you the truth. I never imagined it ending like this; I never thought that we . . . that what we had would end here. But I guess this is where it started, huh?" He tried on a smile that was more of a grimace. She could only stare at him, numb.

"There's only one way to say this, and you're going to find out anyway, so it should be from me. Cathy is pregnant."

"She's what? How can she be?" Stupid questions, she knew, but they came out without thinking.

"I'm sorry, Marci. I always tried to be honest with you about my relationship with my wife."

My wife.

"There's more. She knows about us. I mean, not you specifically, but she knows that I was unfaithful." *Past tense.* "She knows that I have been having an affair with another woman. Apparently, she has suspected something for a while. But she followed me on Friday night—"

"Followed you? To my apartment?"

"Yeah, but she doesn't know who you are. She's agreed not to try to find out, and I've agreed . . ."

"To end it," she finished for him.

"Yes."

"She's pregnant," Marci said, more to the floor in front of her than to Doug.

"Yeah. Ten weeks. No one knows yet except family." *Was that excitement she detected in his voice?* He had always wanted children. She realized that soon he would be showing pictures of a sonogram around the office and half the women in the building would be pestering him to know everything about the baby. Another person was now in their little drama.

As if reading her thoughts, he went on. "So obviously this changes things for me. A lot. Even if I was thinking about leaving Cathy—"

"Even if? Even *if*?" Her anger came from nowhere and surprised even Marci. "I think we both know damn well you were doing more than thinking."

He looked taken aback, but maintained the icy calm veneer. "All right, fine. Even *though* I was thinking about leaving her, I can't do that with a child in the picture. I was a child of divorce myself. I could never abandon my child, Marci."

"Well, who the hell asked you to?" she hissed at him, standing and tossing aside the stupid legal pad.

How dare he take the high road with her? As though she had lured him to her bed single-handedly and tried to pry him away from his family? As though she would hear the news that Cathy was pregnant and insist that he leave her anyway? Bad enough she was ignored for days and then dumped across a desk under fluorescent lighting, but having to watch him paint himself the hero in the process was disgusting.

"So this is where you have been for days? This is why you haven't called? You've been out shopping for cribs, and it just now occurred to you that you might need to mention to me that it's over?"

"It's not that simple," he said.

"Oh, really? Well, do explain the complexities to me. Or do you think I'm too stupid to understand?" Her bitterness was unexpected, invigorating.

"No, Marce." With an exasperated sigh, Doug put his elbows on the desk and his face in his hands. He stared at the pile of papers beneath him for a while, and she wondered momentarily whether he was actually reading something. She saw traces of silver around his temples she had never noticed before. "No way out," he said, almost inaudibly.

When he lifted his head, he was again composed. The next words sounded as though he'd been rehearsing them. "I know you're upset. You have every right to be hurt and angry. You can even hate me if you want to. I deserve it. But we made a mistake. *I* made a mistake. And as much as I care about you, I have to do the right thing by my marriage and my family. You're a good person, and I know in time you will understand that this is the only way."

She wanted to throw things at him. Didn't he understand that his composure hurt her more than anything? He'd had five days to come to terms with this; she was learning everything now. It was unfair that he was asking her to rise to the occasion and be the bigger person. She had always known the end of their relationship was inevitable, and she feared it might not be pretty. She had imagined tearful good-byes in the car on a rainy night as they came to terms with the idea that it couldn't go on. She had even considered a raging battle in which Cathy stormed in on them one evening and all hell broke loose.

But never—in any of her morbid fantasies about the end—never did Doug extract himself like this. To be mentored through the moment in this condescending way, as though she could not grasp his moral obligations, as though they had not been partners in everything until now, was beyond insulting.

He had given her permission to hate him. And right now, she did.

Marci stood up. She had to get out of there. She needed to run and scream and cry, but she had nowhere to go and no one to cry to. The only person she gave a shit about in this town had just dumped her on his way to cigars with the guys.

"Doug," she said, not sure what to say next, only that she wanted his attention. He looked up with raised eyebrows, and it hit her. "Fuck. You."

She spun on her heel and walked out, grateful that her purse was on her shoulder and not back at her darkened desk. If she sat right now, she might never get up again. Doug had made no move to follow her, but she took the stairs rather than wait for the elevator just in case. She was unsure whether she was really trying to escape or hoping he would follow her, but either way there was no going back.

As she descended all fourteen flights of stairs, the missed opportunities of the last six months came to her in waves, as though her unlived life was flashing before her eyes. Nights out with girlfriends she had canceled last-minute when Doug found himself free. Three blind dates from which she'd excused herself, and a couple of nice guys she'd met on eHarmony who never stood a chance after the first half hour. She remembered leaving one date alone at the table four times during dinner to text Doug from the bathroom. He must've thought she had food poisoning or something. Jeremy's frequent and kind offers to take her to parties with his friends or catch a movie on a rainy afternoon. And Jake . . .

All of it wasted time. She was thirty years old and exactly nowhere. She had stayed on at a temp job for far too long on the false hopes of breaking into the business *(yeah, right),* and waiting for a future with a man who had chosen his future more than a decade before. Only now did she realize that this had been her secret hope—hidden even from herself—that somehow things would work out for them. Despite all efforts to pin herself down to reality, she had been carried away by the fantasy anyway. *What a sappy fucking fool I have been.*

She looked up and realized she'd gone down a level too far; her car was back up the stairs on P1. The stairwell now held the humidity of the Austin evening and smelled vaguely like urine. It occurred to her for the first time that she was alone in an almost-deserted office building at night, paying not even a little attention to her surroundings. What's worse, if she were kidnapped or killed, no one would know until she didn't show up for work tomorrow morning. Everyone who loved her was back in Atlanta. Everyone who had reached out to her here in Austin had been kept at a distance and trained to respect her privacy.

When she emerged into the parking deck, clutching her purse, she saw him. He was walking to his car with his beat-up leather briefcase in one hand and his phone cradled under his chin. He had his back turned to her and was too far away for her to hear him, but she could guess who was on the other end of the line. She backed into the shadows and waited for the familiar black BMW to pass her, oblivious, on its way out. She made her way to her car, put on the seat belt, locked the doors, and cried with her head on the steering wheel.

8

Fuck him. That's right. Couldn't have said it better myself. I wish I *could* say it myself."

Suzanne's outrage did little to ease Marci's pain, but it was
nice to have someone on her side, even a thousand miles away.
She was glad she had broken down and told Suzanne about
Doug on Sunday, though at the time she had been thinking of
it more as some sort of step toward legitimacy than a protective measure for herself.

For over an hour, she listened vaguely as Suzanne alter-
nated between asking Marci whether she was okay and de-
scribing in detail the horrifying things she would do to Doug's
genitals if she had access to them. It occurred to Marci that in
a previous life her best friend might've been an accomplished
torturer of spies and heretics. She replayed tonight's conversation with Doug over in her mind, looking for some clue that
would make the whole thing make sense.

She did not expect to sleep that night, but by the time she
had hung up with Suzanne and forced herself through her
nightly routine, her eyes were so tired and puffy from her tears
that she could barely keep them open. A mercifully dreamless
sleep took over and held her until the 6:00 A.M. alarm.

She debated not going in to work on Thursday but needed

the hours because her rent had gone month-to-month and was more expensive. Besides, she felt she had something to prove to Doug: she was strong enough to carry on without him. She wanted to prove it even if she didn't feel it. A thick layer of concealer helped disguise the evidence that she had been crying all night. She dug out a brightly colored scarf to detract attention from her tired face.

It was amazing how the rest of the world continued normally when her life was in ruins. The usual e-mails were in her inbox, the same small talk with Jeremy and Victoria, the same choices for lunch. She found that anger was the best friend she had at the moment; it kept the spiraling depression at bay. The stubborn desire to be as unaffected by Doug as possible actually made her focus better on work. She plowed through her data entry in the morning and actually managed to finish a couple of minor projects that had been lingering on her desk for a while. Though she was always alert for his approach, Doug did not pass her cubicle, and she made none of her usual excuses to go to his side of the office.

The day passed. Victoria stopped by Marci's desk on her way out that afternoon. "Got a minute?"

"Sure," Marci said. She instinctively went to hide whatever was on her screen and then realized there were no covert e-mails from Doug. There would never be again.

"I was wondering whether you had lunch plans tomorrow. There's something we need to discuss." Victoria's tone was neutral but serious sounding.

"Um, sure. I mean, no. No plans."

"Great. It'll be us and Candice from HR. You know Candice?"

Marci nodded.

"Great. We'll do eleven thirty at Carmelo's. I'm taking the morning off for something personal, so I will meet y'all there."

"Okay. Thanks, Victoria."

Victoria gave a noncommittal wave and swept out of the office, leaving Marci to wonder once again what was coming next. On the drive home, her brain excavated a memory of Cathy and Candice chatting chummily one day when the former had stopped by the office several weeks ago. Could it be that Cathy did, in fact, know who she was and was exacting her revenge by getting Marci fired?

She reminded herself that temp employees could be let go without cause and there would be no need to call a meeting with her if that were the case, much less a meeting at Carmelo's. They would simply call the agency and say that Marci was no longer needed.

Despite this very sensible reassurance, however, she did not sleep at all that night. She had learned that the worst she could imagine was not always the worst that could happen.

Friday morning, Marci used up the other half of a tube of concealer and stopped for a cappuccino with a double shot on the way to work. Between the caffeine, lack of sleep, anger, nervousness, and depression, she spent the morning trying to keep herself from bursting into either tears or hysterical laughter, never knowing which might be coming. With Victoria out, Marci was unsure whether she was meant to ride with Candice or take herself to the restaurant, and each time she stopped by Candice's office, she was on the phone. At 11:15, she tried again and found the office dark and locked. Clearly, she was expected to make it there herself. Carmelo's was just a few blocks away, and she couldn't afford to park twice, so she set out on foot.

After walking a few minutes, she glanced down at the Post-it on which she'd scrawled the address and realized that, while she was right that the restaurant was on Fifth Street, she was on the wrong side of Congress. That meant backtracking what she'd done and walking an additional five blocks in the opposite direction, and she had only five minutes. There was nothing to do but run for it, in the ninety-plus degree weather. Her sandaled feet pounded the hot sidewalk, breasts bouncing painfully as she went. A homeless man pushing a cart covered in antigovernment signs cheered for her wildly as she passed him. She felt ridiculous, but could think of no better option. *At least if they are firing me, they can add "lack of punctuality" and "slow runner" to the list of reasons.*

When she got to the restaurant, she was soaked through with sweat and completely out of breath. She steered herself to the restroom to see how she looked and almost wished she hadn't bothered. The concealer had caked with the sweat and made it look like her face was covered in mud. Her fuchsia T-shirt showed enormous sweat rings under the arms. She rinsed a paper towel in the sink and tried to clean up her face and then stood under the hand dryer with her shirt lifted to try to dry her shirt. It seemed to work, but it also made her face red and sweaty again. It was 11:43, and she needed to get to the table, but she wanted to give the dryer just a couple more minutes to work, hoping to make the sweat rings less visible.

This is why, when Candice walked into the restroom, Marci was standing with her shirt lifted high and hot air blowing over her body. Candice's face registered shock, just as one would expect, but like any well-bred Austin woman, her words were polite in the face of even the oddest behavior. "Hi, Marci. We didn't see you come in."

"Hi, Candice," Marci said, smoothing her shirt. She was glad she'd worn a nicer bra today, at least, instead of the beige standby with the fraying straps. "Hot today, isn't it?"

"It is," Candice said, still looking at Marci with something of an appraising look, but not cruelly. It was as though she was just sort of vaguely wondering what planet Marci was from, but not with any strong feelings that she should return there immediately.

"I'm sorry I'm late," Marci finally managed.

"Oh, it's okay," Candice said. "Frank was late, too. We're in the weird little nook by the bar." She gestured toward the back wall and stepped into one of the stalls.

Frank? As in Frank Dodgen? Holy crap.

Marci took a last glance in the mirror and smoothed her hair. The sweat rings were mostly better, she decided. Maybe not immediately noticeable if she kept her arms at her sides. The rest, well, it was what it was. At least the restaurant had soft lighting.

Frank greeted her warmly and shook her hand as she approached the table, but Victoria gave her an admonishing look behind his back. In response to both, she repeated, "I'm so sorry I'm late. I . . . went the wrong way."

"Fine, fine," Frank said, and then, to the waitress, "We'll have a bottle of Chianti for the table, please. Okay, ladies?" Candice was taking her seat, and the three of them nodded their assent.

After a few moments of staring at the very pricey menu, unable to concentrate, Marci was relieved when Frank tossed his menu on the table and said, "Well, let's get right down to business, if that's okay with you girls. I'm not one for a lot of bullshitting, as you know."

The waitress seemed to sense that this was her cue and interrupted to get their orders. Victoria and Candice both ordered Caesar salad with grilled chicken, so Marci followed suit, even though she was starving and would've preferred one of the grilled panini. Frank ordered an enormous sandwich with every kind of meat known to man.

"Well, Marci, I imagine you know a little about why we're here already," he said, and she glanced at the other two women, both of who wore neutral expressions. She did not. He went on. "I've talked with Doug Stanton—"

Marci let out a gasp that Frank did not seem to notice. She thought Candice glanced at her but couldn't be sure. She tried to keep her focus politely trained on Frank while her insides turned to knots.

"—and he shared with me your portfolio of work. It's good, Marci. Really good. I can tell you that Doug doesn't get excited about new talent easily, but he has basically insisted that we create a position for you. And looking at your work, I'd say he's right."

Marci could not believe what she was hearing. Was this really happening? Was she being offered her dream job?

"So, of course, Victoria, I'd like to know from you what you need Marci to do in terms of transitioning out of your department. Of course, we'll make sure we get another administrative worker. Candice, you'll talk with the temp agency? I'm sure we have to jump through some hoops with them, but we've given them enough business over the years; they ought to make it easy for us to hire Marci without paying an arm and a leg."

It was all but settled in Frank's mind, apparently. She had wanted this opportunity for years, and here it was. Solid, no interview necessary. Doug had made it happen. *Doug* . . . Was this his way of making it up to her? Buying her silence at work?

"Now, of course the pay won't be much at first. More than you make now, I imagine, but it's entry-level, keep in mind. Of course, if you're good, you'll do well and you'll be able to write your own check in this town. Kids who come through our office are never at a loss for job offers."

Hearing herself referred to as one of the "kids" was odd,

but that was definitely an improvement over "the temp." She would be moving out of her isolated cubicle and to the open, well-lit creative side.

Near Doug. Jesus, surely she wouldn't be working directly with Doug? Just being on that side of the office was going to be hard. Did he seriously think that she wanted to sit *closer* to him while she watched him get on with his life? Listening to the office buzz about his new baby, watching Cathy traipse in and out with her developing belly? Her excitement about her career faded into a fog of anger and resentment, and she had trouble focusing on what Frank was saying.

"Marci?" Frank said, obviously aware that he'd lost her. "What do you think?"

"I'm, wow. I'm overwhelmed," she said, and then added, "It sounds like such an amazing opportunity."

"Well, it will definitely be a learning experience," Frank said. "But listen: I don't want to put you on the spot today. I'm sure you have a boyfriend or husband you need to talk it over with." He winked at her kindly. He knew damn well this was the opportunity of a lifetime and she didn't need to talk it over with anyone, but he wanted to pretend that she had some power in the situation.

Frank was slightly older than the other three partners, the only one who had not gone to college with them. He had sort of a "good old boy" reputation, but Marci could see that what he contributed to the team was deeper than that. His no-nonsense style seemed to keep the firm's artistic temperaments in check. He was also consistently kind, from what Marci had gathered. There was something to be said for that.

They spent the rest of lunch making small talk—company business, vacation plans, free concerts at Zilker Park. Of course, even in May, it was never too early to begin speculating about Longhorn football. Marci tried to show as much interest as possible in all these topics but found that she most often felt she was floating above the conversation in a weird sort of haze.

Victoria gave her a lift back to the office, and on the way she apologized for not giving Marci a heads-up about the job offer. In uncharacteristic disclosure, she then began rattling on about everything she had going on in her personal and professional life, everything from a botched six-week relationship that had ended this week to her ancient cat's inability to control his bowels and her unwillingness to put him down. It was more detail in one ten-minute trip than Marci had gleaned in the previous ten months working with Victoria. It seemed the job offer from Frank Dodgen had inducted Marci into some sort of exclusive club. The whole experience was surreal.

At Victoria's request, she spent the rest of the afternoon bringing all her current projects to a stopping place and preparing instructions for the next person. "Even if you don't start the new job Monday, I'd like to make sure we're prepared for the next temp." Marci had completed all of this by 3:00 P.M., and rather than wait for quitting time, she updated her timesheet to pay herself for the time she'd spent waiting for Doug Wednesday night and left the office without a word to anyone.

She could not go home, not now, so she went to the Speakeasy instead. She paid the exorbitant fee to park on Fourth Street and climbed the long narrow stairs to the rooftop portion of the bar. It was nearly deserted, but the bartender was already setting up for a long, fair evening outside. In a few hours, Austin's young professionals would pay fifteen dollars each to crowd this patio and look out over the city and the river to the south.

For now, she sat alone in the glaring sunlight with a dirty vodka martini and laughed sourly at her life. How had she gotten here? Painfully, she looked back at all the moments when she could have turned around, saved herself some of this pain and heartache. Each time the opportunity had arisen, she had plowed forward to her own doom.

Like the first kiss. She remembered it with crystal-clear precision: they had been standing behind Doug's desk, going through papers together late one evening while he tried to reorganize his files to make room for a new credenza with less filing space. *Brought together by furniture,* she thought bitterly, and pointed at her glass to signal the Speakeasy bartender for another martini.

Her memory brought up the smell of vinegar, the odor lingering in Doug's office from the sub sandwiches he'd ordered for the two of them and Elena while they worked. Elena had gone home more than an hour before, but being a temp who had no life and craved overtime, Marci had agreed to stay with him until everything was done.

While they worked, she and Doug talked about books and Southern culture versus Texas culture. They had both noticed that everyone north of the Mason-Dixon seemed to lump Texas in with the rest of the South, or even the Southwest, but the reality was that—culturally, ethnically, artistically, and even geographically—Texas really was a world of its own. He explained his impression of Georgia as a place full of barefoot rednecks with Confederate flags, or aging debutantes living in mossy mansions. She laughed at both stereotypes, and told him anytime he wanted to see the *real* South, she'd be happy to give him a personal tour. It wasn't like her to be so flirty—that was more like Suzanne—but there was something about him.

In the instant he had leaned toward her over a pile of papers, Marci had known. In slow motion, his face gravitated tentatively toward hers, and a little voice had warned her that this was wrong. She knew in that moment she was becoming someone she had never wanted to be, the girl everyone was rooting against in all the movies and soap operas. Ironically, it was the fear in his eyes, the battle she could see in his face that drew her inextricably closer. She had leaned into his kiss, closing the door on resistance.

That stupid kiss would've been the time to turn around, she mused, playing with the speared olives in her drink. Just pull back, appear shocked, let him apologize, and walk out of the office. But there had been other moments, too: times when he had neglected her for days and she had almost gathered the resolve she needed to end it. One rainy night in his car she *had* ended it, only to find him standing on her porch an hour later, soaked to the skin and pacing back and forth, his curls matted down over his forehead pathetically.

If I had been a little stronger, any of those moments, if I could have listened to my own judgment, I would not be here now. My suffering could have been my choice, and perhaps even healing now, instead of this.

She thought about Frank Dodgen and the job offer: everything she'd been hoping for, the entire reason she had been wasting away in that particular cubicle for the past ten months. Yet it tasted bitter to her now. Why had the job suddenly appeared *now*, when Doug knew how long she'd wanted it? It occurred to her that perhaps he could have gotten this job for her months ago, but of course it was safer for him when she was on the other side of the office and he could pretend he thought her name was Megan. All this time, reading her writing, giving her praise and encouragement while they holed up alone in her little apartment.

Her phone vibrated on the table. Doug's cell. Calling, perhaps, to announce gleefully that he was having twins? Or that her new job would report directly to him, and that they could work side by side every day, she the doting young protégé and he the patient teacher? Perhaps the next offer would include overtime pay for serving as a babysitter for Doug and Cathy.

She took another swig of the drink and signaled the bartender, whose name she had overheard as Randy. He glanced at the clock, hesitating before mixing her another drink. She remembered Jake tending bar for a year after college and telling stories about the precarious situations when someone was clearly taking in too much too fast, but of course not wanting to put a big tip in jeopardy by turning down a customer. When he brought her the drink Randy said, "Can I get you something to eat?"

"Yeah. I'll have two extra olives."

A concerned look crossed his face, but he said nothing else. Clearly, Randy was choosing his battles. Marci had already resolved to take a cab home, and at this moment she wanted to think as little as possible.

In addition to her intense pain, what she wanted most to avoid was the choice in front of her, if you could call it that. Deep down, she knew that the martinis would take her only so far, and she would have to decide what to do on Monday. Take the job and do her best to ignore the overwhelming heartache? Continue her temp assignment for another week, month, year? Start over at another assignment, trying to explain to the temp agency that she had to leave because they offered her a promotion? None of it seemed acceptable.

Ten weeks, ten weeks, ten weeks. It kept running through her mind, and she imagined with horror a sonogram pinned to the bulletin board in Doug's office. She remembered when Beth had had her first child a few years back that Beth's name was always printed at the top left corner of the squiggly black-and-white image. Marci had always thought this was strange because the picture was of the baby, not Beth. She could not keep out the image that flashed into her head: a blurry little ghost on black filmy paper and the words CATHY STANTON in neat little white letters.

How big were babies at ten weeks? She knew Beth had told her at each stage how big the baby was, but she could remember none of it. She did remember that ten weeks wasn't really ten weeks, somehow, that pregnancy time was weird. Was it more or less?

Randy dropped off a basket of bread. "It's on the house."

"Thanks," she said. "Do you know what the deal is with pregnancy and weeks?"

"What?"

"You know, it's so many weeks, but that's not really how many weeks. It's some kind of thing . . ." She was surprised at how incoherent she sounded to herself. She didn't *feel* that drunk.

"Oh, you mean the age of the baby versus the gestation age," Randy said. In response to her quizzical look, he said, "I'm a medical student.

"They measure the weeks from the woman's last menstrual period, but the baby itself is a couple of weeks younger than that. You know, because of the time between the period and ovulation."

Marci nodded as though she understood this completely. He continued, maybe happy to be discussing something other than sports or failed relationships. "So if you're twelve weeks along—"

He stopped, suddenly pale, and looked at her empty glass. "You're *not*, are you?"

"Not me. My . . . a friend."

"Oh. So, anyway, if your friend is twelve weeks pregnant, the baby is actually ten weeks old, so she actually conceived ten weeks ago, not twelve." He waited a minute to see whether she was going to ask him something else, and when she didn't, went back to the bar.

So if twelve weeks was ten weeks, then ten weeks was eight weeks....

Her heart lurched. She pulled out her cell phone, ignoring the voice-mail icon, and brought up the calendar, unable to stop herself from counting backward. Eight weeks ago would have been just after her birthday. Doug had given her the necklace, told her he loved her, and, sometime in the next few days, had gotten his wife pregnant. Her stomach churned ominously. She reached for the bread, but it felt dry and chewy in her mouth. She could not swallow.

In seconds, she was up and stumbling toward the dark entry to the narrow stairwell, grasping the railing to avoid falling. Four or five young guys were making their way up to the roof, talking animatedly. At first, they did not step aside for her, and for a second she thought she would fall into them and they would all go careening down the stairs together. But the second guy in line noticed her face and tugged frantically on the sleeve of the friend in front of him. "Move, move, *move!*"

They all plastered themselves against the wall to make way for her, looking horrified, and she could not stop to express gratitude. The pallid old restrooms were almost halfway down the long stairwell. Had they been even three steps farther down, she would not have made it. She had no time to lock the stall door or even wipe down the toilet seat before she fell to her knees, retched, and vomited clear liquid, which burned her throat and elicited sympathetic whispers from a couple of waitresses primping in front of the mirror. "Been there, honey," one said.

Never in her life had Marci felt so alone. When the heaving stopped, she went to the sink and splashed water on her face, pulled herself back up the stairs, and asked Randy numbly for a Coke to wash the bile taste out of her mouth.

"Closing out?" he asked. She nodded.

"I'll call you a cab." It was not an offer, and it did not occur to Marci to object. She took the plastic cup full of soda and walked to the opposite side of the patio, where twilight painted the busy little city in sort of a soft trance. She floated above herself and downtown Austin as she looked over the railing at the traffic below.

As she stared down at people coming and going from work to home and back out to the clubs and restaurants downtown, her body began to lean forward. Somewhere in the back of her brain floated a simple but dangerous message: *It would be so easy. This could all be over.*

A car horn blew, and she snapped back to herself. Her heart pounded. She hurried back to the bar, signed the credit card slip, and followed a hostess, whom Randy had apparently recruited, downstairs to where the cab waited for her.

It took forever for the cab to weave its way off Fourth Street, but once it did she seemed to arrive at her apartment stairs just seconds later. She staggered up, stood mindlessly in the kitchen for a few minutes, deciding whether to eat something, and then just fell into bed without even removing her shoes.

Marci awoke at 1:15 A.M., sweating and stiff from sleeping in her work clothes. When she sat up, her head swam dangerously and the room spun around her. She used her hand to steady herself against the mattress. The phone was not difficult to find, lying in the middle of her bedroom floor. It told her there were now three voice-mail messages, but she did not check them. None was from the person she had to call now.

It was 2:15 in Georgia, she realized as it rang. Too late to hang up now.

"Hello?" Jake's voice was rough and sleepy.

"Hey," she whispered, almost inaudibly. "It's Marci."

"Hey, sweetheart . . . You okay? It's late."

"I know, I'm sorry. Jake, I have to get out of here. I . . ." She teetered on the edge of it, and then courage failed her. "I lost my job," she finished feebly. Her cowardice was ridiculous. Jake was one of her closest friends. She didn't owe Doug anything anymore, least of all discretion.

"What? Marce, you're not making sense. Have you been drinking? Are you safe?"

"I'm fine," she said, failing to convince even herself. From nowhere, sobs engulfed her throat, and she could barely speak. When she managed to get it out, it was barely a whisper. "I just—I just need to come home."

Thirty seconds of silence stretched out; she cried helplessly and half-wondered whether Jake had hung up, or perhaps decided this was too absurd to be reality and fallen back asleep. But when he did speak again, his voice was controlled and coherent. "Can you pack tomorrow? Do you have someone to help you?"

She nodded, and then, realizing this was a phone call, squeaked, "Yes. I'll ask someone."

"Okay," said the voice that had reassured and supported her for more than a decade. "I'll rent the truck and see you Sunday morning."

9

Athens, Georgia—June 2001

One sunny day, early in the summer before her junior year of college, Marci sat at an iron patio table outside Blue Sky Coffee on College Avenue. She was smoking a cigarette and pretending to read *Anna Karenina*. This charade was hardly necessary, both because she had read the book three times in the past year, and because anyone who might care what she was reading had either gone home until September or was at the beach, soaking up the last days of a break before the summer semester started.

These weeks were a quiet time in Athens, when the population of the city shrank by two-thirds and the only residents remaining were the townies, university support staff, and graduate students too busy, or too poor, to leave. For the last two weeks, Marci had been living alone in a four-bedroom apartment off Riverbend Parkway, one of only two people occupying the entire building until Sunday, when a few more of the residents would grudgingly return to take up their studies during summer semester.

Her solitude for the last two weeks had been primarily self-inflicted. Of course, she had the option of going home to her parents' house between semesters or taking the summer off entirely before her junior year, but something pulled her to stay. Theoretically, she was prepping for an intense summer of three full classes, or at least this was the reason she gave her dad to explain that she was not making the hourlong drive to their suburban Atlanta home during the break.

But the reality was harder to explain: it had something to do with the relaxed, chatty demeanor of normally surly downtown vendors and the absolute quiet in the gray dusk of the oversize apartment. This was a college town's twilight time, and Marci felt more at home here now than she did during the crowded football Saturdays or the commotion of the semester.

She couldn't deny that the wedding invitation tucked into the back flap of her book had something to do with her avoidance of home, too. Wedding chatter and forced squeals of excitement were not high on Marci's priority list just now.

She pulled out the invitation and read it again:

> Mr. and Mrs. James Lionel Walker
> request the honor of your presence
> as they celebrate the marriage of their daughter
> Elizabeth Lynn
> to
> William Raymond Sewell, Jr.
> Saturday, August 25th, 2001
> Four o'clock in the afternoon
> First Baptist Church, Marietta.
> Reception to follow.

Leave it to Beth to make sure her wedding invitations were in the mail two and a half months early. Now mid-June, Marci had done nothing about getting the bridesmaid dress Beth had

instructed her to buy. She supposed that now that the invitations were in the mail, there was probably no getting out of
purchasing and wearing the forest-green taffeta explosion Beth
had so proudly shown her in the bridal magazine over spring
break.

It was all so surreal, this idea of the wedding, even though
it was far from a surprise. Beth and Ray had been dating since
their sophomore year in high school, and had been pretty much
"engaged to be engaged" since the senior prom.

When Suzanne and Marci had begun preparations to move to
Athens for college, Beth had opted to stay home and attend
the local community college so she could be with Ray while he
worked at his dad's auto repair shop. When Ray had officially
proposed by tying an engagement ring to an ornament shaped
like a wrench last December, absolutely no one was surprised,
and both families seemed to be celebrating the union without
reservation.

"Huge mistake," Marci said, and tossed the invitation aside.

Only Suzanne knew that Marci felt this way, and privately
they talked about how odd it was to be committing the rest of
your life to someone before you were legally old enough to
drink. Ever since the three of them had met in the sixth-grade
cafeteria nearly a decade before, Marci had admired Beth's
combination of intelligence and practicality. She was the most
centered and confident person Marci had ever met; she seemed
removed from all the awkwardness and struggles with identity
that came with puberty. Marci had imagined Beth could do
anything. She was gifted in math and science, and teachers always mentioned careers like astronaut, engineer, chemist, and
doctor when Beth was around.

And then came Ray. He and Beth were partners in their
sophomore biology lab, through which she naturally carried
him. He was sweet and handsome and well liked. He held the

door for Beth whenever they walked together, no matter how crowded the hallway. When he brought her a cluster of daisies and a romantic mix tape after passing the biology final, Marci and Suzanne (and nearly every other fifteen-year-old girl within earshot) were overcome with jealousy. Beth and Ray had been inseparable ever since.

Marci lit another cigarette and closed the book on the invitation. She sat back in the chair and watched the bikes and cars go back and forth in front of her. She knew she should have been happy for Beth, but she couldn't deny the thought that maybe someone with the potential to be an astronaut-engineer-chemist-doctor was wasting herself going to community college and becoming a mechanic's wife.

She had sunken into a listless reverie, warmed by the sun and dangling the cigarette over the side of the chair, when someone sat abruptly in the chair across from hers. She looked up, shading her eyes. "Don't let me wake you," Jake said, propping his feet on the third chair at their table, pulling out a newspaper.

"Hey, stranger," she said. "I wasn't expecting to see you until next week."

"Came back early for Frisbee practice," he said.

"I thought the season was over." She remembered going with Jake to a particularly raucous party at the team captain's house after the last game.

"Yeah, but there are enough of us around this summer we decided to just play informally. We're going to Auburn in a few weeks to scrimmage with those guys, so we wanted to at least get a couple of practices in first. Suzanne still on her cruise?"

"Yep. You know Suzanne—it's a rough life."

Jake nodded and picked up the paper, so she did the same with *Anna Karenina*. They read for a while in companionable silence until he tossed the paper aside and downed the last of his iced coffee. "Did you take the bus?" he asked. She had. "You want to come to practice with me? I can drop you at home after."

Marci started to refuse, having promised herself she would get in a long walk this afternoon to counteract the cigarettes. The idea of returning to solitude, however, was not appealing. "Sure. What the hell?" She stood and tried to pull her shorts over the waffle pattern the iron chair had created on the back of her thighs.

They hoisted themselves into Jake's Jeep, a rickety old navy blue contraption that seemed barely street legal to Marci. He loved it, though, and refused to give it up despite his parents' frequent offers to buy him the new car of his choice. They rattled through campus and out to the intramural fields at breakneck speed. Marci was a little afraid she would be tossed from the passenger seat, but also invigorated by the wind whipping through her hair and the perfect sunny day around them.

She settled herself on a little hill that rose next to the practice field and watched Jake and his buddies toss the Frisbee at incredible speeds and race to outdo one another. For the first half hour, she kept up the pretense of reading her book, but in reality she found it nearly impossible to do anything but watch what was happening on the field. In part, this was a self-preservation measure, because she had to duck more than once to avoid decapitation by spinning plastic.

There were minor dramas playing out in front of her. Two of the guys—whom everyone called "Nads" and "Truck"—took every possible opportunity to argue about the rules of the game, throwing and catching techniques, strategy, and anything else.

Jake and a few of the other guys used the skirmishes as opportunities to make jokes and small talk at the opposite end of the field. Some seemed aware of Marci's presence. She couldn't help noticing that when the Frisbee came to the area of the field closest to her, there was a good deal more grunting, jumping, and tumbling to reach it. And lots of additional loud cussing when someone missed it.

Once she saw a couple of guys hanging around Jake at the far end of the field. Though she could not hear what was said, she thought they might be looking at her as they exchanged some sort of commentary and laughter. She felt self-conscious, as though she were once again the chubby girl being teased on the playground. She straightened her legs to hide her bare thighs, blushing furiously. But as they dispersed to follow the action downfield, Jake gave her a wave and goofy grin that set her mind at ease.

He had unpretentious good looks—kind of a rough-hewn boy next door, his hair streaked with blond from a week at the beach with his family and a whole spring of driving the Jeep every sunny day. This was not the first time she had noticed, of course. But there was something about the way his T-shirt clung to him as he ran, his tanned skin in the late afternoon sun. As she watched him, a Frisbee skittered to a stop just inches from her. *Snap out of it, Marci, before you get hit in the head.*

After practice, most of the guys collected in a loose huddle near the metal bench, which was littered with gym bags and water bottles. Some of them changed out of sweaty shirts and shorts right there, without regard for Marci's presence nearby, while others relived the practice with excited hand gestures and playful punches aimed at one another. She noticed that Nads and Truck stood at opposite ends of the group.

Jake approached her, smiling. "Exciting stuff, huh?"

"Not bad, actually," she said honestly. "I'm glad I came."

"Good," he said. "So some of the guys are going for pizza and beer, just down the road. No pressure or anything, but we can tag along if you want to go."

"Oh, I don't know." She was wearing the baggy shorts with the hole in the butt and paint splatters on the legs and a tank top that she feared exposed every inch of arm fat.

"Don't let him lie to you," said Truck, approaching them and slapping Jake on the back. "There's all kinds of pressure. We need a woman to keep us under control. You'd be saving us from ourselves. You have to come."

Jake raised an eyebrow in her direction. "Well?"

"Okay, fine," she said. "But you have to take me home so I can change."

"Deal," said Jake.

He waited patiently in the shared living room while she changed, obsessing over the right combination of cute and flattering, but without looking as if she was trying too hard. She settled on a denim skirt and scoop-neck T-shirt with athletic sandals. Small necklace, no earrings.

"Why does your apartment smell so nice?" Jake asked as she emerged.

Marci laughed. "Well, maybe because there are four girls living together and we have actually *cleaned* it since our lease started, or maybe because two of those girls are really into that kind of crap." She pointed at a hideous porcelain dish right behind him that was four little naked cherubs dancing around a bowl of apple-scented potpourri.

"Ugh," Jake said reflexively. "I mean, unless you like it, in which case . . . no, I'm sorry. It's just ugh."

"You can say that again," she said. "It's not mine. Ready?"

The Frisbee guys had already made it halfway through their first pitchers when Jake and Marci arrived. They were seated at a long, sticky picnic table on the patio, watching baseball on the big-screen TVs and arguing loudly about something.

Truck and Nads (who, Marci later learned, were actually Travis and Aaron) were at the other end of the table from them, arm wrestling. Obscenities flew around the table in favor of one competitor or the other and grew louder as Travis twisted Aaron's arm down to the table.

"Fucking cheater!" Aaron cried, jumping from the table in outrage.

"What?" Travis grinned. Despite the grime and vulgarity, Marci thought he had kind of a nice smile.

Aaron's face was crimson. "He stuck his hand up my shorts under the table!" The rickety wood table shook as the whole group collapsed in laughter.

"All's fair in love and war," Travis said, making kissing noises at Aaron. "Your credit card, please, ma'am. The next round is on Nads! Or should I say, Nads's mommy! She pays your bills, doesn't she?"

Aaron started to protest but looked around at the group waiting for his response and seemed to change his mind. He pulled out his wallet, slammed down a card, and sputtered away from the table, ignoring his teammates' cries coming from behind him.

"Oh, come on, sweetie, don't go away mad!"

"Hey wait! How come only Truck gets to feel you up? We all want a turn!"

"Tell your mom I said 'hi'!"

When Aaron returned several minutes later, he no longer seemed angry. He started a conversation with two teammates about the baseball game overhead. No one mentioned the earlier incident. *Men are so strange,* Marci thought.

Meanwhile, Truck made his way down to their end of the table and sat across from Marci, next to Jake. He stuffed half a slice of pepperoni in his mouth and elbowed Jake roughly. "Mmm . . . Didn't know you had a girlfriend, Stillwell." And then to Marci: "Did I meet you at our house party a few weeks ago?"

Before she could answer, Jake said, "She's not my girlfriend."

"Oh, well, then." Truck wiped his hand on his shirt and extended it to her. "Travis Fortner. Nice to meet you, um—?"

"Marci," she said.

"Marci," Travis repeated, holding her gaze.

"Easy, Truck," said Jake.

"What? Any friend of yours is a friend of mine, Stillwell." He winked at Marci. Another argument broke out at the other end of the table, and Truck got up with his beer glass. "Ah . . . Duty calls. Nice to meet you, Marci."

Marci smiled back. She watched him inserting himself into the loud conversation down-table, feeling he would do little to settle anything. Soon another scuffle broke out, and several guys jumped to avoid a spilled pitcher of beer. The restaurant manager came over to tell them all to settle down.

"Hey, want to get out of here?" Jake asked, throwing cash on the table.

"Sure," she said.

Instead of taking her home, Jake suggested a visit to a new bar downtown where a friend of his was working. Buzzed from the beer and relieved to be in friendly company after so many days alone, Marci was up for pretty much anything. Jake pulled sandals and a button-up shirt from the back of the Jeep and made his grubby practice clothes into passable bar attire.

"Sorry about the guys," he said as they settled on barstools in the back corner of the bar. Dark and nearly deserted, the bar thumped with insistent techno music and disco lights, as though a horde of people were going to show up any moment for dancing. "They can be pretty obnoxious and sometimes don't notice when there's a lady around."

Hearing Jake refer to her as a "lady" was weirdly sweet. "It's okay," she said. "I thought it was fun."

Jake's friend brought them two bottled beers and two shots of something that tasted like Lemon Pledge. Marci shuddered as it went down. She had not planned to drink so much, but it seemed rude to turn down free drinks, especially because he had been kind enough not to check Marci's ID. She was the last of her friends to turn twenty-one and often felt she was holding them back.

"Well, just don't pay any attention to Truck, okay?" he said as they slammed the shot glasses back on the bar. "He's kind of a player."

"Why are you worried about it?" she teased. "I'm not your girlfriend."

"No, you're not, but you're my best friend, and I don't want you getting hurt."

"I'm your best friend, really?"

"You are, by a long shot," he said. "I thought you knew that."

He looked at her for a minute and then slapped his hand on the bar. "Speaking of long shots, let's have more of that lemon stuff, huh?"

They talked for a while about the bar (pretentious yet grimy), the Frisbee team (fun but rowdy), and the upcoming summer semester (grueling but nice to have more credits going into fall). Before each drink was empty, another appeared in its place. After a third round of lemon shots and beer, Marci began to complain about Beth's wedding. "I just don't understand how she can choose to do this, to make such a big decision about her life before she's even old enough to *drink*."

She gestured broadly at the bar in front of them, as though Jake needed illustration for what she meant by "drink."

"I agree totally," he said. "That's why I'm not even going to date anyone seriously until I'm at least twenty-five. And I am not getting married until I'm thirty."

"You're not going to date until twenty-five? Jake, that is a waste! So many women would want to *be* with you."

"Well, I didn't say I was going to be a monk or anything. I mean, I'll *date*. I am just not going to get serious with anyone. I don't want to be one of those guys who marries some girl he met in high school or college and spends the rest of his life wondering what else is out there. You know?"

"Yeah," she said. "I really want to live *my* life first. I don't want to marry a mechanic and stay in my hometown forever. That just feels like settling, you know? I mean, no offense to Beth and Ray, but what about seeing the world and going to college and expanding your mind?"

"Totally," Jake agreed, emphatically swigging his beer.

"Plus there's the dress," Marci said, feeling free now to say what was on her mind, especially because Jake and Beth had never met. "They're so green and so puffy. I mean, I'm puffy enough as it is. And I know I will have to lose weight to fit into it. I always try to do that, and then I can't, and I end up with a girdle so tight I look like a sausage."

"I don't think you should lose *any* weight," Jake said, slurring only slightly. "You're perfect just the way you are." He put his hand on her cheek, and she patted his belly playfully.

"Easy for you to say. You don't have to squeeze your gut into a girdle."

"You're perfect," he insisted, now with both hands on her face.

Marci felt herself moving toward him in slow motion and

saw his expression change. The kiss tasted like beer and Lemon Pledge with remnants of the dirt and sweat from Frisbee practice. They looked at each other, surprised, and then kissed again with renewed fervor. As they kissed, Jake slid off his seat and moved closer to her. He wrapped his arms around her and let his hands linger on the small of her back. She clasped her hands behind his neck. Marci had seen couples making out in bars before and had always resented the public display. Now that the tables were turned, it was pretty fun to be the disgusting ones. She cared about nothing except getting closer to him.

The bartender returned briefly to take their glasses and whistled lewdly. "Atta boy, Jake," he said. Their laughter at this separated them, and they looked at each other, appraising and embarrassed. Part of her knew that this was weird, suddenly making out with her friend after two years. She ought to have felt uncomfortable, but happy didn't seem to be leaving room for it. For the number of drinks they had both consumed, his eyes seemed remarkably clear as he looked down at her, his hand on the side of her face.

"Is this weird?" he asked, reading her thoughts.

"Totally," she said, grinning. *God, what would Suzanne say?*

"I agree," he said, and leaned in to kiss her again. The thump of the music grew distant. She closed her eyes and inhaled him with every breath. After a few minutes, he whispered throatily, "Cab to your place?"

"Mmm-hmm," she said, nuzzling into the crook of his neck. He paid the tab and guided her outside with his hands on her hips.

In the dark backseat of the cab, Jake's hands wandered beneath her shirt while they kissed. Marci could barely control her excitement. She had always been attracted to Jake, and once in a while she had a fleeting sense the feeling might be

mutual. But he had never acted on it, and she had not allowed
herself to entertain the idea for long. Not so much as a kiss on
the cheek until tonight.

In the parking lot of her apartment, the middle-aged driver
heaved an annoyed sigh while Jake fumbled in his pockets for
the fare. When the cab pulled away, they walked hand in hand
to the front door of her dark apartment, stopping to lean against
it for a few more minutes before she located her key and let
them in. Inside, she wasn't sure what to do. Offer him a drink?
Put on a movie? Abandon all pretense and head straight for the
bedroom?

She had brought guys back to the apartment before, of
course, but always while at least one of her roommates was
home and generally after an official date. This was new territory: an empty apartment with someone who needed no introduction to her life. Jake, however, did not seem to feel any
awkwardness. He pulled her shirt over her head and threw it
on the floor, walking her back toward her bedroom as he did.

They undressed each other hurriedly and collapsed onto
her bed. After a few more minutes, she couldn't stand it any
longer. She reached into the top drawer of her night table and
pulled out a strip of condoms. He looked at them with a mis-
chievous grin and then back at her. "Are you sure?"

"*So* sure." Or at least she had been until he asked. She
paused before handing him the string of little square wrap-
pers. "It feels right, don't you think?"

"Yeah. And you're okay with everything? The whole 'no serious dating' thing?"

Even though the conversation had only been a couple of
hours ago, it felt very distant from where they were. Irrelevant
to them. She didn't want to talk about reality now. Hesitation
might mean ruining her only chance to experience this with

Jake, her best friend, who was handsome and funny and naked in her bed. Everything else would have to iron itself out tomorrow. She kissed him in response, and they made love without turning back the covers.

A few hours later, she woke up cradled in his arms and snuggled closer to him. He shifted, kissed her bare shoulder, and slid his arm out from under her. He began getting dressed at the foot of the bed. "Why are you up?" she asked.

"It's morning," he said. "I gotta go home."

"Your car is downtown," she said. "Can't you just stay?"

"Nah, I'll walk. It's a nice morning. You should sleep in." The words were friendly, but his tone was clipped and tight.

"Jake." She sat up. He was apparently focused on finding his sandals and said nothing. "Jake?" The hint of desperation in her own voice embarrassed her.

"Last night was great," he said gently, meeting her eye at last. "Really great. I'm just worried that it wasn't the smartest thing we could've done."

"Why?"

"Because you *are* my best friend, and I meant what I said that I don't want to date anyone seriously at this point in my life."

She resented his assumption that she wanted some kind of serious relationship, even after their conversation last night. On the other hand, she did not want him to leave, especially like this. "Can't we just have fun? Don't friends do that sometimes?" She'd heard about friends with benefits—admittedly not from anyone she actually knew, but still.

"Maybe we could, but . . . honestly, Marce, I don't think you would be happy with that for very long. The way you looked at me."

She felt suddenly defensive. "You were looking pretty intense yourself. I don't think it was *me* who suggested getting a cab."

"I know, I know. I'm sorry. I guess . . ." He studied a fraying spot on the carpet. "I guess I love you too much to be the guy who lets you down."

She slammed her head back against the pillow, regretting it immediately and remembering the lemon shots. She turned defiantly away from him to face the wall.

"If I haven't already," he murmured sadly.

He waited a minute or two for her to respond, but she could think of nothing to say. Everything he was saying made sense; he'd been very clear about it last night, and the way she was acting now only confirmed his theory. She wanted desperately to be casual and light, say something like, "Okay, sweetie, I'll catch you later," and mean it. She wanted to prove to him that she could be his friend and his lover and that it wouldn't be weird. But it *was* weird, and casual was the furthest thing from what she was feeling right now.

Marci heard him pick up his keys off the floor behind her. A few seconds later, the front door creaked open and closed, and she was alone again in the empty apartment.

10

Suzanne had been the one originally to meet Jake two years earlier, and had tried desperately for a couple of weeks to add him to her growing list of conquests. The three of them had all been in an enormous section of English 101 freshman year, taught by Cyrus Somebody, a moody TA who dressed in head-to-toe black every day and offered them extra credit if they attended his readings at local poetry slams.

Cyrus seemed to resent the fact that teaching basic composition to the great unwashed student population was among his duties, and he had a particular vendetta against athletes and members of fraternities and sororities. These students often found their weekly papers were returned to them not only with grammatical corrections but also with bright red insults that bordered on personal attacks. Although Jake was not in a fraternity and played only Ultimate Frisbee, he seemed to have been lumped into this category, too, because Cyrus frequently peppered his papers with comments like "sophomoric," "illogical," and even "shrug-inducing."

One day a few weeks into the semester, after Jake had been shot down for an in-class comment that was "obvious and pedestrian," Suzanne dashed out of the classroom behind him, dragging Marci behind her with a half-open backpack. By the front steps of the building, she managed to catch up to him and pull on the zipper to his bag flirtatiously.

"I didn't think there was anything obvious about what you said at all. I think that TA has a total chip on his shoulder, don't you?" When Jake stopped and turned to face them, Suzanne put on her most charming smile, generally known throughout the Southeast as irresistible.

"Yeah. Thanks," Jake responded. "I just wish I didn't have to worry that chip on the shoulder was going to cost me an F in his class."

"Oh, me, too," Suzanne commiserated. In truth, she had an 89 in the class because she and Marci had been religiously attending the awful poetry slams since the first week. Not only did the extra credit help, but Cyrus had begun to go easier on them as soon as they'd appeared at the coffeehouse for open mike night. It usually cost them two cappuccinos apiece just to stay awake for the whole thing, but it seemed to be worth it, at least for Suzanne.

Marci, who had a 97 and did not need the extra credit, was focused on Jake. He was leaning against the brick and concrete half wall next to the stairway, looking handsome and wind-swept as he listened to Suzanne politely. Marci noticed that he was still tanned from a summer outdoors and the mild fall they were having so far. The morning was cool and cloudless, and shade from the mature trees that surrounded the English building kept the sun from being too glaring. Set against the backdrop of a perfect fall day, Jake seemed to fit in completely with the surroundings. Marci was suddenly very glad she had accepted the scholarship to come to Georgia rather than splurging on an out-of-state school.

Suzanne's lilting Southern accent was denser and sweeter

than usual. "I do, too," she was saying. "I worry about it every single night . . . I can't sleep a wink." Suzanne had placed her hand congenially on Jake's chest, a signature move of hers—*make body contact as soon as possible; it makes them feel close to you*—and Jake did not seem uncomfortable.

"You know I can always help," Marci said, and for a split second she thought Suzanne was annoyed at being interrupted. If this was true, she didn't show it for long, and she embraced Marci in a sudden hug. "Oh, Marci! You're exactly the person we need. You should tutor us! You have amazing grades in this class and Cyrus likes you, while Jake here and I are both struggling."

"That would be awesome. Oh, and, nice to meet you," Jake said, with his hand out to Marci.

"You too," she said. "I'm Marci. Well, I guess Suzanne already said that . . ." She trailed off awkwardly. He smiled.

"Oh, my gosh, Marci, please tell me you'll tutor us in this horrible class. I can't fail; I just can't!" Suzanne was gushing with Scarlett O'Hara drama. Marci fought the urge to laugh at this ridiculous display. *Oh, well,* she thought, *I guess this one is off the table for me. What else is new?* Going to college with your best friend had its drawbacks, especially when that friend was a perky blonde size 6 who could out-charm any debutante in the state.

As it turned out in the coming weeks, however, Jake was off the table for Suzanne, too. In the frequent joint study sessions at the library that followed, she had tried every trick in her considerable repertoire. Everything from lip gloss and tight sweaters to a dramatic breakup with a fake boyfriend. None of it worked on Jake. He was kind, funny, and clearly enjoyed being around them, but he gave zero indication that he was interested in either of them. Politely ignoring Suzanne's embarrassing efforts to fall on top of him, he managed to knit himself into their social circle as they met nearly every day to discuss literature over dinner or drinks.

In a couple of weeks, Suzanne had given up on Jake and moved on to the far more lucrative conquest of her art history teacher, who incidentally *was* a fan of lip gloss, tight sweaters, and college freshman melodrama. Thanks to Marci's keen eye for editing and symbolism, all three had improved English grades. And thanks to a couple of late nights on campus and some thinly veiled suggestions about going to the administration and/or Dr. Kimball's wife, Suzanne more or less ensured she would never have lower than a B in art history.

Marci enjoyed the friendship with Jake. None of the guy friends she'd hung around in high school had come to UGA, and it was nice to have some testosterone around to balance things. Jake had a way of getting straight to the point about things, which Marci really liked. He seemed to say exactly what he was thinking without preface or apology.

Jake was also obsessed with movies, and he constantly dragged anyone who would go to the student center to watch artsy pictures and foreign films. Suzanne and Rebecca both complained about this and often found reasons to opt out, but Marci usually liked whatever he chose. She had never been much of a movie person growing up, and had more or less failed to see anything beyond the big box-office hits and whatever came on channel 17 on weekends. Learning about the whole world of independent films made her feel very grown-up and collegiate.

Fall of their sophomore year, Marci and Suzanne had moved to their apartment on the east side of town with two other girls from the dorm, while Rebecca went to the sorority house and Jake opted for a cheap apartment off Atlanta Highway with some other film guys. The distance did not impact their friendship, though: Jake's routine calls for dinners, drinks, and movies continued unchanged. In fact, he seemed to appreciate Marci and Suzanne more, compared with his pretentious roommates. "If I have to hear one more time that Akira Kurosawa is a genius or that Stanley Kubrick is overrated," he would say, "I'm going to jump off my balcony. Seriously."

"That's nothing," Marci said. "Rebecca has been intolerable since she moved into the Delta house. She keeps dragging us to parties and expects us to keep up with all the silly gossip. There are at least four Jennifers, and they're all blond."

"That's confusing," Jake said.

"Yeah, don't tell her, but Suzanne has started labeling them so we can keep them straight. 'Slutty Jennifer,' 'Anorexic Jennifer,' and worse. It's terrible, I know."

This would have mortified Rebecca, who idolized her sorority sisters without reservation. The Deltas, and the social connections that came with them, were Rebecca's ticket to everything she wanted. She downplayed her origins as daughter of a mail carrier and a housewife in Birmingham. Their senior year in high school, she had moved in with an affluent Georgia aunt who was a past sorority president at UGA, to establish residency and improve her chances of being accepted into one of the better houses.

This left her with little in common with Marci, who had no interest in climbing through the social strata and only minimal understanding of the world Rebecca inhabited. Suzanne, however, had all the apparent qualities every sorority would want. She was beautiful, charming, decidedly Southern, and a legacy Alpha Chi. That she had decided not to rush, despite handwritten invitations from the chapter president and even a few alums, surprised even Marci.

All of this social maneuvering had never seemed to impact Jake, who remained a fixture in their lives and on their couch all the way through sophomore year. Their easy friendship had continued, through midterms and finals, and through Suzanne's and Rebecca's leaving town that summer. Right up until the night of too much beer, lemon shots, and a racy cab ride back to Marci's apartment.

11

The night after Marci's drunken liaison with Jake, Suzanne and Rebecca returned to Athens. Jake called and invited them all out for tacos, as though nothing had happened the night before.

At the restaurant, he hugged Marci tightly and kissed her on the forehead, smiling in a way that was completely disarming and that ruined her plan to hate him forever. While they waited for a table, he said quite normally how much the guys liked hanging out with Marci and that he hoped she would come to some of his summer games. He added to Suzanne and Rebecca, "Of course, you girls are welcome, too. The guys always love a female audience. It makes us act like idiots." He winked at Marci on this last comment, and she looked away quickly.

A couple of hours later, as the apartment door closed behind a departing Rebecca, Suzanne rounded on Marci, still holding a leftover enchilada in a takeout box. "Oh my God! You had sex with Jake!"

Marci felt the blood rush to her face. "No, I didn't!"

Then, under Suzanne's pointed stare, she let out a distressed moan. "Oh, God. You can tell. How stupid am I? It's totally going to ruin our friendship. I was so drunk."

"Never mind that. How was it?"

Marci's blush deepened.

"Oh, my," Suzanne said. "That good?"

Marci nodded reluctantly. "Such a bad idea."

"*Totally* bad idea," Suzanne agreed, though her voice was still exuberant. Marci couldn't tell whether she was impressed that Marci had managed to snag a guy who had rejected Suzanne or just pleased with herself for figuring out a juicy piece of gossip. "I'll get the ice cream, huh?"

"Please."

Saturdays in Athens were always more colorful and laid-back in the summer. The townies, who typically stuck to the more outlying bars and restaurants to escape the crowds of the school year, ventured downtown to help fill up the patios and slurp frozen cocktails. Besides the college-student uniform of frayed khakis and tattered baseball caps, now there were the black fingernails and nose rings of the local goths, and Hawaiian shirts and sandals sported by middle-aged residents, some of whom had started as students a decade or two earlier and never left. During summer semester, even the most swamped and ambitious students seemed to feel they were due a few hours to relax on Saturday night.

Suzanne, Rebecca, and Marci had spent the afternoon watching the Frisbee team scrimmage against a club from Valdosta, who were smaller in number and less organized than the UGA group. After an easy couple of victories, Jake's team invited their opponents, and the girls, out for a night on the town. They crowded a pizza place for dinner and then made their collective way to an equally cheap and dirty bar known for its pool tables, nickel drinks, and loose interpretation of underage drinking laws.

Drinks were definitely in order tonight. So far, Marci's

semester had been more or less disastrous. On top of the awkwardness with Jake, she had managed to get the one Spanish 201 teacher on campus who actually expected students to do voluminous amounts of work in order to complete his class. Spanish homework. In the summer. While most of her peers were meeting with their TAs at the local Mexican restaurant to do "informal conversational practice" over margaritas once a week, Señor Vasquez was about a hundred years old and expected translated portions of great literary works every class. Introduction to World History was going to require more reading than any English class she'd had so far, and the professor of her Southern Writers class—whom she worshipped and desperately wanted to impress—had been calling her Melanie for the last two weeks.

The girls crowded around a tiny high table in a corner while the guys took over two of the pool tables and strutted for one another like peacocks with pool cues. They did shots between turns and sang along to the house band playing all the college bar standards: "Sweet Home Alabama," "American Pie," "Piano Man." There were awkward, drunken attempts to flirt, mostly with Suzanne, who seemed pleased with the attention but was keeping her options open.

One or two of the guys allowed themselves to be redirected to Rebecca when Suzanne went abruptly to the bar, excused herself to the restroom, or pretended to be deep in a previous conversation with Marci. Rebecca showed a similar lack of interest, however, having set her sights on a Valdosta player in a Sigma Nu hat across the room. Marci, positioned at the least accessible spot at the back of the table, figured that by the time they would consider talking to her, they weren't ready for strike three. This explanation was somewhat plausible and kinder to her ego than the nagging suspicion that she wasn't the kind of girl men came to talk to in bars.

The only exception, apparently, was Travis, or "Truck." He had glanced at Marci periodically, smiling or winking as he leaned in to make a shot. He was good at pool; he and his partner had been holding the same table against several challengers.

After a few more subtle attempts to do so, Rebecca managed to draw the attention of the Sigma Nu by accidentally walking behind his outstretched cue with her drink, which poured all over her in the ensuing accident. He apologized profusely for what was clearly her mistake, pawed at her chest with bar napkins for longer than was strictly useful. When he finished his game, he returned to their table and bought the three of them an apology round. For the rest of the evening, he did not venture far from Rebecca's side; by midnight, they had found a cozy spot in an empty booth to exchange pleasantries.

Jake spent a good bit of time at their table, too, and when Rebecca relocated with the Sigma Nu, he took over her seat for a while. Marci tried not to let her bitterness show, but the wounds of the previous weekend were still fresh, and she found herself ranging from frosty to downright hostile whenever he was nearby. This left him oscillating between normal, avoidant, and awkwardly solicitous.

"I'm getting another beer," he ventured at one point. "Do you guys want one?"

"Whatever," Marci said coldly.

"Well, I don't mind. I'm going to the bar. It's my treat."

"Fine."

"Bud or Miller?"

"Whatever." With a nice eye roll for effect.

"Um, okay. Suzanne? Anything?"

"No, thanks, Jake. Thanks for offering." Suzanne's voice was sympathetic, which Marci considered disloyal under the circumstances.

He walked away looking dazed and took his time getting back. Marci noticed that he stopped to talk with teammates and to chat with a couple of girls who were too dressed up for such a crappy bar, obviously drawn in by the concentration of guys. She watched as the brunette in a low-cut tank top twirled her hair and laughed at something Jake said. She couldn't help noticing that Jake's return smile seemed genuine. "Dear God," she muttered, staring at them.

"Sort of makes you wish you hadn't been such an ice queen, doesn't it?" Suzanne piped up helpfully.

"Thanks a lot, Suze."

Suzanne looked as if she wanted to say something, but Truck appeared at their table just then and sat down unbidden. "Hey," he said cheerfully. "Finally lost. Well, to be honest, I threw that last one. I like pool, but I have other interests, too." He leered at Marci as he said this, and Suzanne coughed as she excused herself again. With all her feigned trips to the bathroom that evening, Marci thought a careful observer would be concerned that Suzanne had a bladder infection.

"So, Marci, are you seeing anyone?" Truck asked before Suzanne was even two feet away. Marci was flattered by the attention and thought he was attractive, but wished he weren't making his intentions quite so obvious.

"No, I'm not. Are you?"

"No. I've dated lots of girls lately but haven't found anyone cool. Not like you." She wondered what was cool about her and how Travis had managed to unearth it in the ten minutes of time they'd spent together.

Normally, she would have called this kind of bullshit for what it was and suggested that he go find someone less intelligent or more gullible. She was considering saying something exactly to that effect when she glanced over and saw Jake staring at them. Knowing it was wrong on every level, she put her hand on Truck's arm the way she had seen other girls do and laughed uproariously at nothing. He looked confused for only a second before he began to laugh, too, perhaps concerned that he had said something unintentionally funny.

Across the room, Jake freed himself from the brunette and returned to the table. "Here's your beer, Marce," he said, taking Suzanne's empty chair and sliding it closer to her protectively. "Hey, Truck."

"Stillwell," Truck said, keeping his eyes on Marci. Applause broke out at the pool table closest to them as a guy in a tattered flannel shirt sank the second-to-last ball of what had obviously been a perfect game. Travis stood and stepped closer to register his opinion on which pocket the guy should choose for the final shot.

"I need to talk to you," Jake murmured while Travis was momentarily distracted.

"About what, Jake?" Marci's voice was as bright and innocent as could be.

"Don't do this. Don't"—he paused—"*whatever,* with Truck."

"Why not? Am I in danger?"

"Of course not," he said. "But you've been drinking and you're pissed at me, and I get that. I just don't want you to do something you'll regret later."

"Something I'll regret or something *you'll* regret?" she challenged. Her boldness pleased her. The concern on his face made her feel powerful.

"Both," he said flatly. Her heart jumped. The flanneled guy banked the eight ball off the side and into a corner pocket. The bar erupted in cheers.

"Well, Jake," she said in a teacher's voice above the din. "Unless there's someone else here who can make me a better offer, I guess I'll just have to make my own decisions."

Jake looked wounded, but before he could respond, Travis

returned and put his arm around her affectionately. "That was awesome. Guy could be on the semipro circuit."

"I'm exhausted," Marci said. "I think I'm going to go outside and wait for a cab. Anyone want to keep me company?"

Travis looked pleased at this sudden window of opportunity. "Sure," he said. Then, turning to Jake, he added, "If that's okay with you, dude."

"Is that okay with you, Jake?" Marci feigned sugary innocence.

He gave her an icy stare for a moment, finally shrugging in resignation.

"See you later, then," Marci said, and turned on her heel. She waved at a perplexed Suzanne, who was standing at the bar nursing something pink, and followed Travis the Truck into the night air.

When she woke with her head throbbing the next day, she realized with a groan that Jake had been right. She *did* regret bringing Travis back to her apartment, for a number of reasons.

First, the slamming front door at 3:00 A.M. as Suzanne came home reminded her that she had the keys to Suzanne's car in her purse, which meant Suzanne had not only stayed sober for no good reason, she'd had to take a separate cab home. Plus, she'd be charged double by the parking people for leaving the car overnight. In both the money she'd have to fork over and the time it would take to soothe Suze's irritation with her, it was going to be an expensive mistake.

From the moment she'd begun descending the stairs from the bar toward the downtown sidewalk, she began to hate herself for what she'd just done to Jake. She had been hurt and angry, but now she'd added petty and malicious to the list. While they waited for a cab and Travis pushed his beery tongue into her mouth, she had looked around to see whether Jake had followed them down the stairs. He hadn't; so she wondered if she should just go back up herself. Pride held her, however. She already felt childish and ridiculous. Going back on her huffy exit from the bar was too embarrassing to consider.

Travis was another issue. From everything Marci had heard about him, primarily from Jake, he was a player and reveled in one-night stands. He was handsome and confident, and Marci had seen him brushing off attractive girls all evening. In all her hesitations about her own behavior and assumptions that Truck was a temporary solution at best, she had never questioned whether she would *enjoy* her time with him.

This turned out to be a major oversight. When they got back to her apartment, Marci could not help remembering with shame bringing Jake here a week before under far better circumstances. She and Travis had raided the liquor cabinet and consumed shots of Suzanne's expensive vodka with squirts of lemon juice. They had eventually made their clumsy way to the bedroom, where Marci was prepared to lose her regrets in simple animal sex. This part would be easy.

Or so she thought. Travis turned out to be a very sloppy drunk, evidenced first by peeing all around her toilet, including on Suzanne's fluffy rose-colored bath mat (*add that to my tab,* she thought the next day). When he emerged from the bathroom and collapsed onto the bed with her, he struggled to get his shorts off and scarcely attempted to undress her at all. She tried to feel sexy and remember that she was enjoying this, but with each moment that passed it became more challenging. Truck was annoyed when she insisted that he use a condom and fumbled so much to get it on that he was unable to use it for its purpose anyway.

Marci was ready to give up and escape into sleep. But Travis insisted on spending the next forty-five minutes trying every way imaginable to arouse himself. This involved Marci doing a lot of unpleasant work while he apologized, swore that this never happened to him, and said, "you're so pretty," in a way that was more creepy than convincing. Finally, he let out a frustrated sigh and rolled over without another word. Within minutes, he was snoring louder than anyone she'd ever heard.

She was relieved when she awoke hours later to find him gone, and completely shocked when he called that evening to ask her out to dinner, "to make it up to her." She returned his call, knowing they would certainly cross paths again and to thus avoid being entirely rude, but pleaded a previous engagement to get out of dinner. Over the next several days, he continued to pursue Marci in a way that surprised her enormously, given his reputation and their embarrassing first experience together.

Eventually she consented to a few awkward dates with him, more out of kindness than desire. Selfishly, however, she enjoyed the impact this seemed to have on Jake—making him surly whenever she mentioned going out. She was pretty sure Jake knew as well as she did that nothing serious would develop between Travis and her, but his discomfort with the idea was a bit gratifying.

Over a couple of weeks, this became the only source of tension between them as their friendship returned once again to relative normalcy. Her anger with Jake dissipated with each interaction. They never talked about what had happened between them or about the confrontation in the bar, but came to a silent understanding: their friendship would not withstand pressing the issue further.

12

One Sunday in late June, Marci broke down and made the trip to Atlanta to the bridal shop to order Beth's forest-green monstrosity. The salesgirl tsk-tsked as she pointed out that Marci was the last bridesmaid to order—even flighty Suzanne had managed to stop by—and that she would have to pay a rush fee to ensure "timely delivery." Baffling, because the wedding was still almost two months away, but whatever. Anything for a friend.

Normally comfortable in a size twelve or fourteen, Marci discovered that bridal-wear sizes were painfully smaller than real-life sizes. Why the wedding industry collectively decided to take one more knock at a girl's self-esteem on the most beautiful day of her life, or her friend's life, was incomprehensible. As though the stress of a wedding didn't break you down enough.

Once she and the clerk had wrangled her arms and torso into a floor sample on the third try, the disapproving noises resumed. "Hmm . . . I'm thinking the sixteen is going to be a little snug through the middle. You'll have to order a size eighteen and alter down, because you're a little thick through here. The alteration fee is sixty-five dollars."

"But the dress is only a hundred and five!" Marci protested.

With alterations, rush fee, and the shoes dyed to match, the whole Emerald City ensemble was going to cost her more than $230.

"It's either that," the saleslady chirped, patting Marci's constricted belly, "or skip dessert for the next two months!" Marci left the shop further in debt and ready to wear the first size 18 dress of her life.

Back in Athens that evening, she sat at a high table by the window of the Globe Bar and complained about the dress incident to Rebecca and Suzanne.

"The whole wedding industry conspires against women," Suzanne said. She'd helped plan an older cousin's wedding the summer before and had resented every minute of it. "They sell you on the idea of this 'perfect day' and then make you feel like crap about yourself if you don't get everything just right. It's all about getting women to spend money by playing on their insecurities, if you ask me. Everything's marked up like two hundred percent for weddings, too. Bullshit. Total bullshit."

"Wow, Suzanne, you're starting to sound like one of those überfeminists in the women's studies department," Rebecca teased. "Maybe you ought to slow down on the rum and Diet Coke."

Suzanne scowled. Marci sensed a far less pleasant tirade brewing beneath her best friend's flawless exterior, fueled by Captain Morgan and ready to fire at Rebecca. It was a catfight in the making, and Marci had no desire to play referee between those two sets of claws. She intervened quickly with "Well, I certainly don't think that awful dress was worth two hundred and forty dollars—do you guys?"

Suzanne slowly softened her glare, which Rebecca had yet to notice because she had been examining a flaw in one of her fingernails. They both shook their heads. Rebecca, who was not in the wedding but had seen pictures of the dresses in Beth's catalog, took the reins. "Definitely not. I mean, y'all know I love Beth and all . . ." she prefaced.

Suzanne and Marci glanced at each other. They didn't know that she "loved Beth and all," because Rebecca had known Beth only during their senior year and never really seemed to click with her. Rebecca did not seem to notice their exchanged eye roll and went on unimpeded. "But, seriously, doesn't she know that forest green went out of style like ten years ago? And those invitations were so tacky. I guess that's what happens when you marry young like that; you haven't grown into good taste yet."

Marci regretted bringing up the subject of the dress entirely. She had just wanted to bitch about the whole experience for a bit and throw back a couple of sympathetic tequila shots with her girlfriends. And while she agreed about the dress and even the invitations, something about hearing it from Rebecca's mouth made her bristle on sweet Beth's behalf. It was like when she and Nicole were kids. Marci could pick on her little sister relentlessly, but if anyone else so much as called Nicole a name, Marci ran to her sister's defense. She had a sudden desire to tell Rebecca to shut the hell up.

Fortunately for all three of them, Jake appeared in the doorway of the bar before the conversation could go any further. He gave the bartender an easy wave and signaled for his usual pint of Guinness before sidling up to the empty chair between Rebecca and Suzanne. He paused at the empty shot glasses in the middle of the table. "Didn't know we were doing the hard stuff tonight or I'd have ordered one myself," he said. "What's the occasion?"

"We were just talking about weddings," Suzanne said before Rebecca could speak.

"Jesus Christ."

"You said it," she agreed, raising her glass to him before taking a sip from her drink.

"Did you know," Marci added, "that Jake doesn't want to get married?"

"Why not?" said Rebecca.

"Neither do I," said Suzanne.

A cloud passed over Jake's face as he looked across the table at Marci. *Good. Let him be hurt a little.*

"I never said I didn't want to get married. I said I want to wait until I'm thirty."

"Thirty is a good age to get married," Rebecca said. "But I'm going to get married at twenty-six so I can spend four years living in New York and traveling with my husband before we have children."

"What if you haven't met the guy you want to marry by twenty-six?" Suzanne asked.

Rebecca didn't miss a beat. "Well, I'll live in New York and travel by myself for a couple of years, and I'll meet my husband on a beach in Spain or something. And if that doesn't work, I'll go to my backup guy."

"I beg your pardon?" Suzanne looked baffled. "'Backup guy'?"

"Yeah," Rebecca said. "Roger Simon is my backup guy. We grew up together in Birmingham. He was my big brother's best friend and has wanted to marry me since the fifth grade. He's in law school now at UAB, so he'll be a lawyer, at least. If I'm not married by twenty-eight, I'll marry Roger. Plenty of time to get settled and have our first child by thirty."

No one said anything. Marci couldn't believe that Rebecca had so much of her life planned already, never mind the fact that poor Roger was her consolation prize if she didn't meet Señor Right on a beach in Barcelona. Marci could barely plan from one week to the next, much less think about what her late twenties would hold. Thirty was so far away; how could anyone decide now what they would want then? Apparently, Jake and Suzanne were equally caught off guard by these declarations, because they both stared pensively at the center of the table.

Rebecca took the last sip of her amaretto sour and slid off her barstool. "Well, I need to go. I have an early class in the morning and a rush meeting tomorrow night to get ready for. Kiss, kiss!" Suzanne rolled her eyes at this affectation as Rebecca strolled out of the bar without paying her part of the tab.

As annoyed as Marci had felt with Rebecca that evening, her absence left a tension lingering over the table. She wondered whether Jake knew that Suzanne knew what had happened between them. After a few minutes of silent sipping, Suzanne was the first to speak. "It's actually not a bad idea."

"What?" Jake and Marci said in unison.

"The whole backup-guy thing. I think I've actually heard of that, people choosing someone who they like and respect who they'll marry if they don't meet someone else by a certain age. Like thirty or forty or whatever."

Marci was shocked to hear this, particularly from Suzanne, who had no interest in marriage. "Who would do that? I mean, if you like someone enough to marry them ten years from now, why not just marry them now?"

"You mean like Beth and Ray?" Suzanne argued. "I thought you felt it was too early to get into a serious relationship."

"I do, but . . ." Marci stuttered.

"I get it," Jake said softly. He did not meet Marci's eye.

"You guys should do it!" Suzanne said abruptly, as though she were suggesting they all run next door to the Grill for a burger.

"What? No. That's stupid." Marci squirmed in her seat,

careful to look directly at Suzanne and not across the table. She was angry with Jake now. Why would she want to marry him in the future?

"No, it's not," Suzanne said, quite seriously. "I mean, you never know what's going to happen in the next ten years, do you? Maybe you'll both be happily married to other people, but if not, you can marry someone you already love and respect. By thirty, your biological clock will be ticking!" This last was directed at Marci, because for some reason, guys did not have biological clocks.

"What about you? You have a biological clock, too. Why don't you two do it?" Marci sputtered defensively. Of course, all three of them knew the answer to this. Suzanne and Jake had never connected, while just a couple of weeks ago, she and Jake had certainly demonstrated that they at least had the *potential* to be more than friends.

"What about Truck?" she added weakly. She hadn't actually talked to Travis in nearly a week, but Jake didn't need to know that. He seemed sulky after she said this, which pleased her.

Suzanne scowled. "Oh, come on, like you're really going to marry that Neanderthal! And anyway, if you do, certainly you'll decide that before you turn thirty, won't you?"

Marci took a long gulp of beer from her glass. Only she had objected to Suzanne's suggestion; Jake had not weighed in at all. Was she being petty?

As if sensing a chink in Marci's armor, Suzanne renewed her assault. "Jake, you'd marry Marci if you were still single in ten years, wouldn't you?"

He looked at Marci for the first time, expression inscrutable. "Yeah, I think I would."

Suzanne stopped a passing waitress and asked for a pen. "Let's go ahead and make it official, then. Come on, Marce, what do you have to lose? It's not like this will hold up in court or anything."

"Fine," Marci said. *Whatever they want. It's not like this is meaningful or anything. Just a joke.* Jake would be married in ten years anyway, to some blond heiress his parents had chosen for him, and she'd be . . . she had absolutely no idea. "Fine. But I need another shot of tequila first."

13

May 2011—On the Road

The cell phone vibrated on the seat next to Marci. *Doug again.* She ignored it and focused on the U-Haul in front of her, the back painted with a mural designed to make it look like the door was actually half-open and someone's neatly stacked boxes and lamp were in danger of falling out onto US-79 any moment. Marci knew that her belongings were not so neatly packed as the painting, given that she'd had only one day to get everything into boxes before Jake arrived with the truck. Still, the precarious-looking illustration made her even more anxious than she was already feeling.

The side of the truck was no better, depicting a meteor crashing into the earth somewhere in Iowa and creating a vast crater with the explosion. Small print provided some information about the significance of this—ADVENTURE ACROSS AMERICA!—but she had not read it when she and Jake were loading the truck early this morning.

She'd spent the day before terminating her lease with the apartment complex and packing furiously with her friend Wanda, who had gladly accepted pizza and a listening ear as payment. Wanda was the biggest gossip Marci had ever known.

They'd worked together a few years ago on a temp assignment with adjoining desks and had become intimate friends by the sheer force of Wanda's constant stream of self-disclosure, narration of everything she knew about the office where they were working, and, when the former two yielded nothing of interest, her opinion about everything she'd read in that week's *People*.

As they had stowed Marci's life haphazardly into boxes, Wanda had figured out after an hour of probing that Marci had no intention of explaining either the sudden move or her obvious tears. Giving up, Wanda had deluged her for the next five hours with gossip from the large company where she was now working as a receptionist. It apparently did not matter that Marci knew no one at the company and could not keep the various names straight. Wanda still gave her an exhaustive list of who was sleeping with whom, who was likely to get promoted, and even who she suspected was stealing the coffee creamer.

Marci did not listen, exactly, but she was grateful for a companion who could keep herself entertained while taping boxes and wrapping glasses, and she was doubly glad not to be alone. Wanda had stayed until nearly 10:00 P.M., leaving amid many hugs and promises to stay in touch after Marci was in Atlanta. With her sheets packed away and pictures off the walls, Marci had fallen on the couch after the last box was sealed at 2:00 A.M. She slept with the TV on all night for company.

Jake had arrived at her door around 9:00 that morning, as promised. Apparently, he'd taken the first flight in from Atlanta and a cab straight to the U-Haul place. How he had organized everything so quickly the day before and how much all of this was costing him, Marci had no clue. She couldn't ask. They had loaded the truck in near silence, talking only enough for Jake to ask her questions about the few items she had not packed: some were riding in her car with her and others were going to Goodwill.

Now it was nearly noon, and they had yet to stop for gas or food. The morning was especially cool and clear. They had chosen the back way to I-20, avoiding the Dallas / Fort Worth area and instead taking a greener, more peaceful route to Shreveport. It was how she always drove home to Atlanta. She loved the East Texas backcountry; the trees and hills and lakes were not the desert that most people imagined when they thought of Texas landscapes. Today Jake was sharing her path, navigating the awkward orange-and-white box in front of her, leading her home.

As she expected, her phone buzzed as they neared Shreveport, Jake this time, and they agreed that it was time to gas up and eat, and that she would follow his lead. He chose a clean-looking truck stop off the second exit they encountered. From somewhere he produced a lock for the U-Haul's back gate—another detail taken care of for her. She felt more gratitude for Jake than she could say.

They ate a greasy lunch in a discolored pink Formica booth, surrounded by souvenirs and supplies for truckers. The restaurant smelled like stale cigarettes and fried chicken. Marci could get through only about half her burger before losing her appetite. Jake did not ask questions, nor did he attempt to make small talk. This was something she had always loved about him: he did not feel the need to fill silence. Her phone buzzed once while they ate, and Jake looked at it but said nothing. As soon as it was done ringing, she turned it off.

They gassed up the truck and looked at the map after lunch. Jake guessed they could be home by 11:00 P.M. Georgia time if they only made one more quick stop around Meridian, Mississippi. "That's about halfway home," he said, "and we'll cross the river about halfway there."

Back in the car, she put in her favorite Old 97's CD, turning up the volume impossibly loud. She sang along, almost yelling in self-pity, letting the tears flow freely.

> *Valentine the destroyer*
> *Valentine you belong*
> *In the stars*
> *Where you are*
> *Always rollin' on*
> *Cried, I've cried*
> *Till I couldn't carry on*
> *It's a lonely, lonely feeling*
> *When your Valentine was wrong . . .*

By the time they neared the Mississippi a couple of hours later, she had listened to the whole CD twice and made a decision. She called Jake and told him she needed a quick pit stop, but not to wait for her. "I'll catch up to you before Meridian," she said, and he agreed reluctantly. She slowed until the U-Haul was out of sight, leaving the horizon just minutes before the enormous span of bridge that went over the river.

She had to cross the river before exiting and then spiral down to the frontage road to head north on Highway 61. She worried briefly that she wouldn't be able to access the river quickly and thought about scrapping the idea altogether to catch up with Jake. But before she could find a good place to turn around, she saw a sign for Riverfront Park on the left, pulled in, and parked her little Corolla.

The necklace was in her glove box, where it had been since Doug had made his announcement a few nights before. Had it really been less than a week since that horrible night in his office? It took a couple of minutes to cross the grassy area and make her way down to the river. As she got closer, the earth became squishy beneath her sandals and her feet stuck in the mud when she stepped. Two elderly black men in wading boots and with fishing poles watched her with apprehension as she sucked and squished her way down.

They seemed to be watching to make sure she didn't plan to get *in* the river, and when she stopped about six feet from the water's edge, they went back to watching their bobs. Even though it was often referred to as a geographic dividing line for the country, and she'd read books about how big the mighty Mississippi was, Marci was still amazed by its sheer enormity in person. She could easily imagine being swept away by the current. Looking left, she wondered morbidly how often people jumped from the I-20 bridge.

She fished the necklace out of her pocket and studied it, tracing a thumb over the turquoise oval. This moment called for dramatic finality, some sort of catharsis. Poetry, even. She wished she could remember a beautiful Irish funeral dirge from her British literature class or an appropriate Bible verse. Even the lyrics from an 80s power ballad would do. Nothing came to her. In the end, she settled on "So long, fuckwad," and launched the necklace as far into the river as she could manage.

It made a not-very-satisfying plunk as it hit the water, barely audible above the sound of the river and the cars speeding along the interstate downstream. Within seconds of it hitting the water, she could no longer see it and had no idea whether it had sunk to the bottom or floated toward the Louisiana delta. As she squished back up the bank, she imagined that some poor little girl downstream would find the necklace while playing by the riverbank one day and Marci's heartache would be someone else's greatest treasure.

It turned out that climbing back up the bank was not as easy as squishing down to the water. Her feet sank deeper under the effort of propelling her body weight uphill. Had it been this steep on the way down? She groped for clumps of grass to pull herself up as her left sandal was suctioned completely off her foot by the mud. As she turned to reclaim it with her toes, she slipped.

There are times in a girl's life when falling face-first into the mud might be fun. A soggy touch football game with friends. Making mud pies with the kids. Maybe even a wild day at the spa. But halfway through a thousand-mile trip, with everything she owned packed away in boxes?

Marci pushed herself up to her knees and crawled the rest of the way up the bank to more solid ground. She stood awkwardly and waved off the two fishermen, who had turned toward her in stances of reluctant concern. Brownish-red mud stuck to her palms and knees, and a large smear of it coated one side of her shorts and T-shirt. Her feet were more or less covered, and she was nearly an inch taller where it caked to the bottom of her sandals. It was in her mouth, too, tasting coppery and gritty.

She attempted a dignified smile at a picnicking family as she skated over the grassy bank, wiping her feet as best she could as she went. The little park had a water fountain with a low spigot for dogs' bowls, which she used to wash her mouth, feet, and now-ruined sandals. When she got to the car, she realized that throwing her suitcase of clothes in the back of the U-Haul had been a miscalculation. She had no spare clothes in the Corolla.

Fortunately, she had wrapped some fragile items in beach towels to pack them. Marci unwrapped a tacky but beloved garage sale lamp, which featured a porcelain mermaid she lovingly referred to as Zelda, and used the towel to dry her feet and wipe most of the solid mud off her skin and clothes. She unwrapped another towel from her framed college diploma and laid it across the driver's seat. She set the diploma and the lamp on the floorboard. "Sorry, Zelda," she said, and set out to catch up to Jake and the U-Haul.

It took only twenty minutes to regain her position behind Jake, who had obviously slowed a bit waiting for her, despite her instructions to the contrary. She flashed her lights as she approached the U-Haul from behind, and Jake sped up again to their previous pace. She dreaded the next time they would stop, when she would have to explain her mud-covered state.

In the meantime, the unanswered voice mail icon on her phone seemed to glare at her from the passenger seat, so she listened to the first two seconds of several voice mails from Doug, deleting them as she went. They all started the same way: "Hey, Marce"—and then the sound of her finger tapping the delete button. In her fervor, she nearly erased a message from her mom, who had apparently called while the phone was off.

Knowing that Elaine was likely pacing around the kitchen with the phone in her hand, as was her habit anytime either of her daughters was on the road, Marci returned the call immediately. She tried to sound as upbeat as possible as she updated her mother on where they were and how far they had left.

"Are you sure you don't want to come here, honey?" her mom asked for the thirtieth time in the last two days. "Won't you be putting poor Suzanne out?"

"No, Mom. Thanks, but I think it's better if I stay with her for now." Suzanne knew what had happened with Doug and was already preparing for when Marci arrived that evening. She had even taken the next day off so they could do whatever Marci needed. There was no way she could begin to tell her mother what had happened, and no way she could be around her in this weepy emotional state without arousing suspicion. Suzanne's was the safest place by far.

"Well, don't you be a bother," her mother chided, as though Marci were eight years old and going next door to visit Mrs.

Williamson, who had an old-fashioned typewriter she always let Marci play with, not to mention an endless bowl of Andes mints on her coffee table.

"Don't worry; if Suzanne gets tired of me, I'm sure she'll call you to come pick me up."

Her mother pretended not to hear this. "How's Jake?"

Even though Marci had been near Jake all day, she realized she had no idea how he was doing. They'd barely talked, and it had all been about getting Marci home. "He's fine," she said shortly, hoping to avoid follow-up questions.

"Well, it sure is nice of him to go to all this trouble to help you out." *As though I don't know this already.* "You're lucky to have such a good friend in your life. Your father and I were just saying how wonderful it is that you two have managed to stay in touch all these years."

"It is," Marci agreed.

"We were also wondering how you can be just friends with such a nice guy. Jake's cute, don't you think, honey?" *Oh, God. Not this. Not now.*

Before Marci could answer, however, she thought she heard her father's muffled voice in the background. "Hold on, honey. What, Arthur?" Her mother sighed after a slight pause. "Daddy says we shouldn't be talking to you while you're driving. It's dangerous. Keep your hands at ten and two, sweetheart! Call us when you get to Suzanne's, okay? No matter how late!"

She hung up, grateful for her father's interference as usual. Ahead, she could see the outline of Jake's face in the truck's side mirror and noticed he was singing along to the radio. It was the first time all day that she smiled.

14

As miles and miles of Mississippi rolled underneath her, Marci found her thoughts drifting back and forth between the man driving the truck in front of her and the man she was leaving behind. Somehow, she didn't think her painful relationship with Doug would heal the way things had with Jake. At the time, however, the heartache had seemed intense enough.

A week after they had signed their "contract," Jake had received a late acceptance letter to film school at NYU, where he had been wait-listed since the middle of freshman year. He had come to Marci and Suzanne's apartment in person to tell them he was leaving before the start of the fall semester.

Despite their disappointment that he'd be missing football season at Georgia for the next two years, his parents had agreed to support him in New York anyway. In return, he'd promised to come home for Thanksgiving and go to the Georgia–Georgia Tech game with his father. He was also planning to be home for the longer, if slightly less religious, break at Christmas.

As he broke the news to her and Suzanne, Marci saw that he was making an effort to control his excitement. He was going right into the documentary film program because he had already completed most of his core classes. The admissions officer mentioned that the committee had been particularly impressed with his sample submission—a film he'd made the previous year about an Athens musician and former heroin addict who was living with AIDS.

Marci had always thought the film was one of the most amazing things she'd ever seen, so at least the people at NYU knew what they were talking about. She felt intensely proud of Jake and shared his excitement, despite the fact that somewhere in the distance she could hear the sound of her heart breaking.

Suzanne, on the other hand, expressed with vigor many sentiments Marci was holding in by grilling Jake aggressively. How long had he known this? Was he sure he had to go? Wasn't the film program at Georgia just as good? What on earth were they supposed to do without him for the next two years?

He endured the inquisition patiently, and by the rehearsed nature of some of his answers, Marci wondered whether Jake's mother had asked the same questions. When Suzanne had finally decided that he could not be prevailed upon to stay in Athens, he turned to Marci. Her heart raced, and she felt that what was passing between them in the silence was something like this:

I'm happy to go, but sad to leave you.

I know. I'm devastated, but also so excited for you.

If I were staying here, maybe . . .

Yes, maybe.

What Jake said aloud, however, was, "Are you going to be okay?"

So much for imagined conversations. He said it with a tone of concern, but Marci could not see past the fact that Jake thought *she* would not be okay without *him*. What about him? Was he going to be okay? Or was it so obvious that because he was handsome and funny and going to live his dream in New

York that he would be fine, and that she was the one who'd be left behind in this little college town to pine away for him?

"Of course I will," she said a little too brightly. "Truck will take care of me."

She regretted immediately bringing up Travis. Jake's face fell, and he murmured something that sounded like "Yeah, right."

Marci tried damage control. "I really am very excited for you," she said, crossing the room to hug him tightly. "And we will miss you terribly. We're just going to have to pack lots of fun into the next couple of weeks, okay?"

He patted her back before releasing her. "Thanks," he said.

Looking back, Marci remembered very little about the ensuing two weeks. The reality of finishing the summer semester, transferring schools, and preparing to move to New York meant that Jake was busy most of the time. When he did have time to meet the three girls out for a drink or dinner, they talked about NYU's famous professors and their credits, classes he was struggling to decide between, and films he needed to see. There were maps of the city, pictures of campus, Broadway show schedules, lists of equipment to buy. They helped him pack what little would fit in his tiny space at NYU. And he was gone.

Marci had lingered in her sickly relationship with Travis for the first few months of her junior year, ending it just after she saw Jake at Thanksgiving break. By Christmas, however, Jake was dating some bohemian art student from New York who had blue streaks in her hair and talked about Marxism at dinner. By the time that had ended, they heard that Jake was staying in New York for grad school.

Meanwhile, Marci took her new English degree straight back to her parents' house and got a job in the lingerie department at a clothing store. Suzanne took her résumé and her high heels to every museum and gallery in town, eventually snagging a job as an assistant to the special events coordinator at the High Museum of Art.

"It's not related to art *exactly*," she explained to Marci over their weekly Saturday coffee date, "but at least I get to work in the museum. It's a foot in the door."

"Hey, at least you're not spending your life looking at people in their underwear and trying to get bras back on those stupid plastic hangers," Marci countered. "I don't have my foot in any door except the dressing room."

A few months after graduation, a regular customer suggested that Marci try a temp agency if she wanted more regular hours with better pay. She jotted down the name of a friend who worked in staffing on the back of a receipt, and in a couple of weeks Marci had entered the world of answering phones, sorting files, and being referred to by nearly everyone as "the temp." She learned to buy panty hose on sale and keep a bottle of clear nail polish in her purse for runs. She brought a tiny notebook with her to every assignment so she could write during the inevitable downtimes.

What she loved about temping was the constant change. She got to meet lots of people and experience various working environments up close and personal without commitment. She could leave at 5:00 P.M. and not think about work again until she returned the next morning. Social pressure to hang out with coworkers at lunch was minimal, so she would find a tree-lined spot to park her car, eat a sandwich, and write. At night, she went home to her parents' house and sacked away savings for her secret dream . . . to move away from Atlanta and find her true self somewhere out West.

She and Jake stayed in touch, usually by e-mail. He came home from New York a few times, and they would all get together, sometimes with the dating partners that floated in and out of their lives, sometimes without. By the time Jake moved home to Atlanta, Marci had loaded up her car and moved to San Francisco. She leased a tiny apartment in the Mission District, sight unseen, and took four months' worth of rent and utilities with her. She felt very Jack Kerouac, ready to become the next great American writer.

She managed to stay for nearly two years. One short-lived boyfriend, seventeen temp assignments, four magazine articles, and three bounced rent checks later, she packed the car again and headed home. She'd stopped when she reached Austin, the city that seemed a perfect compromise between San Francisco and Atlanta, geographically and culturally.

In Atlanta, Jake was working for a small production company that made commercials for local businesses. In his spare time he freelanced on a few music videos for little punk bands and shot game footage for some local sports teams. Suzanne got promoted to special events director at the High, Beth and Ray had two kids, and Rebecca worked some sort of office job no one really understood. Now it was Marci coming home to visit, and little crowds of friends appearing at restaurants to welcome her when she did.

Only once in the past decade had anything happened to remind Marci of their encounter in Athens that summer. She'd gone home for the winter holidays in 2006, including the obligatory New Year's Eve madness. The whole group had come together and paid a ridiculous cover charge to get into a bar they probably would've passed up any other night. It was festive enough, though, and while certainly filled to the brim with partygoers, it was the only place within a five-mile radius that didn't have a line out the door a mile long.

They'd been drinking cocktails and dancing all evening, and at 11:45, they switched to the free champagne. It tasted like SweeTARTS mixed with diet soda, and as they sipped it they made repeated drunken toasts to their friendship and world peace. Beth and Ray were enjoying a night out without the kids by overindulging and making out on the dance floor. Rebecca was dancing with a boorish guy she had met at work, whom she had to lure to the dance floor after talking him out of a fight with the bouncer.

Suzanne was at the bar, talking to the bartender, leaning over in a way that ostensibly allowed her to hear him better, but not coincidentally highlighted her ample cleavage and low-cut shirt. She'd been there for more than two hours, coming back to their table for little spurts of time with her bounty of free drinks. As midnight drew near, she actually hopped up on the bar and swung her legs over it with the bartender's assistance, ready for a well-earned kiss at the stroke of midnight and probably violating several laws about alcohol service in the process.

As the crowd counted down to 2007, Marci smacked Jake on the chest and pointed at the spectacle of Suzanne behind the bar, laughing. When she turned to him, however, he did not laugh, but pulled her close and kissed her deeply. She felt awkward that she had failed to mention a guy she'd been seeing in Austin for a few weeks, but decided that it was a harmless New Year's Eve kiss, and what Burt the math teacher didn't know wouldn't hurt him.

"Happy New Year," Jake murmured in her ear. "I love you."

She remembered gaping at him, trying to figure what to say or how to say it, but Beth and Ray had invaded their table with an exuberant but off-key version of "Auld Lang Syne" and broken the spell. The evening drew to a close shortly thereafter, as they piled into a couple of different cabs, and Marci returned to Suzanne's for the evening. She was on a plane back to Austin the next afternoon. By the time she and Jake had seen each other next, some occasion in late spring that same year, it seemed too late to mention it. Marci had dismissed it as friendly indiscretion, attributable to bad champagne and the sentimentality of the new year.

That was four years ago. Since then, nothing had happened between them, until the kiss in the bar after Nicole and Ravi's bachelor party. Another kiss in a bar. It occurred to Marci, as she followed the U-Haul off an exit ramp for gas, how many significant moments in her relationship with Jake had occurred in bars.

Maybe that's all there was to it. Maybe they were friends who occasionally got drunk and made out, or promised to marry each other later, or whatever. Maybe all of Jake's suggestions about the two of them had been spurred by, if not attributable completely to, the influence of alcohol. It certainly explained the lack of discussion afterward. How did she know the birthday e-mail wasn't a silly joke he'd thought of after sharing a bottle or two of wine with a large-breasted debutante?

As she pulled her car up to a gas pump and waved to Jake on the other side of the parking lot, she told herself that this was entirely plausible. There was no use in thinking about it right now anyway. She was covered in mud, her heart had just been broken by a guy two states away, and the last thing she needed to worry about was whether this friend was just a friend.

15

*W*hat happened to you?" Jake asked when she emerged from behind the car. The mud had dried on her clothes in a bright red-brown smear.

She'd been thinking about how to answer this question for the last two hundred miles and had come up with nothing. "I slipped."

"Where?"

"By the river. I—I had something I needed to do."

He looked nonplussed for a minute; she could see questions lingering in his expression. But he decided against asking, apparently, and settled for wiping her cheek with his thumb. "It's dried here. You'd better check the mirror inside," he said. He added with a grin, "You're such a klutz."

They got to the gate of Suzanne's apartment around 11:00 P.M. Georgia time. The three of them unloaded the immediate necessities from Marci's car and, once Marci had showered, gathered on Suzanne's living room floor for a beer. Jake would be sleeping on the couch and then helping get Marci's stuff into storage and the truck to the U-Haul place the next day.

"I'm sorry you both had to take off work tomorrow," Marci said as the three of them sipped from the cold bottles.

"What are friends for?" Suzanne said. "Mondays are a slow day for me anyway."

"No problem," Jake said. He thought for a minute, weighing his words. "I'm not going to press you, Marce, on what all this is about. I just need to know one thing. Are you safe?"

"What?"

"I mean, I don't need to know what's going on or who this guy is. If there's a guy. I just need to know that you're safe. You know, because you're running away . . ."

The question embarrassed her. It had occurred to Marci how much she was asking of her friends, but she had never stopped to think they might think she was in danger. She wondered how long Jake had been waiting to ask this question.

"Oh, Jake," Marci said, putting a hand on his. "Yes, I'm fine. There's no danger, honestly."

"Good," he said with a tone that meant the matter was closed until she chose to bring it up again. After all the crying in the car, she had thought she would have no tears left. Yet looking at her two best friends sitting there with their beers, rescuing her without questions or judgment, she wept with gratitude anyway.

For the next few days, Marci more or less lived in her pajamas. She had managed to assist with unloading her things and taking the rest to storage, but after that she'd collapsed into a pile on Suzanne's couch and stayed there, only sometimes making her way to the guest bedroom or the shower. Suzanne brought her a cup of coffee before heading out to work each morning, and that same cup was often still half full next to her as late as two or three in the afternoon, when she would pad to the refrigerator for a can of Diet Coke.

She watched TV nearly twenty-four hours a day—lots of

crime dramas, but also a variety of soap operas in both English and Spanish. "Do you even understand what they're saying?" Suzanne asked her one afternoon. Marci shrugged. *Who needed to understand?*

In the evenings the Diet Coke was replaced with a glass of red wine, as Suzanne joined her on the couch and forced her to eat something while they talked or watched reality TV together. Marci's family called daily, to see how she was doing and to not-so-subtly remind her that Nicole would be coming down next week to start the wedding preparations in earnest. Jake called a couple of times to check in but kept these conversations short, respecting Marci's need for space. "If he was sitting where I'm sitting, he'd be respecting his own need for space," Suzanne teased, kicking Marci gently with her socked feet. She had been patient with her friend, withholding comment on both Marci's approach to mourning and her lack of personal hygiene all week.

By Saturday morning, however, Suzanne had apparently reached the breaking point. At exactly 7:30 A.M., she yanked Marci off the couch, despite protests that she was missing a particularly good episode of *True Crime*. She piled her into the shower and threw the ratty pajamas in the washing machine. Suzanne then produced a simple skirt and top from a shopping bag and tore off the tags while Marci showered, ignoring her friend's protests. She literally sat on Marci's lap on the toilet and forcefully applied makeup, muttering to herself about lip lines and untended brows like a psychopathic Avon lady.

They went to Suzanne's favorite breakfast spot, where Marci was forced to consume a no-yolk vegetable omelet and Bloody Mary for good measure. They went for manicures and massages and then to Lenox Square Mall for a couple of hours of shopping. Despite her constant protests and whining that she'd rather be home in her pajamas, Marci had to admit that it was the best day she'd had in a long time. By dinner, she felt ready to talk. She bent Suzanne's ear for nearly two hours about Doug, Cathy, and everything else. Now it was time to stand up again; falling apart with her best friend had been the first step.

Nicole's wedding was two weeks away. Given the elaborate Indian traditions they were trying to combine with the Thompsons' somewhat milquetoast Presbyterianism, Nicole had her work cut out for her. She had taken a month's leave of absence from work to manage the festivities and the honeymoon. Ravi was joining her in a week, and his brother and sister had both been enlisted to help with the preparations.

Ravi's mother was still refusing to attend the ceremony or even speak to Nicole. Ravi came from a very traditional family, and his marriage to a family friend had been arranged since his infancy. He had foiled his parents' plans for him from the start, however—first by choosing journalism over medicine in college and next not only by dating Nicole but also by choosing to marry her without his parents' blessing.

His older brother, Kal, had also stepped outside the tradition of arranged marriage, but he had wisely chosen to fall in love with an Indian doctor whose family was well respected in the community. His wife, Pritha, had received a slightly frosty reception at first. It had warmed a good bit when the two families met and Mrs. Agrawal learned that Pritha was a third-year resident at Washington's most prestigious pediatric hospital. Once Ravi had chosen Nicole, however, Pritha became Mrs. Agrawal's second daughter overnight. Pritha would teasingly thank Nicole for this from time to time.

Always the optimist, Ravi had assured Nicole that his mother would come around eventually and that she was a stubborn woman but nearly always saw reason in the end. "Nearly always?" Nicole had asked, at which Ravi muttered something about a feud and a sister she hadn't spoken to in forty years. "But that won't happen to us. I'm her favorite," he reported brightly. Nicole confessed to Marci later on that she did not find this all that reassuring.

Still, Nicole could be pretty stubborn herself, and she had tasked herself with throwing the most spectacular Indian/WASP wedding Atlanta had ever seen. She spent hours combing through books and online articles to learn about various traditions and then grilling Ravi and his siblings about which were the most important to their family and which ones could be sacrificed in compromise with the Thompson family traditions (not to mention the fantasy wedding Nicole had been imagining since she stopped thinking boys were icky). She could not control whether Mrs. Agrawal decided to attend the festivities, but she could do her best to ensure there would be as little as possible to complain about if Ravi's mother did.

Marci had observed this process, largely by phone and e-mail, with a kind of awe. Just reading a few articles Nicole had forwarded to help acclimate her to the culture made Marci dizzy. She couldn't imagine trying to glean enough useful information to plan a multiday party and hope to impress her future mother-in-law at the same time. *If it were me, I'd tell Ravi we were going to Vegas or he could take his chances with the arranged marriage.*

Now that the wedding was so near, Nicole was losing her calm resolve, and bridal neurosis was beginning to take over. Marci's first task after Suzanne had helped snap her back to reality was to pick Nicky up at the airport the following day, and Marci could tell right away that the stress was getting to her. Her normally perfect hair was frizzy and disheveled, and there were dark circles under her eyes. Her carry-on luggage consisted of a thick stack of books with tiny Post-its sticking out from various pages, and an enormous navy blue binder marked WEDDING.

She met Marci at baggage claim with her phone already out, talking into the Bluetooth earpiece and pausing for only a second to give her sister a peck on the cheek before resuming a heated conversation with someone Marci could only assume was the caterer. "No, no, that is not what we ordered. . . . Absolutely not—it all has to be vegetarian. . . . Well, I don't care what your notes say, as I told Chris—you know what? If I could just talk to him directly, that would be great . . . Why not? So? I work on Sundays all the time . . . Never mind, I'll just find his cell phone number and contact him directly. Thank you so much for not being even a bit helpful." She tapped the phone off and gave Marci a tired smile. "A little bitchy or Leona Helmsley?"

"Truth?"

"Truth."

"Full-on Leona."

"Yeah," Nicole sighed. "I thought so. Oh, Marci, this wedding is killing me. If you ever get married, you'll understand. It just takes over your whole life."

Marci mumbled something noncommittal. She was beginning to dislike the way people kept saying "*IF* you get married," as though being thirty years old and watching her younger sister prepare for nuptials meant that she was basically ready to be put to pasture.

Nicole made four other calls on their half-hour ride home from the airport: one to the cell phone of the elusive "Chris," two to the wedding coordinator, and one to the photographer. By the sound of the calls, Nicky might've been managing the merger of two multinational corporations rather than a celebration of love between two people. They were just over halfway home when she ended a call and turned to Marci. "So, how are you doing, anyway? I'm sorry about your breakup with that guy. What was his name?"

"Doug." It tasted like saltwater in her mouth. "But it's really not that big a deal." She had told Nicole and her parents the essentials about her flight from Austin, the nothing job, the end of a relationship, but had also glossed over most of the key details. Like the fact that she had been offered a *something* job just days before leaving town. And that she was an adulteress and that her boyfriend's wife was pregnant. *Minor details.*

"Well, I'm sorry. Mom said you seemed pretty upset when— oh, hang on!" She swiped at the ringing phone in her purse and Marci was alone again, surrounded by the sounds of details clicking into place.

Since leaving Austin, Marci had counted more than thirty-two voice mails from Doug. After getting Nicole back to her parents' house and accepting her mother's absolute insistence that she stay in her old bedroom for a few days—"to help your sister"—she went through her phone's overfull in-box and deleted every one. The only one she could not resist listening to was the final message, reasoning that it could represent the last time she would ever hear from Doug.

It was apparently a continuation of a previous message, which she had already deleted.

"Urgh! Your phone cut me off again. Anyway, I don't even know whether you're listening to these messages at all, but it makes me feel better to tell you all this anyway. It always made me feel better to talk to you. I know this whole situation has hurt you most of all, but I hope you'll see that I'm hurting, too, and call me back. Okay? Please, Marci? Call back. Anytime." *Click.*

Doug's voice still ringing in her ears, she stared at the phone for a moment before hitting DELETE. She scrolled through her list of recent missed calls—"D.S." accounted for at least two-thirds of them in the past week—and paused on the most recent call, from 10:00 this morning. Her finger hovered dangerously over the green phone icon. She argued with herself and tried to imagine what Suzanne would say to her right now: "Is there anything he could say to make himself seem like less of a shithead?"

No. There wasn't. Marci clicked the number, but instead of dialing it, she went to the options menu and selected Block. She did not know whether she was strong enough to make this choice every day, so she decided to take the choice out of her hands. Her phone asked whether she was sure she wanted to block all calls and text messages from this number. She was. *I did it,* she thought. *I am a strong, independent woman who will not be ruled by some charming Texas asshole. And now I need a drink.*

Monday morning, she awoke in her childhood bedroom, wearing an oversize T-shirt of Ravi's he'd left on his last visit—the only thing in the house she could find to sleep in. She'd have to run to Suzanne's today to pick up some clothes, the bulk of which were still in boxes. She had more or less relented to the idea of staying with her parents and Nicole for a few days but vowed to go back to Suzanne's for a couple of nights sometime before the wedding.

"That's fine," her mother said when she announced this plan at the breakfast table. "Just be back by eleven because I need your help with something."

Great. So began two weeks of indentured servitude to the bride and the mother of the bride. Marci took her time at the apartment, indulging in a long shower and enjoying the quiet with Suzanne at work. She allowed herself a few minutes to sort through a couple of her hastily packed clothing boxes, noticing with a smile that all the boxes Wanda had packed contained neatly folded and efficiently packed clothing, while her boxes looked as though she'd just taken piles from the floor and scooped them directly in.

She stopped at a coffeehouse on her way back home, ordering an extralarge raspberry–white chocolate mocha. A couple of years ago, she had made the mistake of calculating the number of Weight Watchers' points this drink represented and found that it was around seventeen, the same as a milkshake and nearly two-thirds of her daily allowance. Today, she didn't care. If she was going to spend the next two weeks running around to the caterer, the photographer, the florist, and the alterations place, she deserved a little indulgence.

By the time she pulled back into her parents' driveway, it was 11:30. She carried a duffel bag and a defensive explanation for her tardiness, but her mother didn't even bring it up. "Oh, good, you're back," she said, not looking up from her task of spreading mayo over ten slices of bread. "Go wash for lunch. Aunt Mildred's expecting you in about an hour."

"Beg your pardon? *Mildred?*"

"Yes." Her mother sighed impatiently. "Mildred. She can't drive any longer, and I have to go with your sister to the dress shop, so I need you to take her to the cemetery."

"Does she have a reservation or something?"

"Very funny, Marcella. She still goes once a week to visit Uncle Herbert's grave. You remember where it is, right? She'll want to pick up some fresh flowers for him on the way over. It'll take you an hour, tops."

"But . . . I thought I was going to be helping with wedding stuff." Marci sounded about twelve, even to herself.

"You are, sweetie. This is what I need you to do today so I can go with Nicky. We have to do the final payment and fittings today, so I've got to be there. I'm sorry; I know Mildred is . . . not your favorite. But you'll be doing me a huge favor."

"Fine," Marci grumbled and went to wash her hands. Suddenly, everything she'd been dreading doing today seemed far more appealing.

Aunt Mildred lived in Peaceful Estates, a huge assisted-living complex with various phases dedicated to people with different levels of ability and independence. On one end were a collection of cluster homes with garages and cute little gardens; in the middle stood a midrise apartment building with smaller but still private suites and a nurses' quarter every few floors. Between these two, there was a small green park with tennis courts, shuffleboard, chess tables, and a swimming pool used primarily by the grandchildren of the residents.

On the other side of the apartment building was a community center, cafeteria, and, finally, a squat brick building on the far right end of the property. This was more hospital-like in appearance and function: it had single rooms, wide ramps on all sides, and two ambulances parked outside. Waiting.

Golf-cart paths and manicured lawns filled in all the rest of the space, other than the parking lot and driveways coming from the cluster homes—TRANQUILLITY CABINS, a wooden sign informed her. As Marci parked her car and headed for the apartments in the middle, it occurred to her that the residents here got to keep less and less stuff, along with losing their independence, as they moved from left to right.

"You're late," Mildred greeted her, seconds after she'd knocked on door 601. "Let's go." She pushed Marci back into the hallway toward the elevator with her big purse. Coach, Marci noticed. Nice. *No, thanks, Aunt Mildred, I don't need to come in and sit down. Freshly baked cookies? Oh, I couldn't possibly, but thank you for your generous offer. No, no, I'm happy to take half a day to do this with you. Please don't mention it.*

As soon as they got to Marci's Corolla, she wished she'd thought to bring her mother's car. She struggled to help Mildred into the low seat and rushed to move her CD case, purse, and a couple of fast-food bags out from under the old woman's clunky black heels. Mildred did not comment on any of this but maintained a death grip on her Coach bag and tightened her lips in obvious distaste.

With a series of vague commands—"Go up a ways," "Turn before the chicken place"—and wild pointing, Mildred directed Marci to the Kroger nearest Peaceful Estates. It took some doing to get Mildred out of the car, and the two made their way into the grocery store to buy flowers. Remembering her mother's command to be respectful of her elderly relatives, Marci reached out to support Aunt Mildred's elbow, but the old lady jerked it away huffily. "Don't be an idiot, girl. I can't *drive*. No one said I couldn't *walk*."

Marci mumbled an apology and remained a couple of steps behind the slow-moving woman for the rest of the errand. "Where's the usual girl?" Mildred demanded as an acne-ravaged teenage boy offered to assist them at the floral counter.

"Um, I'm not sure, but I'm Greg. I'll be happy to help you," he said with a squeak. He couldn't have been older than fifteen, Marci observed. *Poor kid.*

"We'll see about that. I need a dozen mixed carnations with some white Gerbera daisies mixed in. And don't give me any garbage from the front bins that are brown around the edges." Involuntarily, Marci thought of Nicole on her cell phone and shuddered.

"Yes, ma'am," he said, and went to work. For someone so young, Greg proved exceedingly competent and patient. He came back with a bouquet Marci would've thought beautiful on the first try, and then without so much as an eye roll, made three more trips to the floral case to replace individual stems Mildred found unacceptable for one reason or another.

"Fine," Mildred pronounced when he was done. Marci

wanted to break into applause on his behalf, but he maintained the same calm, helpful demeanor he'd had the whole time. "Is there anything else?" he asked. *Dear God, man,* Marci pleaded telepathically, *don't reopen the door. Get away while you can.*

"Yes," Mildred said, her voice softer now and less demanding. "Just a single white rose, please." He fetched this quickly, and once Mildred had refused the water vial on the end and the decorative tissue, they were off.

Shady Heights Cemetery was about ten minutes away. Fortunately, Marci remembered how to get there, and Mildred was therefore silent for most of the trip. Her presence was evidenced primarily by the sudden sucking-in of air and clutching at her bag and flowers whenever they approached a stoplight, another car within fifty feet, or a curve in the road. It reminded Marci of learning to drive, seeing her mother clinging to either a purse or the sides of the seat as though her life depended on it whenever fifteen-year-old Marci was behind the wheel.

When they arrived at Shady Heights, Marci veered left toward the lush hillside where Great-Uncle Herbert was buried. But Mildred laid a shaky hand on her arm and directed her toward the small office/maintenance building at the front of the cemetery and insisted on entering alone. A few moments later, a slick man in his late forties emerged with her, escorting her by the crook of her arm in the exact fashion for which Mildred had just scolded Marci a half hour earlier. He motioned to Marci to follow them as he took Mildred to a large, luxurious golf cart with upholstered seats and a tasteful canvas awning. She got out and sat on the bench seat facing backward, glad that Mildred had someone else to criticize for a while.

But the old lady was quiet as the golf cart zipped up the hill to the large shade tree under which Great-Uncle Herbert was at his final rest. Marci held the flowers and Mildred's purse while the man assisted Mildred from the cart. The white rose still lay on the seat, Marci noticed. She and the slick man remained a respectful distance back as Mildred placed the bouquet in the permanent brass vase on Herbert's grave marker. A blank marker was next to his, where Mildred would one day be buried herself.

Mildred did not spend long with her departed husband but soon picked her way back between the other graves to the golf cart. Marci was surprised, though, when the man did not turn to head back toward the cemetery entrance but continued along the road over the little hill toward the back. She had never been this far into the grounds before. The little road curved farther back than she imagined, toward a little pond and a chapel. They moved slowly downhill and around to the right, veering from the main road before reaching the area closest to the pond.

Here was a cluster of obviously older graves, more modest than their counterparts in the more picturesque parts of the grounds, with no decorative statues or looming family monuments. Mr. Slick pulled the cart expertly to a flat part of the ground. Once he had assisted Mildred out again, he reached into his pocket and pulled out a small cell phone. Glancing at it, he said with only a trace of an accent, "Ladies, will you please excuse me for less than ten minutes, as I must attend to something at the office. I feel you will have no trouble finding the other plot. It is just three rows back and to the left as I described. Forgive me. I promise to return presently."

The other plot? Marci was confused, but while Mr. Slick was obviously assuming she knew what was going on, Mildred was looking away from her, toward the general direction he had indicated. He bowed slightly and revved the golf cart back over the hill, far faster than it had gone before. Mildred had begun a slow totter into the grounds, gripping the white rose, and Marci started to follow. "No, stay there," her aunt commanded, without looking back.

So Marci stood at the edge of the asphalt, nudging the grass with the toe of her shoe and waiting. Her annoyance and boredom at being here were beginning to be outweighed by curiosity about the second grave Mildred was visiting and obviously did not want Marci to see. She wondered whether it would be worth a trip back to the cemetery later just to find out, and whether she would remember how to get to this particular spot if she did. Just then, Aunt Mildred's hunched form began to waver, and she collapsed to her knees with a horrifying thud.

Marci raced to her, panicked, desperately trying to get to her before she fell forward and hit her fragile old head on one of the gravestones. *Oh shit, oh shit, oh shit. Mom's going to kill me.*

But as she got closer, hitting her knee painfully on a headstone as she went, she realized that Mildred was not in danger of falling further. She had not fallen, exactly, but had dropped to her knees, where she now held herself, shaking and sobbing. The elderly voice, always so controlled and stern, was now pitching in moans and cries that were painful to hear. Marci was embarrassed to be there. She was about four feet away now: too far to presume any interaction, but too close to gracefully back away.

Aunt Mildred leaned forward, still sobbing, and with a trembling hand placed the rose in front of the grave of Dorothy Elizabeth Walters. *Who was Dorothy Walters?* The realization hit Marci like cold water. *Dottie.* This was the mystery roommate of Aunt Mildred's who'd been abandoned in favor of traditional marriage and children. She looked more closely at the dates below Dottie's name. March 12, 1919, to December 4, 1948. Not even thirty.

Questions came in a rush. How had Dottie died? Illness? Sadness? Suicide? Had she and Mildred stayed in touch after Mildred married Herbert? Did Dottie marry? How long had it been since Mildred had visited her grave, if ever?

Marci thought of Suzanne and tried to imagine losing her dearest friend, which was horrible enough. But then never acknowledging that loss out loud would make it so much worse. *If it were a friend who were also a lover* ... Tears dripped down Marci's cheeks. Mildred's face was in her hands now, and the shaking in her body had eased. Marci felt a strong desire to go and comfort the poor woman, but could not bring herself to intrude on the moment, much less incur the wrath of having disobeyed explicit instructions.

Soon she heard the buzz of the golf cart just over the hill, and instinct told her that Mildred would not want Mr. Slick to see her in this state. As gently as possible, she called, "Aunt Mildred?"

Mildred did not seem surprised by Marci's presence; she simply nodded and held out her hand to be helped to her feet. Marci obliged, careful not to look her in the eye. Mildred produced a linen handkerchief from somewhere and wiped her face wordlessly. Mr. Slick gave them a practiced smile as he conveyed them back into the golf cart and back to the car.

When they got back in the car, Mildred stared straight ahead and said, "Marcella." This surprised Marci—she had not even been sure that Mildred knew her name. It seemed to be a question, but did not sound like one, exactly.

"Yes, ma'am?"

"Your mother says you're a good girl. Is that true?"

Depends on what you mean by good. "I guess so, ma'am."

"Good. You keep things to yourself, then."

"Yes, ma'am." Marci could keep her mouth shut. She knew something about secret pain.

The ride back to Peaceful Estates was less tense than before, though still entirely silent. Both women were lost in thought, and Marci noticed that Mildred grabbed her purse rather less often than on the way to the cemetery. Despite her dislike of her cranky great-aunt, Marci began to entertain the idea of spending time with her periodically, reading to her or helping her run errands.

Marci had no living grandparents, not since her sophomore year in college, when her dad's mother had passed away. Mildred's own children lived out of state; her only consistent company was Marci's mom and Odessa. Of course, she could be horrible, but Marci felt perhaps she had seen a human side of her today, and maybe that could bring them together on some level. In the movies, hard-shelled old women always ended being secretly vulnerable and sweet.

She held the elevator door for Mildred, wondering whether she had any fascinating hobbies or a memoir that Marci could help her write. It was actually perfect that Marci wasn't working right now so she could visit regularly. Perhaps she could invest in a tape recorder to take down Mildred's stories. Of course, it would have to wait until after the wedding . . .

"Are you gaining weight?" Mildred asked as soon as the doors closed.

"What? Um, no, I don't think so, Aunt Mildred."

"Your calves look heavy. And your face is fat. You'd better be careful, or you'll never get married. Your sister is thin; that's why she had no problems finding a man."

"Uh, okay, Aunt Mildred. Thanks for the suggestion."

"Stay away from bread; that's my advice. And all those sodas and hamburgers you kids eat. You know what they say, 'A moment on the lips, a lifetime on the hips.' "

"Yep," Marci said. *And never mind about the tape recorder, then*. She deposited Mildred back in her plush suite and headed home.

16

uesday before the wedding, Jake called to take Marci and Suzanne out to dinner at a place they'd wanted to try, which advertised its nouveau Southern cuisine. Nearly blind from wrapping tiny handfuls of birdseed in tulle and tying the bags with bits of ribbon, Marci could not get out of the house fast enough.

Barely glancing at the menu after they settled into a booth, she accepted the waiter's first suggestion for a cocktail, a pecan pie martini. It tasted like burned caramel, but Marci didn't care. They ordered a couple of the more interesting appetizers, including green tomato and goat cheese fritters and something called butter-bean kabobs, which turned out to be the aforementioned beans and other tiny vegetables speared on little toothpicks and served with some sort of sweet glaze for dipping. Marci wondered what her rural Southern grandmother, who had eaten butter beans at almost every meal with a glob of mayonnaise on top, would've thought of this rather prissy presentation.

"So how are the preparations for the wedding of the century?" Suzanne asked, helping herself to a fritter.

"Oh, my God." Marci exhaled dramatically. "Who is this crazy person, and what did she do with my sweet little baby sister? She's the devil!" She told them about Nicole's most recent meltdown when the florist couldn't get some particular flowers in on time because of heavy rains in South America. There had actually been crying and pulling of hair (Nicole's own, thank goodness). Marci had never seen anything like it.

"See? This is why I don't do weddings," Suzanne said. "Too much emotion. If the floral arrangements aren't exactly perfect for the grand opening of a car dealership, no one throws a tantrum or threatens to fire me. Hell, chances are, no one even notices."

"It sounds like Nicole is under a lot of stress," Jake said diplomatically. Marci loved how he was always seeing the good in people, even at the worst times. But right now she really just wanted to be pissed off.

"Yeah, well, she's certainly handing a lot of that stress my way," she said, dipping a fritter into some sort of creamy pepper sauce and popping it in her mouth whole.

"Well, let this be a lesson to you," Suzanne said in her best motherly tone. "When you get married, you'll have a simple wedding and be a totally low-maintenance bride, right?"

"*If* I get married," Marci said without thinking. She'd become so accustomed to joking about marriage in this self-pitying way in the last couple of years, she had momentarily forgotten Jake and their decade-old promise. *Damn.*

As usual, Suzanne didn't let the ball sit on the field for long. "Hey, aren't you two supposed to be getting married around now? I seem to remember there was some sort of promise made in a bar back in college . . . ," she said innocently. Marci kicked her shins under the table, hard. Of course, she had told Suzanne everything, and now she was playing dumb and stirring up trouble. Marci could have killed her.

Jake grinned. "We *are* supposed to be getting married this year, actually. I'm up for it, but I think Marci is still too attached to whoever she left in Texas." This last bit held just a hint of an edge to it.

"Well then, Jacob, perhaps you'd better get on the ball and show her why you're better than anyone else. Thirty doesn't last forever, you know."

"Yeah, I guess I'll have to work on that. Let me know if you have any ideas about how to win her over." They were grinning at each other the way they always did when having a laugh at Marci's expense.

"Very funny, you two. Can we move on, please? The real wedding is stressful enough."

They did move on, to a conversation about Suzanne's latest job, a huge convention at the World Congress Center that had her running around like a headless chicken. By far the biggest event she had planned since going out on her own, it required she hire an assistant. For the control-freak Suzanne, delegating to someone else—a bright, motivated college grad named Chad—was about as easy as pulling out her own toenails. Still, she was beginning to admit, albeit grudgingly, that she had never been more organized.

While Suzanne went into a few of the more minute details about the event, which Marci had heard in long form as they had come up in the past couple of weeks, Marci's mind drifted to Doug. She had heard from him only a couple of times since she'd blocked his number from her phone, calling from the office number, which she did not block. He had not left messages, though, and Marci supposed he had figured out she wasn't listening or maybe given up on being able to say anything that would sway her. In a way, she was glad, but it was strange not to hear from him.

Despite her anger, she was curious what was going on in the office and in his life. She wondered how her departure had been received by Frank Dodgen, for example. She knew her hasty explanation to the temp agency that she needed to be home due to a "family situation"—she hadn't said who's family—was thin at best. Of course, she would not call Doug, but there was a tiny seed of regret for deleting all the messages he'd left and the information they might have contained.

Jake was talking about his latest project, following a few top-ranked Georgia high school football players as they went through the college recruiting process. "I have five kids on board for the fall, which I know sounds like a lot," he was saying. "I'll be on the road quite a bit, taping games and doing family interviews and stuff, but hopefully it means at least a couple of them will have great stories for the film."

Suzanne, who hated sports, made a show of feigning interest. "So it's a movie about how these football players decide where to go to college?"

"Well, yeah," Jake said, slowed by the question. "But it's so much more than that. A lot of these kids come from lower-income families in rural areas, and suddenly they're being offered all kinds of scholarships and opportunities and being put on pedestals as hometown heroes. Eventually, I'd love to follow all these kids through college and beyond. There's always a chance one of them could make it to the NFL, and then it gets really interesting."

"Watch out with those potatoes there, Mr. Spielberg," Marci teased him. He had been waving his fork of mashed potatoes animatedly as he talked, coming dangerously close to flinging them onto her shirt.

"Oh, yeah. Sorry, Marce." He put down his fork and went on, not noticing the smiles exchanged by his female companions. "Anyway, there's this one kid, Jamal Anderson—he's a really talented wide receiver from Bainbridge. I think he could be talking to schools all over the country. He has nine brothers and sisters and will be the first person in his family to ever go to college. He works a part-time job and has a four-point-oh average on top of being a State All Star. He runs track in the spring, too. The kid is amazing, and actually a really nice guy, too."

"It sounds fantastic," Marci said, and meant it. Jake was great at shooting commercials and community service announcements, and everything he did was polished and beautiful. But Marci knew his real love was the human side of things, especially with sports.

She was so proud of him, and yet there was a stab of envy, too. She envied Jake's passion for his work, his connection to the kids. More than anything, Marci wanted that same passion about something she *did,* rather than just someone she loved.

On the drive back to her parents' house, Marci mused about how much of her energies in the last couple of years had been divided between figuring out how to get by on a temp worker's pay and investing in a relationship that was doomed from the start. She thought of all the hours she'd spent hiding out with Doug, or waiting for Doug to arrive, or being sad that Doug was not around, or wondering what Doug was doing. In the moment, she'd never felt as if she was wasting her time on him, because when he *was* around, the passion was delicious.

Until a couple of weeks ago, every moment she'd had with him had been equal parts devastation and ecstasy, and she could focus on nothing else. It was like a drug, as though the torrid beginning of the relationship had never faded into comfortable normalcy. Even several months in, she had always put on makeup and shaved her legs when he was coming over. She never made him watch bad television with her or wasted their precious time together by complaining about her family or her job. She didn't fart in front of him or shit in the bathroom while he was at her apartment.

At the time, she'd thought of this as a positive thing; their love always felt new and exciting. They didn't have to deal with the things Beth complained about with Ray: perfunctory sex during halftime of the football game, monthlong periods without any sex at all, spending all their time managing the kids and schedules and finances, bitching at each other about laundry and dirty toilets. Doug and Marci never had to deal with any of that. When she was with him, she felt as if she was the only thing in the world he cared about. And when she wasn't, she was looking forward to the next time she would be. Until now.

She walked quietly into her parents' dark kitchen, thinking perhaps that everyone might be either asleep or watching a movie. She needn't have bothered, however, because as she turned into view of the living room, she saw that everyone was awake, and that Ravi had been added to the group. Her father was the first to notice her; he smiled wanly from his place on the couch. In the middle of the room, Ravi was kneeling on the floor with Nicole, who was obviously sobbing. He whispered to her and stroked her hair while their mother paced in and out of Marci's view in front of them.

For a moment, she debated turning around and going upstairs through the dining room, and avoiding the latest drama altogether. What was it this time? The special vanilla extract being flown in from Madagascar for the cake icing had been waylaid at the border by U.S. Customs? She sighed and moved into the room, clearing her throat to announce her presence.

"Hi, sweetie," said her mother, her tone resigned and sad.

"What's wrong?" The question elicited a loud sob from Nicole, and Ravi held her tighter.

"Ravi's mother is not attending the wedding. He spoke with her this afternoon."

Marci spoke slowly, sensing a minefield ahead. "Um, okay.

I—I thought we already knew that? Hasn't she been saying for months that she wasn't coming?"

This time Ravi answered, over Nicole's head. "Well, yes, but I think I was always hoping that she would change her mind by now. My mother can be very stubborn, but I didn't think she would actually miss the wedding. I've been telling Nicole not to lose hope, but at this point it seems really unlikely she will attend."

"Oh," Marci said. "I'm sorry."

He nodded gravely. Marci was a bit surprised to see Nicole this upset. She'd been very nonchalant about Mrs. Agrawal's refusal to attend until now, so Marci had never explored it with her. Now it appeared that it was bothering her more than she'd let on. Poor Nicole; she thrived on approval, more so than Marci, and failing to earn it from this very important person was obviously crushing her. Marci wanted to say or do something to comfort her sister, but could think of nothing.

Ravi, however, had it covered. He held Nicky by the shoulders, pushing her back from him just a little. He produced a couple of tissues from somewhere, wiped her eyes and (*really gross*) snotty nose with incredible tenderness, and then kissed her eyelids. Watching such a sweet, intimate gesture, Marci felt odd that she and her parents were witness to it. "My love," he said in a soft, deep voice Marci had never heard him use. "This is my mother's mistake. I am sorry for you, and for us, because it is so hurtful. But I am more sorry for *her* that her stubbornness will cause her to miss out on my wedding to the most beautiful woman I have ever met."

Nicole smiled through the fresh tears. Ravi wiped them with the back of his hand and held up her chin as he continued. "We can do anything together, right?"

Knowing her stubborn and petulant baby sister, Marci expected to hear an argument or a "Yes, but . . ." Nicole, however, nodded obediently, her eyes fixed on Ravi's. Marci had never seen her sister so soft and compliant, especially not after mercilessly running down every wedding professional in Atlanta over the last several days.

"We have the rest of my family supporting us, and our friends, and your wonderful family." He gestured to acknowledge the three of them. "And, most importantly, we have each other. We will always have each other, and if my mother cannot see that, it is her loss. Not ours." Marci saw her dad glance over at her mom and give a tiny nod as Ravi spoke. He liked his new son-in-law. Nicole was in good hands.

Nicole was a different person with Ravi in town, and over the next few days Marci found herself wishing he'd flown down sooner. When they returned to the caterer for a second tasting—the first had not lived up to the bride's expectations— Marci went to provide a third opinion. Chris, the heavyset catering manager, looked like a nervous cat as he covered a tiny table with food samples. He was tired and pale, and there were sweat rings beneath both arms on his black smock. He gestured a little too desperately at the first dish, inviting them to try the reworked vegetarian samosas, with more curry and less cilantro.

For her part, Marci could not taste a bit of difference from the first batch of samosas last week, but apparently Nicole was very happy with the changes. She clapped her hands in delight, and gushed about how they were exactly as she'd imagined, helping herself to another bite. Chris let out a sigh of obvious relief and took them through the rest of the wedding meal.

The remainder of their last-minute errands followed a similar pattern. Nicole was entirely pleased with everything, occasionally checking with Ravi or Marci for their opinions as well, but doing so in a way that really only invited compliments and excitement. Things seemed to go by much more quickly than they had over the past couple of weeks. When they stopped at an outdoor mall for ice cream in the late afternoon, Ravi and Nicole held hands and pointed at things in shopwindows. For the first time since high school with Beth and Ray, Marci felt like a third wheel.

The wedding was a two-day affair, short by Indian standards and about fifty times as long as the standard Presbyterian ceremony. Nicole and Ravi had chosen carefully from the traditional ceremonies to combine their heritages as closely as possible, leaving out bits that would most painfully highlight his mother's absence. At the combination engagement/rehearsal ceremony on Friday night, however, Marci caught Nicole surveying the crowd, hoping for a glimpse of her future mother-in-law. To a mixture of community sadness and relief, Mrs. Agrawal did not appear.

Because much of Ravi's family were practicing Christians, the wedding service itself was to be held in the Thompsons' home church at 4:00 on a Saturday afternoon, with a more Indian-influenced reception at an inn down the street that evening. Rev. McClosky, who had baptized both girls and been a friend of the family for decades, would be sharing officiating duties with an Indian minister who knew both Hindu traditions and biblical scripture.

There was a ladies' brunch Saturday morning, and by the time everyone gathered in the Sunday school rooms in the basement of First Presbyterian at 2:30, Ravi's sisters and cousins and Nicky's sorority sisters were chatting easily across the cultural divide. As maid of honor, Marci was charged with escorting Nicole upstairs to the pastor's office: a small, private space with an adjoining bathroom so the bride could get ready undisturbed. In theory. The reality was that every two or three minutes, someone popped into the room looking for something, delivering food, taking pictures, or asking questions.

Even when the door stayed closed for more than five minutes, the hubbub was ever present. Up and down the stairs and in the hallway below, there was a steady stream of footsteps, giggles, and calling out for this kind of makeup, these color panty hose, or a certain shade of nail polish. For the ceremony itself, Nicole had opted for a traditional American white wedding dress. The bridesmaids—all ten of them—would wear a rainbow of elegant saris and bejeweled sandals. Between the ceremony and reception, Nicole would change into her own ruby-red sari, hand embroidered with silver thread.

Marci put a DO NOT DISTURB note on the door and locked it so Nicole could get out of her brunch outfit and into her wedding dress. Assessing her sister for the first time that day, Marci thought she looked sort of pale. No, wait, she looked *green*. "Nicky, you okay?"

Nicole nodded, held up a finger, and ran to Reverend Mc-Closky's bathroom to vomit.

"Oh, no," Marci said, coming up behind her. "Are you really that nervous? Was it the eggs? I thought mine tasted a little undercooked..."

Nicole shook her head and held out a hand to be helped up. Marci wiped her face with a wet cloth, doing her best not to disturb the perfect wedding makeup Ellie had already painstakingly applied. "We'll have to get El to redo your lips, I'm afraid."

"That's okay," Nicole said, color returning to her face. "I'm just glad I got that over with. Don't tell anyone, okay? Promise?"

"Got it over with?"

"Yeah, it only happens once a day, usually," she explained. Marci must have looked as worried as she felt, because her sister immediately followed with, "Oh, God, no—it's nothing bad. It's just that I'm—well, we're—"

"You're pregnant." The light had come on.

"Yes. Six weeks. Please, please, *please* don't tell anyone, okay? I don't want Mom and Dad to know until after the wedding."

"Oh, my God, Nicky," Marci said. It explained so much about Nicole's recent behavior. A thousand questions ran through Marci's mind, everything from how she was going to get out of drinking champagne tonight to where they were going to fit a baby in their tiny walk-up in D.C.

"I know," Nicole said, reading her mind. "But isn't it wonderful?"

This wasn't the word Marci would have chosen, exactly, but the look on her sister's face said it all. With the color back in her cheeks and her hair swept up gracefully, Nicky looked beautifully adult. Like a mother. The smile took up her whole face; she was radiant.

"Of course it is," Marci said softly, taking Nicole's hand and squeezing it. "Thank you for trusting me with it."

"Ravi is over the moon. He's the only one who knows. It happened when we were home for the bachelor party, actually."

"Ew! In your childhood bed? Was I at home when this happened?"

"Worse," Nicole laughed. "At the hotel! With all those people in the room!"

"Oh, my God—I don't think I want to hear this. What are you, an exhibitionist? Gross!"

"Don't be silly. We went to the *bathroom*." She said this with a "well, duh" tone that Marci remembered hearing frequently during Nicole's teen years.

This brought up more icky mental images than Marci could handle, as she fought off her curiosity about whether the bathroom meant the shower, the toilet, or just the vanity counter.

"Shhh . . ." she said to Nicole and to her own brain. "Don't tell me anything else. Let's get you ready so you can give this baby a daddy."

They hugged awkwardly and stepped out into the office to begin the excruciating process of wrestling Nicole into all the undergarments that would be holding her together under the enormous dress. It was not until Marci had zipped up, fluffed, and powdered the rosy bride; stood for seemingly hundreds of pictures; and walked as gracefully as she could down the aisle in the sandals that did not want to stay on her feet that it occurred to her that her niece or nephew would be just over a month younger than Doug's child.

Between the ceremony and reception, all the bridesmaids and Nicole were painted with henna by four of Ravi's very talented aunts and cousins. Because the henna lasted for about two weeks, Nicole offered that anyone uncomfortable with painting could abstain, but no one did. Most of the girls stuck to having their hands and arms decorated, first with henna and then with a seemingly endless supply of noisy metallic bangles. But a few brave souls, plus Nicole and Marci, had henna applied to their faces as well. The effect was exotic, and gorgeous.

When they arrived in the limos at the Waterford Inn, just a few miles from her parents' home, Marci could scarcely believe the transformation. In the front, it looked like the same antebellum mansion she had always admired as a child. The long driveway, lined with oaks and Spanish moss, took them up a hill nearly a quarter mile from the road, where it circled an old fountain that still functioned and had been fitted with lighting. The house itself was two stories, a faded mossy green, with six enormous columns out front holding up the second-story wraparound porch, and still seeming to defy Sherman and his cohorts to set foot on the property. When she was very young, she'd always imagined the mansion was haunted by the ghosts of Southern belles and Rebel cavalrymen.

Once they entered the inn, however, everything looked different. Red, gold, and purple drapes had been hung in nearly every room, creating an almost tentlike feeling and making the prewar American furniture look out of place. Wonderful, pungent smells from the kitchen filled the entire downstairs as Chris the caterer worked his magic. They could hear the sounds of laughter and clinking of glasses from the back of the house. With the long wait between the ceremony and reception, Nicole had ordered that everyone start eating and drinking before her arrival.

Ravi was waiting for them when they got halfway to the kitchen. He took Nicole's hand and steered her upstairs, where they would have a few moments of alone time before making their grand entrance into the party. Traditionally, this was probably the time for the consummation of the marriage. Funny, Marci thought, because the bride was already knocked up, but tonight it was just a moment of rest to fuel the anticipation of Nicky's appearance and give the bridesmaids time to hit the bar before the first dance.

The beautiful day turned to a beautiful evening, and even though the sun had not yet set, the volume of pine trees around the yard made it seem darker than it was. The reception was staged outside on the mansion's back lawn, where several tents had been erected with more red and gold drapes and zillions of little white lights. The ancient swimming pool was also lighted and filled with floating lotus blossoms. The large back deck now boasted the bar and the DJ booth, and a temporary wooden dance floor had been set up on the lightly sloping back lawn surrounded and crisscrossed by paper lanterns. The fantasy atmosphere captured the magic of the day. *No wonder Nicole spent so much time on the phone,* Marci thought appreciatively.

She located Suzanne and Jake, stationed beneath one of the regal oaks behind the dance floor. As Marci made her way over, Beth and Ray joined them, as did Rebecca and a tall blond man in an expensive-looking suit. Of their group, Rebecca was the only one who'd taken advantage of the "and guest" option on the invitation.

When invitations went out, Nicole had e-mailed Marci in Austin with her list of Marci's friends who were invited to the wedding, and Marci had gently hinted that if Nicole needed to trim the list, Rebecca wasn't *strictly* necessary. But Nicole had fond memories of visiting Rebecca in the sorority house when she went to Athens as a high school junior.

When Marci arrived at the group, Suzanne pressed a cocktail into her hand and Jake kissed her on the cheek. "You look amazing," he said, admiring her pale blue sari and the henna design on her face and hands.

"Cool, huh?" she said, showing off her arms while the bracelets jingled.

"Very, um . . . exotic," Ray said as diplomatically as he could. "It's not permanent, though, right?"

"Don't mind him," Beth said, elbowing him in the ribs. "We don't get too many Indian parties out in the boonies. Ray's not exactly accustomed to appreciating other cultures."

"Sure I do," Ray said with a grin. "Fixed a carburetor for a guy from New York just last week. We even got past the language barrier."

"Well, I think it's sexy," Jake said. Marci wished she didn't blush so easily.

"Marci, have you met my date, John?" Rebecca interrupted. "He's a dentist, just like your dad!"

"Hi there," John said. "Congratulations."

"Isn't he adorable?" Rebecca said, smacking him lightly on the torso. "Don't you think so, Jake?" She batted her eyelashes inexplicably and rocked a little on her heels. Obviously Rebecca had been making the most of the open bar. A brief awkward pause was fortunately relieved as the DJ announced Ravi and Nicole's exit from the house.

Except for the notable absence of Ravi's mother, the evening was perfect. The DJ combined beautifully the standard American wedding reception fare ("YMCA," "Chicken Dance," "Twist and Shout") with fast-paced Indian music. The latter brought all of Ravi's side of the family to the floor in synchronized displays with lots of arm motions. As the evening wore on, they were joined by increasing numbers of white guests spurred on by the welcoming smiles of the family and copious amounts of alcohol.

Even Marci's father, who seldom drank more than a single beer or glass of wine, indulged in several cocktails over the course of the evening and was persuaded to join the dancing by two of Ravi's more attractive and giggly teenage cousins. In fact, the only person who did not dance at some point in the evening was Aunt Mildred, who kept her usual post on the bench seat nearest the door, ready to complain about the skimpy outfits of the young girls and the demise of true Southern gentility to anyone foolish enough to sit next to her.

Marci and her friends were huddled around a poolside table, where they had been camped out for much of the evening talking between dances. As the event wound down and the older relatives of both sides yawned, stretched, and made their way to the newlyweds for final hugs and pieces of advice, the remaining guests crowded the dance floor for drunken swaying to low-key ballads in both English and Hindi.

When the initial strains of "Wonderful Tonight" echoed over the water from the dance floor, Ravi and Nicole extracted themselves from a crowd of older women and made their way to the floor. Rebecca jumped from her seat, nearly knocking it into the pool, and grabbed John by the hand to head to the floor. Beth looked at Ray, who shook his head. "Oh, come on," she whined. "We're never out without the kids."

Ray relented and let his wife lead him to the floor. Marci turned to Jake and Suzanne, ready for the next conversation, but Suzanne was staring across the pool at Sanjay, Ravi's very handsome friend from college. He looked especially good in the white linen caftan he wore tonight, which highlighted his dark skin and easy height. "Mmm . . . ," Suzanne said, chewing the straw in her empty rum and Coke glass. "I wouldn't mind making *his* mama mad."

"Suzanne!" Marci said in exaggerated outrage. But Suzanne was already pushing out of her seat and adjusting her top so it showed more of her cleavage. In seconds, she had sauntered to the other side of the pool and was chatting with Sanjay, who looked not at all unhappy to have his conversation with another friend interrupted.

"Guess it's just us," Jake said. "Wanna dance?"

"Sure," Marci said, feeling a little wobbly-kneed as he took her hand. To distract from this, she asked the question that had been on her mind since her arrival. "So what's up with Rebecca?"

Jake snorted. "I know! Weird, right? I'm not sure, but I think . . ." He trailed off.

"What?"

"I think she's actually trying to make me *jealous*. I know it's crazy, but over the last few months, since before you came home, I've noticed that she's been going out of her way to spend time with me and stuff. I didn't think anything of it at first, you know; we've been friends for so long and all, but . . ."

"Wow."

"Yeah. She asked me a while back to go to this concert with her—in a couple of weeks, actually—and I said yes because it was before she was acting so intense. Now, though, I sort of feel as if she thinks it's a date or something. I wish I could ask you guys to come, but I think it's sold out."

He put his hands on her waist as they swayed, and she realized both how tired she was and how good it felt to be held. They moved closer as the music transitioned from Eric Clapton to a mournful Indian artist belting out a beautiful melody. Marci put her head on Jake's chest, and he moved one hand to her neck, cradling her against him. "You do look really great tonight," he said softly.

He didn't wear cologne, but she could smell his shampoo or deodorant, clean and masculine. It mingled with the fragrance of the blooms all around them, and the thick, humid scent of a summer night in Georgia. Out of the corner of her eye, she could see Nicole and Ravi, their faces pressed together at the forehead, whispering softly to each other. *They are going to be parents.* The thought was still a little unreal. Some part of her would always think of Nicky as her lanky little sister with braces and acne.

Directly in front of her were Rebecca and John, dancing awkwardly. Behind them, Suzanne had managed to persuade Sanjay into one of the larger pool chairs and was already curled up on his lap, laughing dramatically at something he'd said. Marci felt adrift at sea; life around her seemed to be standing still and sailing onward all at once. She needed an anchor.

She turned her head to face Jake and kissed him lightly on the lips. He smiled. "What was that for?"

"Jake." She took a deep breath. The words were tensed on the catapult and ready to come out, waiting only for her brain to signal that it was time to speak.

"Marci," he said playfully, mocking the seriousness of her tone.

"Jake, what if I said yes?"

17

September 2011

The next couple of months passed in a blur. The march of time seemed marked by something significant every week. Nicole called to say they had heard the baby's tiny heartbeat. Ravi got a long-hoped-for promotion at the station, allowing them to upgrade to a two-bedroom apartment in Georgetown. Suzanne dated and discarded two more men, not including poor Sanjay, who had been deserted entirely the day after the wedding. Marci's mom was busy planning a sixtieth birthday party for Marci's dad, which he did not want but pretended to be thrilled about for his wife's sake. And, of course, there was always Georgia football.

Marci had, incredibly, almost forgotten during her time away how seriously her parents took the University of Georgia's football season. It was more like a religion in their house than a pastime. As they packed the ancient family minivan with red and black everything—lawn chairs, tent, even the portable grill with an enormous red and black G on it—she tried to remember if her parents had been this fanatical about Georgia games when she was in college. Whether it was blocked from her memory by embarrassment or vast quantities of alcohol, she could not be sure.

Now, of course, they were tailgating with the Stillwells, whose considerable financial means took the art of school fanaticism to an entirely new level. They made the trip to Athens around midday on Friday before the Saturday home game. They had a circuit of favorite restaurants and bars they systematically visited while waiting for space to begin clearing in the student parking lots, so they could set up their camper and adjoining tent well in advance. Everyone went out to dinner and had a few drinks, and then Jake, his dad, and the other men all returned to sleep in the RV while his mom and the ladies spent the evening in Athens's nicest downtown hotel, which the Stillwells had reserved for every home game weekend until 2020.

The Thompsons had been invited to join this overnight ritual, but thus far they had continued their own family tradition of waking at the crack of dawn and driving up to Athens just in time for breakfast. The two families would meet by midmorning at the Thompsons' tailgating compound on the North Quad and then sit in lawn chairs watching the day unfold while Kitty Stillwell—clad head-to-toe in Georgia gear, including earrings, sandals, and purse—popped in and out of the RV with more food than anyone could dream of eating.

Marci liked to watch the North Quad of campus fill with partiers as the hours wore on, particularly for late games when there was more time for the consumption of alcohol. It was people watching at its best and worst: the sororities and the fraternities who all dressed up for games as though they were going to a cocktail party rather than a sporting event, middle-aged drunks reliving their wonder years at the university, people playing corn hole and cards and Frisbee on the grass.

Sometimes she'd focus on the quad full of people and try to picture it on a quiet spring day when she was a student here, remembering her religion class in that building or taking a nap between classes on that bench. It was difficult to imagine it was the same place.

She was lost in one such reverie when Jake came from behind her and put his hands on her shoulders. "Hi, honey," he said. "Honey" still sounded weird to her, coming from Jake. "Your dad and I were just going to walk downtown for a bit. Do you want to go?"

"That's okay," she said. "I'll hold down the fort here."

Jake and her dad had become very close since their engagement. This made her happy but was also a little surreal. She'd never had a boyfriend who had met her parents more than once or twice. Obviously Doug had not met anyone she loved. With Doug, she couldn't even have dinner in a public place.

Jake, on the other hand, had known her parents and friends for more than a decade, and he fit into her life like a puzzle piece. Her family adored him. His parents had been welcoming, especially Jake's dad, who admired her aspirations to be a writer. They had come together easily, but it was an adjustment being part of a relationship that was so . . . legitimate.

Her mind frequently wandered back to the night they got engaged, and the decision that had changed her life so completely. She did this with something that was not quite excitement, not quite regret. It could best be described as sort of an observant awe, as though she had spent the last three months sitting in a theater, watching her own life with passive interest and wondering what would happen to the main character next.

At Nicole's wedding, almost immediately after Marci had mentioned Jake's proposal—*Had it really been a proposal? Or more like calling in a bet?*—Jake had had no time to respond. As if on cue, her mother had appeared to herd them off the dance floor as the entire party sent off the happy couple with well-wishes and birdseed and catcalls.

As guests filed out, Jake had helped Marci and her parents direct all the packing and loading of the rented equipment, the wedding gifts, and the leftover food and cake. He helped with the lifting of boxes and shuffling of cars, and it was nearly 2:00 A.M. by the time they were alone again, with Marci driving him back to his truck at the Waterford Inn.

At first the silence was almost unbearable, but finally Jake spoke. "So earlier . . . was that you or the gin and tonic talking?"

She didn't know. "Both?"

"Well, you can take it back now that you're sober, you know. I won't be hurt."

"What if I don't want to take it back?" she said, and her whole body tingled. She loved Jake, of course. In one way or another she always had. Now it had occurred to her that they really *could* do this, and it felt like the answer to everything. She could put Doug behind her and have the happy ending every girl had always wanted.

But was it the right happy ending? And what if he didn't want her? What if he'd been joking about the whole thing or had changed his mind after seeing the train wreck that she was when she left Austin? What if she'd just made a pathetic idiot of herself by bringing it up?

He was quiet for the rest of the ride. She gripped the steering wheel, uncertainty eating away at her. A voice inside screamed: *Take it back! Make a joke! For God's sake, do something!* But words failed her. As each mile slipped away under the wheels, the opportunity to change her mind seemed to disappear, too.

When they pulled up next to his truck at the Waterford Inn, he turned to her in the darkness. She turned off the engine and faced him. "Okay," he said, as though getting ready to direct the action in one of his films. "I'm going to ask you this, and I don't want you to answer right now. Go home, sleep, think about it, and call me tomorrow. Don't do this unless you want to, unless you really want *me*. I will always be your friend, no matter what. Okay?"

She nodded. *Unless you really want* me. Was he referring to Doug?

"I never told you this," he went on, "but leaving you behind to go to NYU was one of the hardest things I've ever done. Did you know that?"

No, she didn't.

"Yeah, I turned around twice on the drive there. I even went to a pay phone off the interstate and dialed your number. But I thought I was too young to feel about someone the way I felt about you. And I guess in a way, I was right. That's part of the reason I went. I was afraid if I stayed in Athens, we might end up together and then break up. I couldn't stand the idea of losing you like that. Do you know what I mean?"

He took her hands in his.

"And it's kind of been that way ever since. I watched so many of my friends move in with people and end up never speaking again or, worse, getting married and having custody battles over their kids. Fighting over their DVD collections and Pottery Barn furniture, making stupid rules about who could go to their favorite restaurant and when. Two of my friends in grad school actually went to court fighting about their dogs. Their goddamn *dogs*, Marci."

It wasn't funny, she knew, but she couldn't help imagining two adults in a courtroom with treats in their pockets, trying to get the dogs to choose them.

"I dated these women, all perfectly nice for the most part, and it never ended well. I'd date a classmate or coworker, or even just the really nice girl at the coffee shop . . . we'd date; then it would fall apart, and I'd lose what I had to start with. I lost friends. I lost colleagues and collaborators. I had to switch coffee shops twice."

"Sounds like I'm going to have to chaperone you whenever you get coffee from now on," Marci said.

"Yeah, maybe," he said, picking up on her playfulness but not losing momentum." Anyway, I kept thinking that if I kept you at a distance, kept you as my friend, at least I'd get to keep you. You know?"

She realized that she *did* know. Looking back, with each failed relationship on her part or each girl who came and went through Jake's life, she'd always felt a bit relieved that they still had each other. Looking back, she supposed wrapped in that relief was also hope that their turn was still to come or, at least, was out there and still possible. Now here it was, right in front of her.

"But I guess over the last couple of years, whenever we've seen each other, I . . . Well, I guess I started feeling like maybe those other relationships didn't work out because they weren't *you*. I haven't said anything because the timing never seemed right, and I knew you were involved with someone in Austin."

She sucked in a breath. Not now. *Anything but Doug.*

"You don't have to tell me anything about it," he said, seeing her flinch. "Just tell me that it's over."

"It's over." She knew that much.

"Good." He nodded, closing a mental door. "Marci, I've loved you for a long time. You're my best friend. I'm sorry I don't have a ring, but . . ."

"Yes," she said, cutting him off. She couldn't bear to hear the actual words. "Yes."

"Really?"

"Yes." Tears flowed down her cheeks, and she hugged him

tightly. A few minutes later, she followed his red truck—which had replaced the decrepit blue Jeep only a couple of years earlier—down the inn's long driveway. As he turned toward the interstate and she headed home to her parents' house, she tried a few thoughts on for size.

There goes my fiancé. That's my husband. My husband's truck. Weird.

18

He had come by the following evening to talk to her parents and present her with his grandmother's engagement ring—a beautiful antique with one large diamond and a circlet of tiny sapphires in a dark silver band. "My mom said it needs to be polished," he said. "But I wanted you to have it right away."

Everyone seemed thrilled with their engagement, and no one seemed to particularly regard it as news. Her own parents, of course, loved Jake and were as thrilled as they could reasonably be in their postwedding stupor. "Just wait a year or so, okay?" her dad said in a tired voice. "We have to regain our strength." Now that she had seen the excess of her sister's nuptials and actually had to start thinking about wedding plans herself, she hoped her mother's joke about spending everything on Nicole had been just that.

Other than Rebecca, who referred to their decision through gritted teeth as "a little sudden," all their friends were excited and, again, not terribly surprised. Even Suzanne gave a little squeal when Marci told her and actually offered to help with the wedding plans. "There's a first time for everything," she said.

Jake's parents were kind and warm and welcoming to her. His older sister, Leah, had been married for several years and had three children already, so the pressure on Jake to settle down and make grandchildren was somewhat minimal, other than the unspoken understanding that he *would* carry on the family name. But he was over thirty now, and Marci suspected his mother had begun to wonder whether he was in danger of becoming a confirmed bachelor.

So even though being presented to his family as his fiancée that summer had been intimidating, it was not the scary experience she would've pictured after first meeting the Stillwells a decade earlier. Now they were all tailgating together, and her mother was helping Kitty make snacks in the RV, just as if they were old friends. She could hear them chitchatting and laughing from her seat under the tent.

She took another swig from her can of Bud Light. Strange: under no other circumstances would it be socially acceptable to drink like a fish before noon in front of her parents *and* future parents-in-law. Across the quad, she could see Jake's dad, Robert, talking with some old buddies. By profession, he was a high-end insurance salesman, which suited his personable and lively temperament. But Marci suspected that he didn't really need to work at all. Several generations back, the Stillwell family had founded a successful textile mill that had long ago been sold off, but the proceeds of which more or less ensured that the Stillwells would be independently wealthy for generations to come.

This included Jake, of course, though Marci had been absolutely floored to learn it. Nothing about Jake—from his clunky Jeep and ragged khaki shorts to his crazy-serious work ethic— indicated that he was from "old money." He loved to talk about his family but rarely talked about their wealth; when he did, it was always at a distance, as though it had no effect on him personally. Like his dad, Jake intended to work his whole life as though the money weren't there. Marci liked this about him, because even the relatively small excesses of the Stillwells' home and lifestyle made her feel a little ill at ease sometimes. She was glad Jake didn't expect her to be one of Atlanta's white-glove socialite wives.

Robert caught her eye across the lawn and gave a slight wave. He finished the conversation with his buddies, who, despite being in their late fifties or older, all looked rosy-cheeked and young on a sunny football morning. Clapping of shoulders and pretend punching joined the calling of insults as they joked their way out of one another's presence. *Boys never change,* Marci thought with a smile.

Robert plopped down in the camp chair next to her and cracked open another beer. "Crazy, isn't it?" he said, gesturing at the quad crowded with people, tents, and so much red and black clothing it was dizzying.

"It is," Marci agreed. She was not sure what to say next. Insurance was not exactly a profession that lent itself to easy small talk ("So how's business?" "Anything new on this year's actuarial tables?"), and her current state of unemployment was not exactly interesting, either—at least, not in a good way. She knew from Jake that Robert loved history, especially World War II–era stuff, but Marci's knowledge in this arena was scant at best.

So, she went with an old standby. "It's a beautiful day." *Urgh.* How ridiculous that she had to resort to talking about the weather. He must have thought she was about as deep as a puddle.

But to him, this seemed as good a place to start as any. "It sure is." He looked straight up as though confirming it. "This is my favorite time of year. Cool, crisp days . . . football, family . . ."

During the short, awkward silence, Marci mentally willed her mother and Kitty to emerge from the RV and relieve the tension or Jake and her dad to return. But it wasn't long before Robert spoke up. "Marci, can you keep a secret?"

Now this was something. "Sure."

"You can't tell anyone, not even Jake or his mother."

"Um, okay," she said hesitantly. She wasn't sure how comfortable she was with this.

"Here it is: I hate football."

"Sir?"

"I have had season tickets to Georgia games since two years after Kitty and I graduated. We've been to almost every home game and a few away games over the years, because that's what you do when you're a Georgia alum, especially someone in my line of work. And, of course, when Jake got old enough and we saw how interested he was in sports, I wanted him to have this experience. And I've learned to appreciate it the way you learn to appreciate ballet or opera if you see enough. But as for the game itself, I really can't stand it."

"Wow," Marci said, dumbfounded. She had known men with various levels of knowledge and interest in sports, but had never known a middle-aged straight man to openly admit hating football. Jake knew every statistic there was about Georgia football, not to mention a dozen other sports teams, and his walls were lined with autographed balls, helmets, and jerseys. He and Robert talked for hours on end about the game: the players, recruiting, and so on.

"Jake's old enough to get tickets for himself, and Kitty could probably care less whether we do this every year or not. But do you know why I keep coming out here?"

"No, sir."

"Because I love my family. This is the best time we all have together. It's something that connects us. Jake loves this stuff, and it's nice to have something to share with your son. I know so many fathers who feel totally alienated from their kids after years of working all the time and kids moving to other cities. I'm lucky that my son will still sit and talk to me about something. You know?"

He had the same endearing way Jake did of pausing in his little speeches to make sure she was still listening. "Plus, Leah's husband, Dave, and their kids, my grandkids—they love it, too. I take the little ones to the zoo and the movies and whatever they're into at the moment, but in no other place do we get this kind of face time: relaxing, playing, enjoying each other, being on the same team."

Marci wanted to get up and hug him. "Well, maybe it's not all about football," she said.

"Exactly. But they think it is, so this is just between us, okay?"

"Yes, sir."

"And don't call me sir. We're family now. It's Robert or Dad, okay?"

"Robert," she said, smiling at him. "Dad" just didn't feel right. They sat in companionable silence until Jake and her father returned a few minutes later from their walk around campus.

"Hey," Jake said, kissing her lightly. "Have you seen how much campus has changed since we were here? Every year there's some new building or some new *complex* of buildings. It's crazy."

"Welcome to old age, kids," her dad teased, clapping Jake on the back. "It always feels like the world is leaving you behind. Now, Marcella, I'll take that chair if you don't mind."

Arthur and Robert smiled at each other as Jake took Marci's hand and helped her out of the chair. They strolled around the North Quad, dodging beanbags, footballs, and stumbling sorority girls as they went. Jake told her about the changes on the campus since they'd been at school here, and particularly since Marci had moved away. She listened distractedly, feeling oddly out of place back at her alma mater, and even holding Jake's hand. Still, for the rest of the afternoon's festivities and the game that followed, she kept Robert's sweet little secret tucked away in her pocket.

19

The fall passed quickly. It seemed there was something every weekend to keep them busy. Twice a month they were in Athens for football games, and many of the other weekends, Jake was all over the state working on his recruiting documentary. His early interviews landed him a small grant from a film institute, so now he was filming the guys at their high schools. Sometimes Marci would go with him for a Friday night game and sit huddled in the stands beneath a blanket watching the action.

She'd had half a dozen temp assignments, some of them lasting two or three weeks, some shorter. And in one recurring nightmare, she served for three days at a time as the secretary to a temperamental construction manager who kept driving away the permanent candidates for the position with his expletive-filled tirades that often ended with flying coffee cups and office supplies, and nearly always ended with the secretaries in tears. He didn't bother Marci as much; she'd worked for worse, but she had no interest in the permanent position.

Jake had suggested a few times since their engagement they move in together, but the timing never seemed right with all the work he was doing on the weekends. Truthfully, Marci could have moved in gradually and stayed with him more than a couple of times a week, but she was still enjoying living with Suzanne and having a place to go home.

"So you're ready to be engaged, but not ready to live together?" Suzanne had asked after one of Jake's stronger hints that she should move her boxes to his place.

"I know it sounds crazy," Marci said. "But that's how I feel."

"No, that's not crazy, honey. Neither is marrying someone because you wrote something on a napkin ten years ago. It's all totally sane and usual, if you want my opinion."

"It's a good thing I asked for your opinion," Marci fired back.

"Sorry, sorry." Suzanne backpedaled. "You know you can stay with me as long as you want. There's always a bottle of wine with your name on it here."

So Marci would spend a night or two each week at Jake's huge loft apartment overlooking the city, where they'd cook dinner and watch a movie or go out to one of the ethnic restaurants in walking distance. Typically, she forgot at least one thing she needed to get ready for work so she would dash home early in the morning to shower and dress. Sometimes he stayed with her and Suzanne, though this was less frequent because he felt he was imposing on them in their smaller space with two people and more stuff.

Marci was faced with her first year of attending two Thanksgiving dinners. They started at her parents' house for a lunchtime meal, where everyone wore blue jeans and sweatshirts and no one was exempt from helping her mother prepare the table. Nicole and Ravi had flown down from D.C., and both seemed basically fat and happy. Nicky was nearly six months along; they were having a little girl, whom Ravi lovingly referred to as "Princess" whenever he touched his wife's protruding belly. Nicole's thin face was starting to swell along with the pooch she carried in front. With a little extra weight and her hair cut in a neat bob, Marci thought Nicole looked more like their mother than ever.

Ravi was enjoying his new position as a producer for two of the weekly news shows. He joked that being behind the camera meant he was free to enjoy his sympathy pregnancy weight. They loved their new apartment, which was in a building full of young families and across the street from a nice park. Nicky babbled for half the meal about the school districts, the commute for each of them, looking for a nanny, and the drama of preschool waiting lists.

The only fly in the ointment was still Ravi's mother, who had found fresh kindling for her anger when she learned that Nicole had been pregnant before marriage. At his father's urging, however, she had made one visit to their new apartment for a dinner that Nicky obsessed over for a week. Ravi seemed to consider this a good sign, even though she would speak to him only through his father and only in Hindi and did not speak to Nicole at all, other than to thank her coldly for the invitation to her home.

"Hang in there," Marci's dad told her. "She'll come around once she gets a look at that grandbaby." Their mother said nothing but stood rather suddenly to refill everyone's sweet tea.

Later that evening, their second Thanksgiving at the Stillwells' was a whole new world for Marci. It was much more formal than her family's tradition, and she found it almost painful to pull on her nice slacks and heels with a belly already full of turkey and sweet potatoes. Jake wore a navy blazer and tie and drove to his parents' house in silence. Since she was already nervous, the quiet in the car made Marci fidgety. She bit her nails and changed the radio station every thirty seconds. On her final stretch to the radio knob as they entered the Stillwells' neighborhood, Jake grabbed her hand. "Relax."

"Easy for you to say," she murmured. He pretended not to hear her.

They were greeted at the door by Leah's six-year-old daughter, Jasmine, who wore a puffy velvet dress with ribbon trim and shiny patent-leather shoes. She threw herself into Jake's arms as soon as the door was open. "Gobble-gobble, Uncle Jake!"

"Hey, gorgeous!" Jake lifted her in his embrace and spun her around so that her shoes flew behind her, coming dangerously close to knocking over an expensive-looking vase of flowers in the foyer. Marci stood awkwardly in the doorway, holding a bottle of wine, afraid to get in the way of the flying feet.

Jasmine giggled wildly until Leah approached from the next room. "Jake! For God's sake, she's hyper enough. Put her down!"

"Time for landing," Jake conceded. He settled Jasmine on her feet and leaned against a nearby washstand to recover his equilibrium. "Hey, sis."

Leah leaned forward to allow him to kiss her cheek, maintaining her scolding expression. She turned to Jasmine, who was red-faced and breathing hard. "Go out to the sunporch with your brothers and the other kids. Now. Hello, Marci. Welcome to the House of Chaos."

Aside from the sound of the kids playing at the back, the house was anything but chaos. Every piece of furniture, banister, and door frame in the large old home had been polished until it gleamed. Each surface was covered with a combination of crisp white linens, flickering candles, and centerpieces made of flowers mixed with gourds and fruit. *Kitty must have been working on this around the clock for a month,* Marci thought.

Farther inside, the atmosphere was more like a cocktail

party than a simple family gathering. In addition to Jake's parents and Leah and her family, the Stillwells' guest list included several other couples who were either old friends or long-standing clients or both. Their enormous dining room table had to be extended with a second to accommodate sixteen adult place settings, each of which included three Waterford plates, a wine- and water glass, and thick floral-patterned napkins held by sterling silver rings.

Several people Marci did not know were clustered around Kitty's beautiful grand piano, though no one was playing it. Others hovered in the well-appointed dining room, waiting for the signal to take their assigned seats. A smaller table had been set up in the kitchen for Jasmine and her twin brothers, Caleb and Carson, along with a few other kids.

Although the Stillwells did not have regular help, Kitty had employed three women to assist with preparing and serving the meal. They wore simple gray dresses and slipped in and out of the rooms with trays of food and drink while party chatter filled the entire downstairs. Marci wished fervently that she had ironed her shirt. Better yet, she wanted to be at home with her father in her sweatpants, making leftover sandwiches and watching football.

Unlike the Thompsons' more traditional roasted turkey, Kitty's menu included fish and quail, with side dishes that vaguely recalled the usual feast. Green beans almandine, sweet potato soup, oyster dressing, roasted pears, figs stuffed with goat cheese, and tomato-onion focaccia, with pumpkin crème brûlée for dessert. Everything was delicious, Marci had to admit, and everyone seemed nice. She had trouble, however, keeping up with the lively conversation going on around her.

"No, no, annuities are *not* the way to go. If you'd set foot in my office once in a while you'd know . . ."

"Can you believe we brought back six rugs from Turkey for less than four thousand?"

"You should all stay at our cabin in Blue Ridge next summer. The fishing is amazing."

"Barbara just loves her new decorator; remind me to get her card for you . . ."

"Leigh Ann doesn't golf, but if there's shopping involved . . ."

Marci focused primarily on her food, while Jake chatted intermittently with the couple on the other side of him. After a while, she was drawn in as the conversation turned to their wedding.

"So when is the big day?" a chipper blond woman asked them both. Marci had been introduced to her but forgot her name entirely. "Of course, we'll be on your invitation list, won't we? I couldn't bear to miss it! Are you going to have lots of people or keep it small?"

Fortunately, the lady did not pause between questions to wait for answers, because the truth was she and Jake had not even discussed the size or location of their wedding, much less begun to prepare a guest list. Marci struggled with how to answer, and was rescued as always by Jake. "We are still working on all of that. We're not in a rush."

"Good thing," said the blond lady's husband, a bearded man who seemed underdressed in an UGA polo. "Enjoy being young and single while you can."

His wife sent a playful smack his way. "Oh, shut up. You'd be lost without me, and you know it."

"Yes, dear," he said, grinning at Jake. "I just meant it's good to focus on your career before marriage and babies and all that. Right, Marci?"

The blond woman glared at him and turned back to Marci. "So what do you do, anyway, Marci? Jake's never told us."

"I'm between assignments."

"So you're a filmmaker, too?"

"No, I'm . . . I guess you'd call me an independent contractor."

"What kind of contracting?" the bearded man pressed.

"Well, you know, office work, phones, that sort of thing."

"So you're a temp?"

"Well, yeah. Right now I am."

The blond woman looked as though she smelled something unpleasant. "So is that just since you moved back from Texas? You probably had a real job before that, right?"

Marci reddened and toyed with her dessert spoon on the table. Jake put his hand on hers. His tone was definitive and clear. "Marci's a writer, actually. A really good one."

"Ah, well," the bearded man said, as though the matter were settled. "Excellent, then. Great."

The conversation turned to football. Jake squeezed her hand as he debated with the man the most likely outcome of Saturday's game against Georgia Tech. The blond woman entered a conversation with someone on the other side of her, but Marci thought she noticed a probing glance or two thrown back in her direction.

"You'll get used to it," Jake said as they waddled arm in arm out to his truck after dinner, going back to his loft for the evening. "Once you get to know everyone better, it will feel less intense."

"Yeah," Marci said softly.

"You okay?" he asked.

"Sure, it's just . . . I think that woman thinks I'm marrying you for your family's money."

Jake laughed. "That's ridiculous."

"I know, but . . ."

"And *if* she thinks that," he continued, "it's probably because that's why she married her husband, and she assumes that every woman thinks the same way."

He kissed her lightly on the cheek, dismissing the subject, and opened the passenger door of the truck for her. Marci said nothing else about it and watched the streetlights and scattered cars passing all the way back to the city.

20

One cold Thursday night in the middle of December, Marci and Jake were holed up on the couch at his apartment, watching *North by Northwest*, which Jake had been appalled to learn she had never seen. Suzanne had been out of town all week in some sickeningly warm and sunny location, at a corporate retreat she'd helped organize. With no Suzanne at home, Jake leaving the next day for a final weekend of taping before Christmas, and the holidays making everything feel cozy and festive, Marci had spent several nights in a row at Jake's without feeling trapped or anxious.

She had just finished an assignment filling in for a receptionist at an accounting firm where more than half the staff was out on vacation. She had made thirteen dollars an hour and read three novels between calls. Even with Friday off, for once she was actually disappointed that the assignment was over.

She lay now in her sweats and one of Jake's old Ramones T-shirts, her hair pulled up in a ponytail and head resting on his chest. An empty wine bottle and the remains of Chinese food lay scattered on the coffee table. Despite her interest in Cary Grant and whoever was chasing him, Marci's eyes grew heavy with the rhythmic sounds of Jake's steady breathing. *Maybe I can do this forever*, she thought sleepily.

She woke to the sound of Jake at the front door, talking to someone. From her position on the couch, she couldn't see him, only the light in the tiny hallway that ran along Jake's bedroom between the front door and the rest of the loft, which was all one big room. She sat up and squinted at the clock beneath the TV, frozen on a shot of Mount Rushmore. It was nearly ten o'clock. Apparently, she had been dozing for a while.

Who was here at this time of night? Jake had neighbors who might have been coming or going, but most of them knew he wasn't a night owl. *A fire?* She felt a tiny surge of panic but decided the voices were too muted and calm for that kind of emergency. As she stood to investigate, she heard her name. "Marci's sleeping," Jake said rather firmly. "Why don't you call her tomorrow?"

Her puzzlement lasted only seconds, giving way to complete shock when she heard the response. "Look, I know it's late, man, and I'm sorry, but it's really important that I talk to her." *Doug Stanton. Six months later. In her city. In her fiancé's doorway.*

She plodded numbly to the door, not knowing what else to do, compelled as much by curiosity as anything else. She put her hand on Jake's back and felt the muscles tense beneath her touch. Coiled like a spring. "I'm here," she said softly. Jake gave her a resigned look and pushed the door open further.

"See?" Doug said, like a child who had just proved his parents wrong. "She's awake." He was wearing shorts and a wrinkled button-up over a Longhorns T-shirt. His blond curls were matted, and there were deep circles beneath his eyes. Still, he grinned at Jake, making Marci want to slap him.

"What do you want?" she said as icily as possible.

"I need to talk to you. Please?"

"I have nothing to say to you."

"I know," he whined. "I get that, babe, I do. But I have some really important things to say to you. Ten minutes. Please? We can stay in the building."

"No," she said.

"Please, Marce? I drove all the way from Austin today, just to talk to you. Please don't tell me I can't have ten minutes."

She looked at Jake, whose face was set hard in an unreadable expression. "Whatever you want," he said flatly.

"You've got five minutes," she relented. "In the building."

Jake exhaled next to her, and she sensed his anger. Anger at Doug, clearly, but maybe at her, too. An ominous feeling rose in her stomach, and she considered changing her mind and slamming the door in the slimy bastard's face right then. But how could she deny him five minutes when he had driven fifteen hours? Seeing him after so long, she was struck by her curiosity, and the absurd desire to run her fingers through his blond curls again. She grabbed Jake's gray hoodie off the hook next to the door and stepped out. "I'll be *right* back," she said. He pressed his lips together into a half smile and closed the door behind her.

She rounded on Doug. "What the *hell* are you doing here? How did you find me?"

"Easy, babe; don't want any of your neighbors to call the police, do you?" He was grinning. Antagonizing her had always been a favorite pastime of his.

She scowled. "Stop calling me that. I'm not your babe. Speaking of that, how *is* your baby? And your wife? How's the happy little family?"

His smile faded. "There is no baby. And Cathy and I are divorced. That's what I came to tell you. It's been final for a month now."

"I'm . . ." she fumbled, stunned. "I guess I'm sorry."

"Don't be. It's for the best, and it's a long story. I've been trying to find you for months. Figured out that you blocked my calls, eventually. I have a new number now, in case you're interested."

Marci glared at him wordlessly. Interested, she was not.

"Finally, I came across your engagement announcement a few weeks ago and tracked down your man's address." *Damn.* They had been putting off that announcement for so long and finally caved to Kitty's pleas for public recognition just before Thanksgiving. "Nice rock, by the way." He pointed at her left hand, which she immediately shoved in the pocket of the hoodie.

"What do you *want,* Doug?"

"All business. Like always. You're so *serious,* Marci," he said, mocking her demanding tone. She did not smile. "Okay, I'll be honest. I want you. I came here to explain everything and to talk to you and apologize. Because I really am sorry, Marce."

She snorted.

"It's true, and I know you don't believe me, and I know I can't explain everything to you in a dingy hallway with your boyfriend listening on the other side of the door."

"He's my fiancé," she corrected.

"Fine. And if this is the only place I get to talk to you, I'll tell you everything right here. But I'd rather us sit down when we're both calm and we can have a few minutes to ourselves. I got a room at the Hyatt downtown for a few days."

"No, Doug," she interrupted. "It's over. I'm sorry about your marriage, but . . ."

"Believe me, you're not as sorry about mine as I am about yours. But it's not too late; you don't have to do this . . ."

"It is too late!" she protested, louder than she'd intended. Her voice echoed in the hallway.

Doug sensed the opportunity and grabbed her hands.

"Please don't give up on everything we had, not now when we could actually be together, finally. After all we went through . . . I mean, can you look me in the eye and tell me that what you have with this guy is as passionate and amazing as what we had together?"

Her eyes were stinging with tears threatening to materialize. *No, no, no, no.*

"Please leave, Doug," she said as firmly as she could, dropping his hands.

"Marci, don't."

"GO!" she yelled, and turned back into Jake's unlocked apartment. She leaned against the other side of the door momentarily in the darkness, breathing hard and waiting to hear Doug's exiting footsteps down the hall toward the elevator. At her feet, a torn slip of paper appeared under the door. The gas station receipt had five words scrawled hastily across the back, reminding her of the Post-it notes he used to leave at her desk.

I am not giving up.

She wadded it and threw it in the bathroom trash can on her way back to the living room. The TV and all the lights were off, the space lighted only by the large strip of high windows across the back wall and the city lights beyond. Jake sat on the couch, staring at the sleeping TV. He had cleaned up the mess from dinner, she noticed.

"Hi," she said softly. "I'm really sorry about that. I didn't think he would know how to find me here."

Jake's voice was equally soft. "This is what you were running away from. Him."

She felt ashamed of her weakness, ashamed that she'd been too afraid to tell Jake the truth in the beginning. There was only one way forward—the truth. "Yes."

"He was married. I . . . I overheard."

"Yes."

"You loved him. You still do."

"I did," she acknowledged, and hesitated before going on. Could she lie and say she'd felt nothing when she saw Doug? That all her anger wasn't based on some kind of feeling? Could she tell her best friend something that she *wanted* to be true and hope it would be enough? No.

"Now." She sighed. "I—I don't know."

"You don't know," he repeated. It sounded cold and awful coming back to her in his voice.

"But I don't want him back; I do know that. I love you—I want to be with you." She meant these words sincerely, but as she heard them, they sounded empty. She could hardly blame Jake for not turning to embrace her.

"This is why you don't want to set a date for the wedding."

"What?" She was genuinely surprised. In the last few months, Jake had brought up wedding dates twice—once while they were half-blitzed at a Georgia game and his mother kept not so subtly mentioning it, and another time just a couple of weeks ago when she'd had a terrible headache. Both times she had suggested they talk about it later, but she had not realized he had taken this to mean she didn't *want* to set a date.

Then again, she realized, seeing the hurt on his face now, she had not brought the topic up again, either. A stack of bridal magazines next to her nightstand at Suzanne's was gathering dust unopened, along with the navy blue wedding binder Nicole had helpfully provided her. Weren't most brides really excited to make wedding plans? What was wrong with her?

She wanted to throw her arms around him and apologize for not being a good girlfriend, fiancée, whatever. She wanted to get out the calendar and offer to pick a date right now if that was what he wanted. Anything to fix this horrible silence. But nothing would come out. She felt helpless against the unbelievable turn this night had taken.

He was quiet for a long time, looking at something in the vicinity of the coffee table without seeming to see it. Finally, he said, "I think I need some time to process this. It's—it's a lot to take."

"But Jake, you knew I'd been seeing someone in Austin, right? You knew—"

"I guess I did, but . . . I don't know. It's different now, seeing him, and you . . ." His face contorted with emotion. "I can't talk about this right now. Can you go to Suzanne's tomorrow?"

"What are you saying? You don't want me here?"

"I just need time."

"Jake, I—"

"No. Marci. I have an early morning tomorrow." He was back in control, his tone almost fatherly. "You take the bed, and I'm going to stay out here."

She reached out and put her hand on his knee, hoping he would turn to face her. He didn't push her away, but he didn't look at her, either. She waited a few minutes without response and then stood to go to his bedroom, where she lay awake for a long time listening to the silence in the apartment, feeling like an intruder. Even though she woke before 6:00 the next morning, when she stepped out of the bedroom, he had already gone.

It was Friday morning, and Marci had nowhere to be. Suzanne was going straight from her retreat to San Diego for the weekend. Marci couldn't face spending a long weekday at home in an empty apartment. She steered the car to the interstate and headed north toward her parents' home instead. Dad would be going into work late this morning. Nicole was in town for a baby shower / Christmas party her friends were throwing because she would no longer be able to travel by Christmas.

When Marci got home, her mother was in the middle of cooking breakfast while her father read the paper by the breakfast window and a pajama-clad Nicole lounged in a cushioned patio chair she'd dragged out of storage and placed in the middle of the kitchen. She looked like a Titian painting with her big belly and her aristocratic recline. None of them seemed surprised to see Marci, even though it was a weekday morning and they hadn't discussed her being there. *I have* got *to get a real job,* she thought.

Meanwhile, Nicky was complaining about the aches and pains of pregnancy, the demands of Ravi's new job (which had seemed very reasonable a few weeks ago), and, of course, Mrs. Agrawal. The latest on that front was that she had sent a large package of baby items to their apartment—including some handmade blankets and clothes—but had addressed the box to Ravi only. She had turned down the invitation to the couples' shower being thrown by their local friends and coworkers and sent the box instead.

"Who does she think she is, sending that to *him*? Like he's the one who's been carrying this child for seven months! She even included soothing foot lotion. Is that supposed to be for him, too? Or is she only acknowledging that my feet and my uterus exist right now? I know she's mad about the wedding and all, but it's getting ridiculous! She won't even give me a chance!"

Their mother flipped a couple of pancakes and clucked her tongue in agreement. "I'm so sorry, sweetheart. It makes me so mad, too, because I would give anything to be up there with you guys, to help you get ready and to babysit and everything. And here this awful woman could see you anytime she wants and she can't get over her stupid pride."

"I wish we had moved here instead," Nicole whined. "Ravi could work for CNN, and you guys could see the baby whenever you wanted."

"That would be nice . . ." Mom said, but trailed off. Marci knew their mother would give her right arm to have both daughters and her granddaughter in the same city with her, but she had always tried to respect their choices and not to pressure them. Marci had appreciated this when she was living in California and Texas. She could see now that it cost their mom quite a bit of effort to pull it off. "So, Marci, how are things with you?" she said brightly, changing the subject.

"Not so hot, actually," she replied, and told them about Doug's appearance and Jake's response, minimizing the length and intensity of her relationship with Doug and leaving out entirely the fact that he'd been married and was now divorced.

"I'm surprised that someone who wasn't even important enough to *mention* to your family would come track you down after all this time," her mother said. She was great at not pressuring. Guilt was another issue altogether.

"That's not really the point, Mom," Nicole said, and Marci shot her a grateful look. "The thing is that Jake is being totally unreasonable. It's not Marci's fault this guy showed up on his doorstep."

"Exactly. And what's with him needing space? One minute he wants me to move in and set a wedding date, and the next minute, he's kicking me out? Is this how he thinks our marriage would be? He'll just send me to Suzanne or you guys whenever there's a problem?" She had actually rehearsed this particular point in the car on the way over and was gratified at how grown-up and reasonable it sounded live.

"Why *haven't* you set a wedding date, anyway?" Nicole said. Marci glared at her. "Right, right . . . not the point."

"Breakfast is served, girls. Arthur, put the paper away."

For several minutes, the four of them ate while Marci and Nicole traded complaints.

"I mean, he knew I had dated other people before him. I

wouldn't be mad at *him* if some girl showed up and tried to get him back."

"She's only met me once! How can you hate someone you have barely met?"

"It's not like I'm still in love with Doug or anything. Jake *knows* that. Why does he need me to say it?"

"Why would she send foot lotion, which is obviously for me, and not even have the guts to address it to me? What is she expecting, a thank-you note from my uterus?"

"I mean, I did have feelings for Doug, and I guess they're not a hundred percent gone. But doesn't everyone have something like that in their past?"

"I told Ravi, I'll be damned if she can come to the hospital when the baby is born. After all this, no way."

"How am I supposed to be honest with Jake when he doesn't even want to talk about this?"

Their mother offered encouraging nods and "mmm-hmms," and the occasional "of course, honey." After some time, she turned to her husband. "You've been quiet, sweetheart. What are you thinking?"

Their father chewed a bite of sausage thoughtfully and took a sip of coffee, before answering her without looking at Marci or Nicole. "I'm thinking, Elaine, that I wonder how two such lovely and kind people as you and I have managed to raise two daughters so capable of utter selfishness."

Silence. The three women stared at one another. Finally, Nicole punched him playfully in the arm. "Daddy, come on! This is serious."

"I assure you, Nicole, I'm quite serious."

"Arthur!"

"Well, you asked me what I was thinking." He turned to face his younger daughter. "Nicky, darling, I love you more than life, and I've always thought that you were an intelligent girl. But if you can't see that poor woman is trying as best she can to reach out to you without giving up all her pride, then you are not as smart as I thought."

Nicole attempted a protest, but he cut her off. "You're a mother now." He patted her protruding belly affectionately. "It's time to learn how to be the bigger person. You go home on Sunday and call Ravi's mom and thank her for the gifts. If she doesn't answer, leave a message or write a note and try again next week. And when the time comes, you do the right thing and make sure she gets plenty of time with her grandbaby. No matter how painful it is for either of you in the beginning. Isn't that what you always did with my mom, Elaine?"

Their mother looked surprised. They had never spoken aloud about this, but hearing it, Marci knew exactly what he meant. She had always sensed a tension between Granny Jane and Mom but had never heard her mother say an unkind word in the old lady's direction.

"And you," he said, turning to Marci. "Jake is a good guy. A good man. He's been a friend to you for a decade. Don't you think, instead of sitting here feeling sorry for yourself, that you owe him the truth about this other guy and your feelings for him, whatever the truth is? Marriage is not easy under any circumstances. Wouldn't it be better to start with your whole heart?"

"But I don't even know how I feel anymore," Marci said weakly.

Her father grasped her hand in his. "I think that's obvious, Marcella. But you owe it to yourself and to Jake to figure it out. Don't you think? You know I love you, but you've always run away when things got hard or confusing. You got a C in that writing class and changed majors; you broke up with that guy Mike and moved to San Francisco . . ."

"Daddy!"

"Seriously, honey. You got a couple of rejection letters and quit submitting freelance articles. Now you know your mother and I support all your decisions, whatever you do, but when was the last time something in your life was worth fighting for?"

He wiped a tear from her cheek with his napkin. "You're a good girl." His familiar words rang in her head, the same thing he used to say to her when she was little and she did anything wrong. As a child it always brought her comfort, like her daddy still believed in her even when she behaved badly. Today it made her feel ashamed. If her father knew all that she had done in the past year, would he still think she was a good girl? Would she still be worthy of his breakfast pep talk?

She thought about Jake turning away from her last night, and fresh tears welled in her eyes. *Who have I become?* She toyed with a half-eaten sausage link on her plate to avoid making eye contact with her family.

His speech over, their father stood abruptly and cheerfully announced he was leaving for the office. Fridays were his off day, technically, but he often went in to catch up on paperwork and sometimes to take his staff out for lunch. Kind father, kind boss.

The three women sat in silence for a while after he left. Finally, Nicole said, "He's right. You aren't being very fair to Jake."

"What? What about you? You're the one denying some poor woman contact with her grandchild!"

"Her grandchild isn't even born yet! And she's not sweet and wonderful and handsome, like Jake!"

"Handsome! I knew you had a crush on him; you always have!"

"I do not! Besides, if you care so much about him, where have you been the last decade?"

The last one stung. Marci was getting ready to fire back that

Nicole looked fat, even for a pregnant woman, when their mother spoke up quietly.

"This is my fault," she said, and both girls turned to look at her. "Nicky, sweetie, I've been letting you do this to Mrs. Agrawal—I mean, not encouraging you to do the right thing, anyway—because *I'm* selfish. I didn't realize until just now that the idea of you having another mother, another grandmother for this precious little one, how jealous I felt about that." She put her hand on Nicole's belly.

"I thought I was supporting you, being on your side, but I realize listening to your father that I was secretly just trying to undermine that poor woman and keep you all to myself. He's right. You have to reach out to her, whatever it costs you."

"But Mom—" Nicole started. Elaine ignored her.

"Marci, honey, I don't know what to tell you about Jake. Only you and he can decide whether what you have is enough to sustain a marriage. But Daddy's right; if you can't give your whole heart for some reason, for *any* reason, you're setting yourself up to fail." More softly, she added, "We've been married thirty-four years, and your father still makes me a better person."

Marci left three messages for Jake that day, but he did not call back. In return, she received two calls from Doug, who both times left the address and room number at the Hyatt Regency. She also got a call from a headhunter named Lynnette, with a potential position as a copywriter for a "big company downtown."

She called Lynnette back, grateful for something to focus on other than her dual heartaches. The position was entry-level, of course, but in a large department with room for advancement. Marci could barely take in the details: benefits,

401(k), something about a cafeteria . . . Was she available Monday at 2:00 P.M. for an interview? Yes, of course.

She numbly wrote directions, and Lynnette went on to say that there would be a lot of competition for the slot from recent college grads but that Marci's "life experience" should give her an edge. Marci didn't think Lynnette heard the chuckle.

Jake was scheduled to be in south Georgia most of the weekend, taping "slice of life" footage of Jamal Anderson and a player named Cedric Williams, who went to another tiny high school in a neighboring county. This meant getting shots of family dinners and the players tossing a ball with their siblings or working at their jobs. And, of course, church on Sunday. December was the last opportunity to get this kind of background footage before all the hustle leading to College Football "Signing Day" began in January.

Marci knew this meant Jake would be busy and that the cell phone reception in the rural counties was sometimes sketchy, so it didn't surprise her not to hear from him. Still, she sent him one text Saturday morning—*"Can we talk?"*—and couldn't help feeling disappointed that he didn't even respond to that. Waiting and hoping to hear from him reminded her of the days with Doug. She vowed optimistically that someday—perhaps even at some point in the near future—she would no longer be spending weekends surgically attached to her phone, hoping to hear from a boy.

Doug, on the other hand, she *did* hear from, and frequently. He was booked at the Hyatt in downtown Atlanta through Monday morning and threatened to stay longer, waiting for her to come see him so they could finish their conversation. All day Saturday, he left her messages nearly every hour, narrating his steps through Atlanta, commenting on the tourist spots and restaurants where he found himself.

"Just leaving the MLK monument. Very historic, very important, very cool."

"Underground Atlanta was a total bust. I can see why they buried it."

"The World of Coke is literally the biggest advertisement I've ever seen. I can't believe they have people *paying them* to listen to their product pitches and try samples. Clearly I am not the talented marketer I thought I was, because Coke has taught me I still have a long way to go."

"Found a great Thai restaurant. Wish someone was here to share the noodles with me."

And so on.

After 2:00, she called back, if only to stop the horrible checklist of Atlanta sights. "Okay, okay. Enough of the 'Ugly Texan Visits the South.' We can have dinner, but that's it."

"Awesome. We'll order room service."

"No way. I'll meet you downstairs in the restaurant."

"Fine. No pressure. See you at seven."

Before she could retort that she *knew* there was no pressure because she was *not* coming up to his room, he had hung up.

Suzanne came home a couple of hours later, and they sat talking about her latest relationship failure: Matt in San Diego. Four days earlier, she had boarded a plane thinking he might be "the one," but by this morning she had insisted on taking a cab to the airport rather than letting Matt drive her, to avoid feeling any more connected to him than absolutely necessary.

"So did you end it?" Marci asked, hugging one of the couch cushions and glad to be focused on someone else's life for a few minutes.

"Not exactly. I gave him the whole, 'I'm easily spooked— don't come on too strong' speech. Told him we shouldn't rush anything and to wait for my call."

"And you'll be calling him . . . ?"

"That's right. Never."

"You're a class act, Suzanne."

"Hey, he's the one who talked to his mother five times over the four days I was out there. I mean, come on!"

"Maybe they have a special relationship. Maybe she's elderly and he needs to check in with her. Sounds to me like a responsible son."

"She has her own aerobics studio! And they talked for like twenty minutes at a stretch. One time I got so bored waiting for them to finish talking, I started doing a striptease in front of him. You know, kind of half joking, half 'pay attention to me, dammit?' He got all freaked out and said *I* was weird for putting unclean thoughts in his head while he was talking to his mother."

"Oh, wow," Marci said. "Maybe this time you did the right thing."

"You think? Anyway, enough about me. How's Jakie doing?"

Marci was quiet for a long minute, and took a deep breath. She told Suzanne everything, starting with Doug's surprise visit Thursday night, ending with Jake ignoring her calls and texts for the last two days. And, of course, her decision to go talk to Doug at the hotel that evening. At this last revelation, Suzanne raised her eyebrows, and Marci quickly tried to explain.

"I mean, he keeps *calling,* and he came all this way to talk to me. I feel like if I don't hear him out and settle this with him in person, it will never be resolved. You know?"

"Not really," Suzanne said after thinking for a minute, "but as you know, in-person, grown-up resolution isn't really my thing." They both laughed.

Suzanne got up to make some tea. "Oh, crap!" Marci said, looking at the clock over the stove. "It's almost six. I haven't even showered!"

She ran to the guest bedroom, where she'd been staying, and started digging through piles of clothes on the floor: things she had washed recently, things that were dirty, things traveling back and forth with her to Jake's apartment . . . She pulled out jeans and a slightly wrinkled V-neck sweater from the "sort of dirty" pile, and then started looking frantically for clean underwear.

By the time she got out of the shower, it was quarter past six. She had skipped washing her hair and so pulled it up into a messy ponytail instead, hoping to make up for sloppy hair by at least getting the makeup right. She leaned toward the bathroom mirror and eyed herself critically, reapplying mascara and comparing two sets of earrings. As an afterthought, she sprayed a bit of perfume on her wrists and rubbed both across the skin exposed by the low-cut sweater. She debated whether to put a tank top on underneath, but decided she didn't have time. "Looks like a lot of trouble for a little resolution," Suzanne commented from behind her. "You look pretty hot for someone whose fiancé is out of town."

"Shut up," Marci scowled. "Don't give me a hard time, okay? I'm nervous enough about this as it is. I just . . . I just want to get it over with." She searched for her favorite lip gloss.

"Mmm . . ." Suzanne murmured thoughtfully, and sauntered back to the couch.

"Can you blame me if I want him to regret dumping me, just a little? What's the harm in that?"

"Nothing."

"It's not like I'm going to sleep with him. I'm going to tell him nothing can happen between us ever again."

"Absolutely."

"If Jake were here, I would do the exact same thing I'm doing now. I'd even offer to take him with me."

"Does that include crop-dusting your cleavage there?" Suzanne teased.

"Shut up."

"Yes, ma'am," Suzanne called as Marci slammed the front door behind her.

The restaurant at the Hyatt Regency was nicer than Marci had anticipated. She felt underdressed in her jeans and sweater as soon as she walked in. It was also too romantic for her taste, with an enormous aquarium right in the middle providing ambient light, and cozy little tables all around, covered in white linen and empty water goblets. She debated suggesting that they go somewhere else, racking her brain for someplace more casual close by, but decided that putting Doug in her car was just getting her in deeper.

He was waiting in front of the hostess stand when she arrived, a few minutes late because of traffic downtown. He hugged her tightly, and she was overwhelmed by the familiarity of his scent and the feel of his arms. She forced herself to push back from him and give a polite smile before they followed the hostess to their table. He ordered a bottle of wine without even asking Marci, saying, "I had a few minutes to look at the wine list," by way of explanation.

As usual, all the speeches Marci had prepared on her way down to the hotel had evaporated from her mind. "So, I gather you enjoyed your tour of my hometown today?" she said, wanting to be the one controlling the conversation but not sure how to start.

"I did, I did," he said. Before she could speak again, he reached across the table and took her hand in his. "Marci, I want to apologize for the other night. I should not have come by so late, and I'm sorry. I just wanted to see you so badly, and I'd been driving all day. Well, I hope I didn't disrupt things with your fiancé too badly. At least, I see you're still wearing *this*." He stroked her engagement ring lightly with his thumb.

She jerked her hand back as though his touch were burning her, but said nothing.

"Trouble in paradise?" he asked.

"What do you want, Doug?" Marci's voice was the coldest she could muster.

"Marce, I'm sorry. I keep stepping in it, and all I really want is a chance to talk to you, to apologize, to try to make things right . . ."

"Which things?" she demanded. "What is it you think you can make right?"

He looked taken aback. Just then the waitress reappeared with their wine and asked for their dinner orders. Marci had not even looked at the menu, but Doug ordered anyway. "I'll have the grilled tilapia, please, and the lady would like the chicken special. Or did I get it wrong?" He looked at Marci playfully.

She looked at the menu, hoping to counter his suggestion, while the waitress fidgeted impatiently. After viewing all the options, she realized that she really did want the chicken. *Dammit*. She traded out the polenta for green beans, just to change something, and the waitress twirled away with a scowl for Marci and a flirty smile at Doug. Some things never changed.

He must have taken Marci's angry outburst seriously, because, like any good salesman, he changed tactics. Moved into small talk. What he'd seen that day, differences between Atlanta and Austin—all complimentary to Atlanta, of course. She watched the fish behind him darting back and forth through the giant tank.

Then he transitioned into office gossip. Cristina—the receptionist who had made Marci jealous all those months ago—and Jeremy were now dating. When Marci asked whether they seemed happy, Doug shrugged. "I think I heard they're living together or something now, so I guess they must be." *Good for Jeremy,* she thought.

Victoria had come out as a lesbian after developing a sudden, serious relationship with a petite blond woman who worked for the paper brokerage down on the fifth floor. She'd cut her hair short ("butch," Doug called it) and had started leaving at 5:00 P.M. every day instead of working her usual long hours. The firm had actually had to hire another person to make up for Victoria's only doing the workload of one person, but no one was complaining. She had been profiled in *Austin Out* magazine as one of the top gay executives in the city, and the firm had several new gay-focused clients as a result. Marci thought of Aunt Mildred with a smile, wondering what she would think of *Out* magazine.

The biggest news was that one of the partners, Jack Lane (the *L*), had resigned suddenly after a spat with the other three during their monthly cigar meeting. Jack was the most artistic of the partners and had a reputation for being temperamental, but he had been gone for two weeks this time and it was looking serious. "So," Doug was saying, "we either have to change the name of the firm or find someone else with an *L* name to join us." He laughed as though this were not a big deal, but his careworn features told another story. Could the firm survive without Jack's creative drive?

She had to catch herself and remember that she didn't care; this was no longer her world. She told Doug about the interview she had coming up on Monday, and he began asking her questions to help her prepare. Marci tried to refuse his help, to say that she didn't need his advice, but the truth was she did. Doug was giving her insight into exactly the kinds of things someone would be asking her on Monday, and suggestions about how to answer them to her advantage.

Only when the waitress came to clear their plates did she realize that she hadn't even had a chance to tell Jake about the interview yet. She tried not to think about how he would feel if he knew Doug had heard about it first.

As if on cue, Doug asked, "Is he good to you?"

Marci smiled. "The best," she said truthfully.

He winced. "Good. You deserve that."

"You've always fancied yourself an expert on what I deserve, haven't you?"

"Do you still have the necklace?"

With the slightest twinge of guilt, she remembered watching it sink into the Mississippi. "No."

"Marci, I know I can't undo everything that happened between us."

"That's the understatement of the year."

"Okay, okay. Can you just retract the claws a little? I know I'm a jerk, but I came all this way to talk to you."

"Fine."

He paid the check. She made no move to offer for her share. "Look, I have something upstairs for you. It's a letter, explains everything—or at least tries to explain everything."

"It's upstairs? Oh, Doug. How convenient. Not to mention predictable."

"It's not like that. I just felt weird carrying it around, vulnerable I guess. There's so much I needed to say to you."

"Why don't you give me the highlights?"

"Please, Marci. I agonized over what to say; I've been working on it for two months. It'll take five minutes."

Five minutes. In Doug's hotel room. "No."

"You don't even have to come inside. You can wait in the hall while I get the letter, and we'll come back down here. Or you can leave. Whatever you want."

When she stood, her head buzzed from too much wine and

the fancy-tiny portion of food. She followed Doug to the elevators, letting him lead her by the hand. They said nothing in the elevator, Doug whistling and Marci staring at the patterned carpet. As he had suggested, she stood outside his hotel room, feeling silly and puritanical. *A few months ago,* she thought, *how much would I have given for a night in a hotel room with Doug? Here we are, and I won't go in.*

He emerged with a small wrapped box and a thickly folded letter. "What's that?"

"Don't open it now. I just wanted you to know you have options. Here." The letter was smooth around the edges, as though he'd read and reread it many times himself.

They looked around awkwardly for a place to sit. It seemed silly to go all the way back down to the noisy lobby. Before he could suggest going into his room, however, Marci sank to the floor and leaned against the wall. She read.

Dear Marci—

At the time of this writing, I don't know if you'll be getting this letter in person or if I'll have to mail it to you. I hope we're together when you read it, because I want you to be able to look into my eyes and see how completely serious I am about every word.

"Oh, please," she said, and rolled her eyes. Doug looked a little hurt but remained silent.

There is no way I can ever make up to you what happened between us during those last days you were in Austin. When I heard that you left town, whatever was left of my heart broke into a thousand pieces because I knew I would never see you again. What hurt even more was knowing that I would never deserve to see you again after all I put you through.

I know that this explanation will not undo the hurt I caused you, caused both of us, but I hope it will help you to understand why things happened the way they did. If nothing else, I want you to know that what we felt for one another was not a lie.

Everything I did and said and felt for you was true, Marci. From our first kiss to that last night together in your apartment, I have loved you in a way that was deep and scary. I never thought about stepping out on my marriage before you, even though I have wondered for years whether I made the right choice marrying Cathy. I now know the answer to that question—I only wish I had figured it out before we met so we could have the relationship we were meant to have.

I meant everything I said on our last night together. Looking back on it, I wish I had not let you make me leave, but just held you all night long. If I had known it was my last chance to touch you, I would not have let go so easily. But when I did leave, as soon as I got down the stairs at your apartment, Cathy was sitting there, in her car. She honked the horn and told me to get in.

Marci remembered now, hearing the horn, oblivious in her bedroom just fifteen feet away. She had thought nothing of it at the time—had no idea it was the sound of her world being ripped apart.

I won't get into details, but it was obviously not a pleasant conversation. Cathy told me she'd been following me for a couple of weeks and had checked our phone bills and saw all the calls to your number. She demanded to know who you were, threatened to leave me and to tell everyone in our families what happened.

As you know, I refused to tell her who you were. But what

you don't know is that I tried to leave her. Right then and there, I decided nothing was worth being apart from you, and that I didn't care about my family's opinion if it meant being stuck in a loveless marriage. I told her I was in love with you, and I told her—finally—that I hadn't felt the same way about her for years. I was terrified but excited. I knew it was going to be an uphill battle, but that everything we had dreamed about together was waiting for me at the end.

I had my hand on the door handle, Marci, ready to come back upstairs to you.

That's when she told me about the pregnancy. She pulled out a sonogram, which later turned out to be a friend's that they had altered to show Cathy's name. She told me that if I left the car, or ever saw you again, she would make sure I never saw my own child and that my parents would never know their only grandchild. I know now that she couldn't have done this, not legally, and it's no excuse. But after surviving my parents' divorce and finally pulling the family back together, I can't tell you what that did to me. My heart is one thing. My kid's heart is something else. I couldn't do that to a child of mine.

Next is the worst part. Cathy made me promise to break it off with you. She threatened to monitor my cell phone activity and credit cards every day. She said if there were any calls, any communication, anything even remotely fishy going on, she would divorce me and take my baby to Beaumont forever.

I didn't know if she knew that we worked together or if she was just guessing, but I couldn't take any chances. I had worked so hard getting you the job at the firm, hoping it would help, in some tiny way, to make up for everything else. Hearing that you turned it down and left Austin made me feel like the worst person on earth.

Marci, I know you can't forgive me for the way I treated you that night in my office. It was all wrong, and I see it now. But at the time, I guess I thought it was the only way to make sure that I didn't lose my family, my child. I thought if you hated me, it might make it easier for you to move on. I guess it worked since you're back in Atlanta now and I heard that you're engaged already.

The rest of the story is just ugly, so I'll keep it short. I started realizing Cathy was not getting bigger, and I confronted her about it. At first she tried to pretend she was just small from morning sickness. Then a few weeks later she pretended she'd had a miscarriage. I was devastated. Finally one of her friends, someone who knows both our families from back home, I guess she felt sorry for me because she called me one day and told me the truth. It was a despicable, hurtful lie. Worse than anything you or I ever told. I didn't love her anymore but I had come to love my child, or thought I did.

By the time I found out the whole pregnancy was a lie, you were long gone and building your new life. I moved out the same day, and we finalized the divorce a few months later. I gave her everything she asked for. None of it means anything to me anymore.

Since then, I have been trying to get the courage to find you, talk to you. I have written this letter twenty times or more. It will never be enough to say it right. I honestly don't want to disrupt your new life, if you are truly happy in it. I just couldn't let you marry someone else without knowing the truth about what happened. And without hearing how truly, deeply sorry I am. I have made lots of mistakes, but hurting you is the biggest regret of my life.

Love always,
Doug

Tears splattered the letter as they fell from Marci's cheeks and nose. She hated him for bringing back all the pain she had left behind her. All the months she'd spent healing were gone, and the wound was fresh again. She hated him and felt sorry for him, too. His pain was clear in the words on the page and the expression on his face when she looked up.

He wiped her tears with his thumbs, cradling her head in his hands. "I'm sorry," he whispered. She had no idea what to say. He pulled her toward him and kissed her lightly on the lips. She felt dizzy and sad and scared.

"You're trembling," he said softly. "Come here." He kissed her again, more deeply this time. A protest rose somewhere in the back of her brain, but communication with her body seemed to be blocked. She moved toward him and kissed him back, putting her arms around his neck. The next thing she knew, he was lifting her off the floor and carrying her through the still-open door to his hotel room. So often she had dreamed about this moment—while they were together in Austin, and even after that, when she lay awake late at night, crying in the enormous guest bed at Suzanne's apartment.

Doug settled her softly on the bed, still kissing her. She was shaking now, almost violently. "Are you cold?" he asked. She shook her head. She thought of Jake, sleeping in a crappy motel off some rural highway, hating her. *And now he has every reason,* she thought vaguely.

Doug handed her the wrapped box. "Maybe this will warm you up."

Hands trembling, she pulled on the baby blue ribbon and opened the package. Inside the velvet cube was the last thing she expected: an enormous diamond engagement ring. Nearly twice the size of the more modest antique on her left hand, it was surrounded by her favorite tiny blue sapphires. She felt dizzy, in shock. She looked up to see that Doug was kneeling in front of her.

"I figured every girl is a diamond girl at *some* point. Like I said, I just wanted you to know that I am a hundred percent serious. And that you really do have options." He took her left hand in his and looked at the simpler ring Jake had given her three months earlier. "I guess I'd better let you decide whether you want to take this one off or not. You can't really wear two of these. It's Georgia, not Utah."

She was completely dumbstruck. Words failed her, and the tears began to flow more freely than before. "Why don't you take some time to think about it, okay?" Doug was saying. "It's a huge decision, I know. I can be back in town next weekend if you want, and you can tell me then. Or, hell, mail it to me if you decide to stay with your Southern gentleman. Just be sure to get the insurance on it. This baby wasn't cheap."

Marci knew his rambling jokes were to cover his nervousness. She had to smile because it was so very rare to find Doug Stanton in this state. He sounded like a complete idiot, which helped counter the feeling she sometimes had when she was with him that he was superhuman.

"I won't mail it," she said, and he smiled back at her. He kissed her folded hands and burrowed his head into her lap, nuzzling his way under her arms. She sighed deeply.

"Doug, the answer is no." She tried to say it quickly, so his hopefulness would not last long. Despite how much energy she had spent hating him all these months, she now had no desire left to hurt him.

"Look, honey, I know you're mad—"

"I'm not."

"Maybe you just need time—"

"I don't need time. I'm sorry, Doug, but our time is over. No matter what our reasons, this relationship was wrong. From the beginning, right until this very moment. I'm sorry about you and Cathy, I really am. But I'm with someone else now.

Maybe I deserve him and maybe I don't. But I know that *he* deserves better than this. I shouldn't be here."

She stood and found that the trembling had stopped and her head was clear for the first time in days. She handed him the velvet box. "Good luck, Doug," she said, and kissed him on the cheek. "Please don't ever contact me again, okay?"

"Marci, what are you saying? Don't you think we should talk about this? Don't you want to take some time to think it over?"

She supposed she never should have expected the great salesman to take no for an answer. She picked up her purse where it had landed next to the bed and turned toward the door.

"Look, Marce—I love you, but if you walk out that door now, I am not coming here again. Do you understand? I'm not playing games here."

When the door closed behind her, she did not look back. "Neither am I," she muttered, and strode toward the elevators.

21

There was a spot on a hill, just south of town, where Marci had gone sometimes with an old boyfriend after college. You could sit in the parking lot of a tiny church and watch the planes taking off and landing at Hartsfield-Jackson, crisscrossing in the sky as they danced in their flight patterns. As soon as she left the hotel parking lot (*$15 for two hours!*), she knew it was where she wanted to go next. It took her a few minutes of experimenting with various familiar-sounding roads and one scary turnaround—watched suspiciously by a cluster of teenagers whose party in the dead end of a residential street she had obviously interrupted—but she eventually found the road that curved uphill to the little church.

As she crunched into the gravel driveway, she was surprised that nothing appeared to have changed in the past eight or so years. In the part of the world where her parents lived, everything had been expanded and updated or torn down and rebuilt altogether since she had moved away. But the rickety old church was exactly the same, except for two new signs that designated general areas of the gravel lot for "pastor parking," and "deacon of the month."

It was quiet, at least for one of the higher-crime areas of town on a Saturday night. The parking lot was deserted, but she could hear the rhythmic thumping of cars in the near distance. She knew her father would kill her, so would Jake for that matter, if he knew she was here alone at night. She just wanted some time to process before heading back to the inevitable inquisition at Suzanne's.

She thought about Vann Peterson—Patterson? No, definitely Peterson—the guy who had brought her here a few times after dates. They had met in a mail room during one of her first temporary office assignments after college and dated for about four months before she called it off. She tried now to remember why. Had it been a good reason, or was it just one of the early examples of her running away?

Vann had been cute, charming, and smart. Like Jake, he was obsessed with old movies, and he was outraged to learn on their first date that she had never seen *Casablanca*. Their second date had been ordering pizza and watching it at his apartment. She remembered wondering whether he might not really be interested in her that night—because, despite her best efforts to make herself available during the movie, he hadn't so much as kissed her until the credits rolled.

On their third date, though, he had brought her here, where he loved to watch the planes take off and guess where they might be going. They sat on the hood of his car and made out for nearly an hour, putting her fears of his indifference to rest, especially when his hand found its way underneath her bra. She laughed at the memory of his sheepish smile when he did this. Why *had* she broken up with him?

It seemed so long ago now, but Marci thought she remembered her friends had suggested he had not been good for her. Suzanne had said something about the way he always steered the conversation back to old movies, Rebecca had noticed his "lack of fashion awareness" or something like that, but it was Jake's take that made an impression.

She remembered with sudden clarity. "He just doesn't seem like the kind of guy who would put you first," Jake had said in a big-brotherly tone.

At the time, Jake had been dating Regan, the microscopic blond girl with huge breasts, and Marci remembered Regan cuddling close to him and gushing, "That's what I love about him, always looking out for his friends. Isn't he just the best?"

Nearly a decade later, she felt a surge of nauseated jealousy remembering Regan smearing her perky self all over him at the table. No one in their little group had cared for her much, either, but, unlike Vann, Regan had not required an intervention to oust. Jake had always managed that process pretty well on his own. In fact, despite a steady stream of beautiful companions over the years, she couldn't remember a time when Jake had dated anyone for more than a couple of months.

A car passed by on the main road, slowing visibly as it passed the church. A black man with a gray mustache and suspenders looked out at her from the driver's seat and came to a slow stop on the shoulder, just past the gravel driveway. She imagined it was one of the church members, wondering what a solitary car was doing here on a Saturday night. She waved at him, but he continued to stare at her stonily. She supposed the fact that she was a white girl in jeans and a Gap sweater with a Toyota Corolla didn't mean she couldn't be a prostitute or a drug dealer.

As she watched him watch her, she knew it was time to go. The man kept his vigil, foot on the brake, until she had reentered her car and pulled out of the driveway. As she coasted down the hill, she saw him in the rearview mirror, backing into the driveway and starting back up the hill.

Returning to the apartment, she hoped Suzanne would be awake so they could talk. She had so much to tell, so much to sort out; what Marci needed most was some time with her best girlfriend.

When she pushed open the door, however, there were two faces staring at her from the oversize leather couch, lighted by the erratic flashes of some movie on TV. Suzanne's eyes were wide in an "I tried to warn you" expression, while Jake looked cold and sullen, still staring at the TV. In that instant, Marci realized she had turned her phone off to avoid calls from Doug after leaving the hotel and had never looked at it again.

"Hey . . . everyone," Marci said lamely.

"Hi, doll," Suzanne trilled, her voice unnaturally high and sweet, even for her. "Jakie and I have just been sitting here watching *Spiderman* for a couple of hours. It's been just like old times, sitting around watching movies, drinking beer. I was just saying that we need to do this more often, just get together and relax like this, you know, doing *nothing,* and I already told him I wasn't sure where you were tonight. But here you are! Okay, then, I'm going to bed! Nighty-night, y'all!"

She was up and off the couch by the time she finished this hasty speech, and her silky pink bathrobe fluttered as she closed the door to her bedroom, leaving Jake and Marci alone.

"Hey," she said. "You're back early. How was your trip?"

"Fine. How was your evening?" He spat the question out as though the taste of it offended him.

"It was, okay, actually," she said, answering genuinely. *Might as well get it over with.* "I saw Doug."

"I guessed that," Jake retorted coldly.

"It's not what you think." *Great, Marce. Really original.*

"Really, Marci? It's almost midnight. And how the hell do you know what I think?"

It was like being hit with a steel pipe. He had never been this angry with her before. In all their years of friendship, he had been the voice of reason, the cooler head. She had only ever seen him occasionally angry with anyone, and had always known she did not want to be on the wrong end of it. During the few times they had fought, he had simply remained calm and waited for her to come to her senses. Now she saw the hurt in his eyes and had to fight to stay where she was rather than run out the door.

"I'm sorry. I went to watch the planes. When I left Doug's hotel—"

"You went to his hotel?"

"Well, the restaurant at his hotel," she clarified, though it felt like a lie of omission. "To explain why I don't want him to contact me anymore."

"Oh, of course, I should have known," Jake fumed. "Whenever I never want to see someone again, the first thing I do is go visit their hotel."

"Well, it's just that he had called me a whole bunch, and after everything we had been through, I felt I owed him an explanation in person, you know? And that I was owed one, too." Jake was silent for a second, and she hurried through the rest of her explanation before he could cut her off again. "Anyway, we had dinner, and he gave me this note explaining everything that happened all those months ago. I told him it didn't change anything and not to contact me ever again and I left. That was hours ago. I went to go watch the planes for a while by myself. I thought you were staying in south Georgia. If I'd known you were here—"

"Jamal was in a car accident and shattered his leg. His career is probably over. The family opted out of the documentary."

"Oh, God, I'm so sorry—" Poor Jamal. And his family. And all of Jake's hard work.

"It wasn't his fault," he said simply. "Suzanne called you. I called you. Three times."

"I turned off my phone. I'm sorry; I just knew he would be calling me, trying to get me to come back, and I didn't want to deal with it. I thought you were out of range, so—"

"What were you thinking, going down to that place alone at night with your phone turned off? Do you have a death wish or something?" His anger was veering toward concern for her safety, and she began to feel relieved.

She took a step toward him. "I'm sorry, it was stupid. I—"

"So you didn't go to his hotel room?"

She froze. His voice was calm, but she sensed the mass of anger just below the surface. "Well?"

Lying had become such a habit for Marci over the past year that the justification sprang to her mind immediately. The truth—that she had gone to Doug's room—seemed so opposite everything she had intended and everything she felt. If Jake knew the truth, they were over. As a couple, and probably as friends, too. She knew this instinctively, the way she knew his gestures when he talked about something important or how he reached for her in his sleep. The thought of losing him now was unbearable.

But if she lied to Jake, she would have nothing left anyway. She looked up and said, "Yes, I did go to his room."

He winced as though she had touched him with a hot poker; his face returned to its previous stony expression. "And you kissed him?"

Marci looked at her shoes. "Yes."

He stood quickly, and for a moment she thought he might throw something at her, or put his fist through a wall. From the other side of the couch, he picked up his duffel bag, her first indication that he had come here intending to spend the night. He had planned to make up with her tonight, and she had been with Doug instead.

"Anything else?" he asked in a controlled voice.

"No." She held her left hand in her right, as though protecting Jake's ring from being ripped off her hand. "Well, he tried to give me a ring. I guess an engagement ring. But I didn't accept it. That's when I left."

"Why not?"

"What?"

"Why didn't you accept?" The malice in his voice was entirely new to her. Someone was ripping her chest open and pulling all the vital organs out right there in the living room.

"Because, Jake"—her voice was desperate—"because I don't love him. I just told you I don't want to see him ever again." She was crying now. She had made her choice tonight without even realizing it, a choice about the rest of her life. And now she was watching it slip away before her. "I love *you*."

There was a long silence. Finally, Jake broke it. "I don't think you even know what that means." His tone was not cruel, but cracked with something he had just begun to understand himself. He was disappointed in her, sorry to have chosen her. This hurt Marci most of all.

"Jake—"

"Don't, Marci. I'm going home."

He walked past her, slamming the door so hard when he left that a picture fell off Suzanne's wall, cracking the glass. When she turned around, Suzanne was in front of her. Marci held out the broken picture in both hands like an animal she'd just accidentally hit with her car.

"I'm sorry; I'll fix it. I'll pay—"

"Oh, honey," Suzanne said, flinging the picture into a nearby chair. "Shut up." She embraced Marci warmly, holding her and stroking her hair for nearly an hour while Marci sobbed uncontrollably into the pink silk.

22

s expected, Jake did not answer his phone the next
day or the day after. Marci could barely concentrate
on her interview for the copywriting job on Monday.

The interviews were held at a large hotel downtown—
thankfully *not* the Hyatt Regency—and seemed very rigorous
to her inexperienced eye. About twenty other applicants were
there for the 2:00 P.M. slot, from what she could see. They were
called one by one to meet with a recruiter individually, who
asked all the standard interview questions Marci had heard a
million times as a temp. She found she was only minimally
nervous. After her weekend fiasco, the job felt less like something she was desperate to get and more like a distraction from
her personal life.

At 3:30 P.M., the entire group sat together for a proofreading
test. Marci finished quickly, looked over her work, and then
stared at the clock for a couple of minutes before turning in her
paper. She didn't want to seem arrogant by turning it in too
quickly, but proofreading numbers, invoices, and correspon-
dence had been the bulk of her various jobs for the last decade.
A couple of the younger candidates cast envious or glaring looks
her way as she shouldered her messenger bag and left the room.

As she got in her car, she immediately wanted to call Jake to tell him how it had gone, and then remembered he wasn't taking her calls. She debated heading south toward his apartment—she still had a key, of course—to force him to talk to her but thought better of it and went to Suzanne's instead.

The next few days she waited and waited. No word from the recruiters; no word from Jake.

By Thursday morning, she was going stir-crazy enough that she got in her car and just drove. She followed one two-lane road and then another, turning north whenever she had the option, singing along maniacally with the radio and only occasionally breaking into tears. She ended up in the tourist town of Dahlonega, where she remembered coming with her parents as a little kid.

Marci wandered aimlessly around the quaint little town square decked out entirely with pine garlands, red velveteen bows, and twinkling lights. She felt out of place. She had no camera, stroller, shopping bags, or sense of purpose. She pretended to be interested in a couple of antiques shops and then stopped in Ye Olde Fudge Market and bought a quarter pound of peanut butter fudge and bottle of milk on impulse. She got back in the car and bit into the fudge—it was glorious—and remembered something Katie Couric said recently about using food to cope with unpleasant feelings.

"You can't block out the world with empty calories," Katie scolded, an apparition in a fashionable suit in her passenger seat.

"Fuck you, Katie," Marci said aloud, and took another, deliberate bite of the fudge. The apparition disappeared in a huff, as though even her own imagination had deemed her hopeless.

When she had made her way through a good bit of the fudge, her stomach began to protest the massive quantity of sugar, and she admitted defeat. She threw the last chunk away, along with the plastic milk bottle. She felt dizzy but steadied herself and got back in the car, heading home.

About three and a half 80s CDs later, she got to Suzanne's, where Rebecca was standing on the doorstep with a large box in her arms. "Oh, hey, Marce. I was just about to dig out my phone and call you. I thought you'd be home today."

Of course you did.

"What's all this, Rebecca?" Marci asked, though she already knew.

"I'm so sorry. I absolutely *hate* that he asked me to do this," Rebecca simpered, though it was clear from her tone and energy that there was nothing she "absolutely hated" about this. "Two of my best friends, heartbroken, and I just can't stand being caught in the middle."

"So Jake sent you with my stuff from his apartment?" This was obvious, of course, and she could clearly see her favorite flannel pajamas sticking up in one corner of the box. But it was as though saying the words might allow her brain to absorb the reality of this. *He had sent her stuff with Rebecca. Of all people.*

"Yeah, I mean, he couldn't figure out what to do—he is a *total* mess right now—and I reminded him that I work nearby. I knew you would both want to save the awkwardness. I mean, I was over there last night anyway . . ."

Marci was grateful to have her key in the door by the time this final dig struck home. If her hands had been free, she might have punched Rebecca outright. She opened the door and Rebecca followed her in, putting the box on the coffee table without waiting for instruction. "I wasn't over there, you know, in *that* way, of course," she was continuing gleefully. "I mean, what kind of tramp would I be? You guys just broke up . . ."

"Some kind of tramp," Marci muttered, but Rebecca did not seem to hear her.

"I just went by to see whether I could help at all. Jacob is such a wreck right now. Do you know he had not showered or changed in days? Well, I insisted, of course, and I made him eat something. I know that's what you would've wanted me to do. You're so lucky to have Suzanne here with you; poor Jacob only has little old me. But anyway," she placed a solicitous hand on Marci's arm, "how *are* you?"

"Not great," Marci said through gritted teeth. She hated how Rebecca had always called him Jacob as though she had a different relationship with him than the rest of the world did.

"Oh, I know. It's just awful. You poor girl. And how humiliated you must feel—a broken engagement! It's like a soap opera, but right here in our little group of friends. Well, don't worry, no matter what anyone says about you, I'll defend you. What are friends for?"

Marci could think of no good answer to this question at the moment, which was fine, because Rebecca was already onto the topic of a girls' night out they had planned for the following week and wondering whether Jake's sister, Leah, should still be included, "what with all the awkwardness and everything."

It was what she should have expected from Rebecca, and yet the reality of her words cut Marci deeply. Until just now, she had not thought of the situation with Jake as a "broken engagement," nor had she thought about what that would mean for their families and friends.

The invitations were not going out. The country club would not be reserved, despite the fact that Kitty had already told everyone she knew. They were going to hate her, as was Leah, whom she had always adored and admired. She might never see Jake's niece and nephews again. She had Christmas presents for Jasmine and the twins in her closet right now—what should she do with them?

And at the heart of it, the core problem: their little group of friends, together for more than a decade, would never be the same. She had torn it all apart with her selfishness.

Marci stared at the floor while Rebecca chattered on about

nothing, taking the rare opportunity to bask in the glow of her passive victory. Marci knew it wouldn't be long before Rebecca made a move for Jake. And unlike Suzanne and Marci, who tolerated Rebecca despite her annoying competitiveness, Jake had never been able to see that side of her.

Jake was hurt and vulnerable. Rebecca was beautiful and had adored him like a puppy for years. If Rebecca played her cards right, she probably had a shot.

And maybe that's the best thing for him. You broke his heart; maybe Rebecca will appreciate him. It's time to get down off your high horse and realize you're not so much better than her, or anyone else.

"So what do you think?" Rebecca was saying, and Marci looked up blankly. "About next Wednesday? Should I ask Leah not to come? Don't worry. I can take care of it; I need to call her anyway. I know she'll understand about the, um, special circumstances."

"No, no," Marci said, finally gathering her wits about her. "Don't say anything to her. I've been meaning to tell you, actually, um . . . that I'm not able to go that night anyway. Something for Nicole . . . it's a . . . thing. So see? No problem." Leah probably wouldn't come to girls' night anyway, after everything that had happened, but Marci wanted to give Rebecca no reason to interfere.

Rebecca clapped her hands at the resolution to the imaginary problem. "Ah, well, that's settled. But we'll miss you!" She jutted out her bottom lip in a show of sadness that Marci would not be present and then announced she was leaving. "Please call me if you need *anything*. I'm totally here for both of you, whatever you need."

"Thanks," Marci said as politely as she could, and closed the door behind Rebecca.

The box on the coffee table was a monument to her failure

as a fiancée, girlfriend, and friend. She wanted to unpack it before she fell apart. Beneath her pajamas were underwear, toothbrush, a stack of CDs, and a few books. When she lifted out some pieces of mail she'd taken to Jake's a couple of weeks ago, her heart stopped as something fluttered to the floor. Their bar napkin, the faded promise they had made all those years ago, had been returned to her, wedged between a cell phone bill and her new library card.

Marci unloaded everything on Suzanne a couple of hours later, from the havoc she had wreaked in the social structure to the idea that maybe Rebecca was a better fit for Jake than Marci was. They were sitting in the Mexican restaurant down the street from their apartment, drowning their sorrows in chips, tequila, and many renditions of "Feliz Navidad." Suzanne took a long swig of her margarita on the rocks before responding.

"Marcella Thompson. I have known you since the sixth grade, and that is far and away the *stupidest* thing I have ever heard come out of your mouth. Honestly, I don't know what to tell you about all the broken engagement garbage, except that if that's what this is, everyone will survive it. Even his parents, even Jake, even you. And I can't tell you what Jake will do or who he will end up with"—she held out her margarita glass dramatically—"but if Rebecca Williamson is better for him than you are, then I will eat my hat."

Marci smiled at her best friend's theatrics. "You're not wearing a hat."

"Then I will eat these very beautiful, very expensive shoes. Happy?"

"Ecstatic," Marci said in her best Eeyore voice. A momentary pause was broken as they dissolved into laughter, drawing sidelong glances from the table next to them.

23

A few days before Christmas, Jake finally returned one of Marci's daily calls. Even then, he managed to call while she was in the shower, during the fifteen-minute window each day that she was away from her phone. His message sounded more tired than angry.

"Marci, it's me. I'm calling you back. Well, I guess that's obvious. Look, I don't want there to be all these hard feelings between us, either, but I just don't know what to do with everything right now. I meant what I said. I feel like I don't really know who you are now. Like maybe I was living in a fantasy, trying to make our lives like *When Harry Met Sally* or something. I thought you were my future, and now I just don't know. But I need some time to sort things out. I guess what I'm saying is I need you to back off. Not forever, but just for a while. I'll get in touch when I can, okay? I love you—"

He said it almost automatically, as he had for months. For years. Then he seemed to catch himself. "Well . . . yeah. I do still love you. You have to know that already. . . ." He paused as though he wanted to elaborate, but then finished hurriedly: "Anyway, I'll call you in a few weeks. Okay? Take care of yourself and wish your family happy holidays. Oh, yeah, congratulations on the job." She heard something like a deep sigh before the click.

Marci stared at the phone for a while, and then picked it up and dialed. "Mom? Yeah, I'm okay. It's just . . . I think I'm going to come home until after the holidays."

She spent Christmas and the days following holed up on her parents' couch, watching bad movies with her dad and grazing from the cookie tins he brought home from work. It always astonished Marci that people brought sweets to the man who filled their cavities, but this year she was grateful. According to her mother's scale, she had put on ten pounds since November, but she told herself that New Year's resolutions were just around the corner.

Through a well-connected client, Suzanne managed to get New Year's Eve dinner reservations at Nikolai's Roof, where they indulged in a six-course meal beyond anything Marci had ever experienced. As each plate was taken away, waiters in red coats brushed crumbs from the pristine white tablecloth into tiny silver dustpans. Marci fought off the ridiculous urge to laugh each time this happened.

"Are you sure you don't want to go out to a club? It's still early," Suzanne said as they finished a roasted pear dish that reminded Marci of Thanksgiving at the Stillwells.'

"No, thanks," Marci said. "It just wouldn't be the same without . . . everyone." Neither of them had talked to Jake or Rebecca. Beth and Ray were also gone; after years of their kids' begging and pleading, they had consented to take their kids to Disney World for the holidays.

"I guess two single girls alone at a bar on New Year's *is* kind of sad," Suzanne agreed. For the past several weeks, she had been in the unusual condition of being dateless and Marci realized she had not even asked about it.

"Not sad, just . . . not tonight," Marci said. The waiter

brought the bill in a leather booklet. "Oh, I can't wait to see *this*." Her new job started next week, and she was sure Nikolai was getting her first week's pay before she'd even earned it.

"Nope," Suzanne said lightly as her manicured fingers snatched the bill. "This one is on me."

"What? Why?"

"Call it congratulations on your new job."

"Suzanne, this dinner had to be more than a hundred dollars!"

"Marci, honey, didn't your mama teach you anything? It's rude to talk about money at the table." She wore that prim little grin Marci knew all too well. There was no point in arguing.

"Thanks," Marci said, and downed the last of the vodka cordial in front of her.

They went back to their apartment and caught the last few minutes of the ball drop in Times Square. Marci thought of the years Jake had been in Times Square with his film school friends and the night four years ago when he'd kissed her at midnight. She had no idea where he was tonight, how he was celebrating, who he was kissing. Regis Philbin was hosting *New Year's Rockin' Eve,* and Jake was out of her life. Nothing was right with the world tonight.

Her new, *permanent* job started the following Monday, and Marci was immensely grateful for something to do all day. It turned out the company, Lambert Publishing, had hired about sixteen copywriters from the enormous pool of applicants she'd seen at the hotel. The recruiter had told Marci confidentially that she'd been in the top three chosen, which made her proud, and also concerned that someone would figure out within the first week that there had been some sort of huge mistake.

Orientation took up the first three days. The tedious experience included listening to long lectures on copier-usage policies and the benefits package and watching videos on sexual harassment and diversity. Because most in her cohort were high-achieving approval seekers in their first jobs out of college, the questions were numerous, detailed, and seemingly endless. Twelve women, including Marci, and four men had been recruited. Most wore freshly pressed and fashionable clothing, which must have been purchased either by parental support or with the last of their recently acquired student loans.

Of the sixteen, at least half were what Marci would call "airtime junkies." They could not seem to pass up any opportunity to hear themselves talk. Marci watched them in irritation and amusement. She knew that at some point in her life she had been just like these kids, desperate for attention and approval, with no clue how the real world actually worked. Her fears about being too old for the job faded as she realized that her relative maturity might be her biggest asset.

Marci drove back to Suzanne's each afternoon feeling more and more satisfied that, after nearly ten years of blowing aimlessly in the wind, her work life was finally heading in the right direction. Once orientation was over, they were broken into small teams and given projects to start on immediately. The creative director asked her to be the team leader for her group. This terrified and thrilled her.

The firm moved at a fast pace, with a sense of urgency she had never experienced in Austin. Women wore full makeup to work every day, and either pressed slacks or panty hose—a far cry from the lightweight skirts and sandals favored in Austin. People walked, talked, and expected things fast. The hectic pace was an adjustment, but for the first time in her life, Marci had a badge for getting into the building with *her* name and picture on it rather than TEMPORARY EMPLOYEE #7 or something similar. She had a desk where she could store things overnight and hang up pictures. But pictures of *whom*?

Despite her turmoil, the routine of going to the same place at the same time each day was soothing. She bought a commuter pass for the highway 400 toll plaza. She purchased a travel mug from the independent coffee shop along the route to work. She also invested in a tiny cooler for taking her lunch to work. She vowed to start paying Suzanne rent and bring lunch from home at least three times a week.

Some parts of her new routine were less satisfying. Several times each day, she picked up the phone and battled against the temptation to dial Jake.

Over the next two weeks, Marci worked nearly a hundred hours. This was partly from a desire to ensure her inaugural project as team leader was an impressive success, and partly as a distraction from the fact that Jake had not called her back.

She had begun looking at tiny apartments in the city, but Suzanne had insisted Marci stay on as her roommate. Marci hesitated. She really wanted to demonstrate her newfound independence by sending out change of address cards for her very own place. But between the rental prices of even the tiniest spaces downtown and how much she enjoyed living with her best friend, she decided she would stay.

They spent half a Saturday at Marci's storage unit, trading out boxes of Suzanne's spare-room junk for more of Marci's things. Suzanne even cleared off single shelves in her linen closet, refrigerator, and pantry for Marci's exclusive use. The bathroom was more difficult, because Suzanne had every bottle, jar, and tube known to woman spilling out of her vanity drawers, not to mention four separate hair-styling appliances. In the end, Marci opted to continue carrying her own toiletries back and forth in a basket, à la freshman dorm, rather than disrupt her friend's beauty routine.

It turned out that Marci's long-term stay was also the excuse Suzanne had been waiting for to redecorate the whole place. Marci discovered this when Suzanne began dragging her to home-decorating and furniture stores every day after work. "Don't you think we need a new couch, something that's less *me*, and more both of us?" "When we have big parties, we're going to need this cocktail service, don't you think? I've had my eye on it for a while . . ."

One freezing Tuesday evening, Marci stood in Pier One, exhausted and bleary-eyed, comparing throw pillows for Suzanne as though she were at the eye doctor. "This one or that one? That one or the green one? Shiny green or fluffy green?" She was fantasizing about clubbing Suzanne over the head with a pillar candle and dragging her to dinner when her phone rang. The number on her cell phone was familiar but not recognizable.

"Marci? It's Leah." She sounded breathless.

"Leah? Hey, what's wrong?"

"It's Daddy. He's collapsed."

24

The hospital was in the northern suburbs, an easy forty-five minutes from where Suzanne and Marci were in Buckhead. Still, Suzanne managed to get them there in less than half an hour. They skittered into the emergency waiting area and found Rebecca there, pacing back and forth and talking on her cell phone. She waved at them soberly as she finished her conversation. "No, still no word. He's conscious, I think, but the doctors haven't said yet whether he's going to be okay. They aren't even letting Jake or Leah in to see him right now. Okay, Mama, I need to go. I'll call you when I hear something."

She hung up and threw her arms around Suzanne and Marci. "Oh, it's so awful. Jacob is completely in shock; he hasn't said a word since we heard. I was just telling Mama that it's so lucky I happened to be with him when we got the call. We had just finished dinner."

"Rebecca, what happened?" Marci interrupted.

"They say he was out working in the garage—you know how he does—and Mrs. Stillwell heard a crash. He fell right into his workbench, knocked everything over. She ran out and found him unconscious, called 911. They don't know how serious it is yet, maybe a stroke. I guess they are waiting on tests.

He's in the ICU now. At one point he was awake, but I don't know now. They're only letting *immediate* family back there."

Marci's heart pounded in her chest. Of course, she had no idea what he thought of her now, but Mr. Stillwell had always been extremely kind to her. And he was Jake's hero. It was unthinkable. She sank into a nearby chair, and Suzanne held her hand while Rebecca made another call.

A few minutes later, Leah came through the double doors with her cell phone. Her eyes were puffy and red, her normally perfect hair falling out of a sloppy ponytail. She almost walked past them in her rush toward the door.

"Leah," Marci said softly.

"Oh, Marci! Thank God you're here." Leah stopped and threw herself into Marci's embrace. "It's Daddy. It's so hard to believe."

Not knowing what to say, Marci just hugged her back and said, "I'm so sorry."

"You have to go back there," Leah said. "He needs you." She nodded her head toward the double doors. Then she squeezed Suzanne's hand and said, "Hi, Suzanne. Sorry, I have to go call Dave and make sure the kids are okay. My damn phone doesn't work in here."

"Leah, I don't know," Marci started awkwardly. Did Leah know that she and Jake hadn't spoken in three weeks? Or did she think they were still engaged? She was suddenly painfully aware of the absence of the ring on her finger. She had stopped wearing it after Jake's last call. Behind Leah, Rebecca ended her call and turned to them with interest.

Leah put her hand on Marci's cheek. She looked exhausted. "We all know what happened, honey. Doesn't change the fact that you're family. Just go back there and tell them that you're my brother's wife. It's down the hall and to the left, waiting room E2."

At the words "my brother's wife," Marci's heart leaped, and she immediately felt ashamed for losing sight of the gravity of the moment. She followed Leah's directions, feeling Rebecca's stare halfway down the hall.

The smaller waiting room seemed to be for immediate families of those in the ICU. Jake's mother sat on a small couch in the corner, looking stunned. She sat perfectly straight, both manicured hands gripping her purse, which sat on her lap. She looked as though she were waiting to be called for a job interview for which she'd been up all night preparing. Jake was next to her, his head in hands, staring at the floor between his feet.

No one had stopped her on the way back, so it had been unnecessary to tell anyone she was Jake's wife. But with no nurses to question her and bring her to the family, she was unsure how to approach them. No matter what Leah said, Marci felt she was intruding on this very private moment after Jake had explicitly asked to be left alone.

Kitty Stillwell looked at her, but her expression did not register familiarity. Her face was barely recognizable as the formidable chair of the Country Club Social Committee. She looked at Marci with wide eyes and said quietly, "Robert."

Marci nodded sympathetically as Jake looked up and saw her standing there. Selfishly, she hoped he would rush into her arms the way his sister had, to allow her to comfort him and share his pain. But he didn't move and said nothing. His face was drawn and expressionless. Her heart ached for him. Quietly, she took the empty seat catty-corner from him, so that their knees almost touched. After a minute, Jake reached for her hand and held it tightly, but he did not meet her eyes again.

They sat in silence for a while; Marci had no idea how long. Leah returned and took the chair on the other side of her mother. People drifted in and out of the tiny waiting room, having hushed conversations and plunking coins in the vending machine for coffee and snacks. Marci wondered how Suzanne was doing in the waiting room with Rebecca but did not want to go find out. Jake was holding her hand.

After a while, a black man in a lab coat, who Marci thought impossibly young to be a doctor, came and sat across from them. He introduced himself as Dr. Williams and looked each of them in the eye individually as he said, "As best we can tell right now, it seems Mr. Stillwell has experienced a fairly serious stroke. Normally, strokes like this one are preceded by more minor events, but either Mr. Stillwell did not have those symptoms or ignored them."

Leah's head dropped to her hands. "Oh, Daddy," she murmured. Jake reached behind his mother to put a hand on his sister's back.

"He is conscious and seems alert right now. We're doing everything we can to keep him comfortable and to mitigate any additional damage to his body and brain. I'm hopeful we were able to act in time that his life is not in immediate danger." All four sighed deeply.

"You can go see him now, for just a few minutes, but I have to warn you that there is some pretty severe paralysis on the left side because of the stroke." He looked at Leah. "Your dad doesn't really look like himself right now. We don't know yet whether the paralysis is permanent. Once he has fully stabilized, we'll move him to a transitional unit and get him started on physical and occupational therapy."

"He's retired," Kitty said automatically, her tiny voice gravelly with disuse.

Rather than explain occupational therapy, Dr. Williams stood and led them toward the hall and Robert's room. As they filed out, he placed a hand on Marci's arm. "You're the daughter-in-law?"

"Yes," Marci said, not at all confident that this was the right thing to say.

"Listen, I know this is difficult for everyone, but they're going to need some help processing everything. Stroke recovery is complicated, and there will be a lot of details and options. I think it would be helpful if you could take some notes and help them sort through it. Sometimes it's easier for someone who isn't a blood relative. Understand?"

She nodded. He pointed down the hall, where a nurse was leading the other three into Mr. Stillwell's room. She walked slowly, giving them time, and then hovered just outside the door as the three of them crowded around his bed. With the slackening on the left side of his face, all the tubes and wires, and the white pallor of his skin, Robert Stillwell looked *nothing* like himself.

Marci watched through the glass as Leah fell to her knees next to her father's bed and buried her head in his hands. Robert put his functioning right hand on top of his daughter's head and seemed to look around at the rest of his family. She could not see Jake's face, and for the moment she was grateful for this. She did notice, however, that Jake's mom hung back from the others, closer to the doorway than to Robert's bed. As Marci watched her, trying to get a hint of her expression from behind, she saw that Mrs. Stillwell was wavering where she stood, leaning—

Marci got there just in time to keep Kitty from crashing into the counter with the hand-washing sink. She braced the tiny woman awkwardly against it, trying to get her hands under Kitty's armpits and yelling for Jake, who seemed to be turning around in slow motion. Marci managed to ease her into a seated position on the floor and then prop the unconscious woman up against her own legs while holding her shoulders. A large woman in scrubs rushed in and snapped at Marci to step back as she took over. Marci pressed herself backward against the door frame, trying to be as small as possible.

"It's all right," the woman said, with some sort of Caribbean accent. "She's only fainted. Here we go, sweetheart." She waved something under Kitty's nose and helped her into a chair in the hallway about ten feet from Robert's room. Expertly, she examined Kitty's reflexes and softly asked her questions. It seemed to take her a minute to be able to focus, and when she did, she threw her arms around the nurse's neck and broke into sobs.

As if responding to a silent alarm, Dr. Williams appeared from around the corner and knelt in front of Mrs. Stillwell. He muttered instructions to the nurse and then continued talking to Kitty, holding her hands. Marci could not hear him, but he saw Mrs. Stillwell nodding gently as she leaned into the doctor. The nurse returned with a small paper cup and a glass of water. Kitty took the pills without protest, and Dr. Williams patted her hands. The nurse stood nearby, her expression neutral.

"I've given your mother-in-law a mild sedative," Dr. Williams said, addressing Marci as he entered the room. "This has been too much strain for her. Someone needs to drive her home and help her get some rest. That's the best thing for everyone now."

"I'm not leaving Daddy," Leah said matter-of-factly.

"I'll take her home," said Marci immediately. She was happy at last to feel she could be useful.

"You don't have to," Jake started.

"Don't be ridiculous," she said firmly. "You need to be here. I will take her home. I need a key."

Jake pulled a small silver key off his key ring and handed it to her. Having something tangible to do made Marci feel calmer, more empowered. She was in temp mode—figure out what needs to be done and do it. She turned to Leah.

"What does your dad need from the house? Will they let him have anything?"

"I—I don't know." Leah looked utterly lost.

"It's okay. I'll ask at the nurses' desk. Is there a bag I can bring things in?"

"Bedroom closet . . . top shelf."

"Now, what about you guys? Don't you at least want a sweater and a pillow if you're going to stay here all night? Has either of you eaten anything?" They looked at her, wide-eyed.

"Okay, we'll see to that, too. Leah, why don't you give me Dave's cell phone number and I'll let him know I will be stopping by to pick up some things for you once we get your mom settled. You wear contacts, don't you?" Leah nodded. "So you'll want a lens case and your glasses, probably."

"Who's going to stay with Mama?" Leah asked.

"Suzanne or Rebecca will. I'm sure either of them will be happy to. I'll be back as soon as I can. Call me if you think of anything else."

Out in the hallway, the nurse helped the already-drowsy Kitty into a wheelchair and led Marci toward the exit. She confirmed that Mr. Stillwell could have a robe and slippers and suggested he might want a framed photograph of his family in the room with him. She told Marci at least three times that no live flowers were permitted in the ICU. On the way out to the waiting room, Marci saw it was nearly 11:00 P.M.

Rebecca and Suzanne had both dozed off in the uncomfortable-looking waiting room chairs. Rebecca's hand was clenched around her cell phone. *Probably hoping to hear from Jake,* Marci realized. Was it possible that Rebecca would one day serve in this role?

Marci woke them and explained the situation. "We need to get Mrs. Stillwell home and to bed, and I think one of us ought to stay with her. I am going to call Dave and pick up some things for Leah. Jake didn't say that he wanted anything, but maybe we should bring a pillow and something to eat anyway."

"I'll go with you and stay with her," Suzanne volunteered. "But I have a meeting at ten tomorrow, so you have to promise to come back for me. At least that way I can crash on the couch for a few hours."

"I can go get Jake's stuff," Rebecca said.

"Do you, um . . ." Marci hesitated in discomfort. "Do you have a key to his place?" *Surely not yet?*

Rebecca shook her head. "I'm sure he'll come out soon to check on me, though, and I can get his key then. It's no problem."

"You can take mine," Marci said, fumbling with her key chain and not meeting Rebecca's eye or looking at Suzanne, who she could see reacting in her peripheral vision. "I haven't returned it to him yet. I guess you can do that for me." She tried a hollow little laugh that had no effect on the awkwardness whatsoever. As she handed Rebecca the key, she was vaguely aware that she was passing off one of her last excuses to see Jake after this.

It's better this way, she decided. *Clean slate. If he wants to see me, he'll see me.* The nurse pushing Mrs. Stillwell coughed loudly, and Suzanne and Marci followed her to the exit. Suzanne went to get the car while Marci waited with Kitty, who had begun to snore softly in the chair. Loading her in the car was easy; she was such a tiny woman. Marci thought about what she'd heard once about men tending to choose wives who remind them of their mothers, and wondered how Jake ever could've thought she fit this bill. She was twice the size of this petite woman. Rebecca, on the other hand, had been a perfect size 2 since puberty.

On the way to the Stillwells' home, Kitty seemed to half wake, and began singing the Supremes' "You Can't Hurry Love," off-key, in the backseat. Suzanne and Marci exchanged covert smiles in the front, a relief after the long night of worrying and waiting.

With Kitty tucked into bed and Suzanne snoozing on the couch, Marci made her way to Leah's house. A bleary-eyed Dave met her at the door with a duffel bag and a pillow. Never much for conversation, he said only "hey," as he handed these items to her and went back inside.

The emergency waiting room was empty when she returned. She made her way back down the now-darkened hall, unobstructed by the reduced staff of night nurses. In the back waiting room, Leah accepted the bundle gratefully. She nodded toward Robert's room, indicating that Jake was with him. "Go on," she said, and settled in with her pillow.

Marci entered the room quietly and took the seat next to Jake by his father's bed. She was exhausted. Robert was sleeping, undisturbed by the soft beeps and clicks from the machines. Jake and Marci sat there for a long time without saying anything; she was grateful just to be next to him.

Around 4:00 A.M., Marci awoke with her head on Jake's chest and a long string of drool pooling on his shirt from the corner of her mouth. She hurriedly wiped her mouth and his shirt, but it didn't seem to bother him. As she sat up, she noticed that he had his arm around her. He shifted to give her space to sit up straight.

"How long was I asleep?"

"About an hour."

"Oh. Sorry."

"It's okay. There's nothing to do right now but sit and stare at him," Jake said morosely. "You should probably go home and get some sleep. I know you have to work tomorrow."

Marci looked at the clock. Four A.M. "Later today," she murmured.

"Go on; we're fine here. When Leah wakes up, I'm going home to shower and sleep for a few hours."

She stood to leave, and Jake grabbed her hand. He looked at her directly with tired eyes. "Thank you for being here."

"Of course."

He held on to her hand. "Marci, about Rebecca—"

"You don't have to explain—"

"There's nothing going on with us. I mean, I know she wants something to happen, but it's not. I just thought you should know." He gave her a grim little smile.

Marci leaned down and kissed his cheek. "Thank you."

25

For the next three weeks, Marci spent most of her evenings, weekends, and some lunch hours at the Stillwells' home or the hospital. She kept a notebook of Robert's progress, medications, and advice from the doctors and nurses. She ran errands for anyone who needed it and sat with Robert and read to him from his favorite war histories while Leah and Jake took breaks for dinner or fresh air.

Overall, his recovery seemed to be going well. He had been moved out of the ICU after a couple of days and, according to his treatment team, showed very positive signs for regaining some functioning on his left side. They had started him on light physical therapy in the afternoons. His speech was deeply slurred even at his best moments, but he seemed able to understand pretty well. At her mother's suggestion, Marci had purchased him a handheld marker board so he could communicate.

Marci's parents came to the hospital frequently, too. Her dad often turned up in the mornings before his first patients of the day. Arthur shared Robert's love of military history and took particular joy in having an excuse to spend an hour a day reading aloud from Robert's books. Her mom liked to come in the early afternoons, when she knew Kitty would be alone with Robert and need support. Each day, Kitty seemed stronger, a bit less fragile, but she was far from herself. Marci wondered a few times what would've become of her if Robert had not survived the stroke.

After a few weeks, the hospital staff began preparing the family for the process of moving Robert home. He had made it very clear, using the red marker and bold letters on Marci's board, that the option of a temporary assisted-living setting was *not* acceptable. So he would have nursing care and in-home physical therapy and would need a special bed on the first floor of their home. Because there was no bedroom on the ground floor of the Stillwells' enormous manor, Kitty's prized drawing room, which had once been featured in *Classic Southern Homes,* had to be appropriated for his care.

The financial cost of the medical equipment and of retooling the downstairs bathroom for Robert's use was not an issue for the Stillwells, but the emotional toll on Kitty was substantial. She cried as the movers came to pack her beautiful baby grand piano into a crate for storage, and cried again when the company delivered the hospital bed for Robert.

Suzanne, Marci, and Leah spent an entire Saturday packing all of Kitty's most precious antiques and knickknacks and, the following Saturday, redecorating the room to look like a cozy bedroom and minimize the sterile look of everything. Suzanne, far more talented than Marci in this regard, even designed and hand-sewed a beautiful cover for the bed, with holes for all the buttons and switches and elastic to allow it to move when the bed was repositioned. This seemed to lift Kitty's spirits tremendously. When she saw it, she cried again with gratitude and hugged Suzanne tightly.

The night before Robert's homecoming, Marci sat with him while the rest of the family members were at the elementary school play in which Leah's daughter was performing. She read to him for a while and then showed him pictures on her phone of the remade drawing room. "And, of course, when you're back to your old self, we can put everything back just the way Kitty had it. I made sure to take pictures of all of it, just the way it was."

Robert half-chuckled and gestured for the board. "U know Kitty," he wrote, and Marci laughed. He took the board back and wrote again. He pointed to Marci as she read it. "Good daughter." For the first time since his stroke, Marci allowed herself to cry freely, with her head buried in Robert Stillwell's hands.

Though she had seen Jake frequently over the past few weeks, they had not talked about their relationship directly, and they had not been physical at all. Marci was doing her best to be Jake's friend and keep a respectful distance from everything else. Inside, though, she was dying to know how he felt about her, what he thought about their future together.

She knew now that she loved him and regretted deeply her indecision when he had wanted to build a life with her. She had begun realizing it before Doug appeared at the door, and the last few weeks had solidified everything. Maybe Nicole was right: she always wanted what she couldn't have and so Jake's rejection had inspired her to go after him. Or maybe she really had always loved Jake, deep down. The experiences of the last few weeks had brought those feelings to a new level, opened her eyes to the man Jake was today, not just the boy she'd fallen for in college.

Either way, Marci had a strong sense that, wherever she was now, there was no going back. Every time she saw Jake, her heart jumped and hope filled her, but she had become a master of discipline when it came to holding back these feelings. Of course, the situation with Robert, not to mention that Jake had told her explicitly to back off, made any sort of expression inappropriate.

Yet she could not help wondering whether Jake was feeling some of the same things. Though he said nothing, she sometimes caught him looking at her. They had eaten dinner together a few times, sometimes in the hospital cafeteria, other times at the Waffle House down the street. Their conversations were kept to the state of his dad's health and some small talk, which she let him lead. One night he observed, when her hands were resting on the empty table as she waited for her omelet and hash browns, "You're not wearing the ring."

His tone was completely neutral, but it was a shock to her anyway. It was as if he'd just noticed that she had new glasses or something. "No. Well, I didn't know. After everything."

"Yeah. I guess so." He nodded gravely. He followed with: "Jamal is going to Georgia next year."

"What?" Marci was as surprised by the abrupt change of subject as she was by the news itself. "I thought he was injured."

"He is," Jake said. "But he's going on a full academic scholarship. I actually sent some film of him to the business school, and they found him some money and an assistantship. It's a really big deal for an undergraduate."

He was beaming. Seeing his obvious pride breaking through the cares of the past several months was wonderful. "Wow. So you got his family to come around?"

"Yeah. I went down there and talked with his dad for a long time. He made me go fishing with him for like four hours. They were so devastated after the accident. I think they turned their anger on me, too. I don't blame them—a rich white kid from the city capitalizing on their son's disappointment . . ."

"But that's not what you were doing!"

"I know that, but you can see how they might feel that way."

"Yeah," she conceded.

"Anyway, the important thing is that Jamal gets to go to college. And they signed back on for the documentary. I think it's going to be an interesting contrast to the players who do make it to the college teams."

Marci sat back and enjoyed the steady flow of Jake's voice as he continued to update her on all aspects of his film. It seemed he had missed having someone listen to all the details of his project, and she certainly had missed hearing him talk so freely. He asked her about her new job and seemed interested in her description of Lambert. They never returned to the subject of the ring or their relationship. Still, she did not sleep that night, analyzing from every angle what the conversation might mean.

Once Robert returned home and a full-time nurse was hired, things settled down for the Stillwells, and Marci was no longer needed. She began to focus again on work: the project she was leading was due in a few weeks, and it had been hard to give the team her full attention lately. She found herself sinking into Suzanne's new leather couch in her pajamas by 7:30 every night, eating whatever could be found in the freezer or ordering takeout, and watching bad television until she fell asleep.

She thought about Jake often, and even called him a few times to check on Robert, but they did not talk for long, nor did they address what was becoming the elephant in the room between them. After a while, Marci grew so restless and desperate for information that she actually called Rebecca and invited her to lunch, hoping she would know more about what was going on in Jake's world.

This turned out to backfire, as tiny Rebecca spent nearly the entire lunch talking about dieting and carbs and her personal trainer. Enjoying a meal with Rebecca when she was on a dieting kick was impossible, so when Rebecca ordered a mixed green salad with grilled chicken, Marci followed suit. She could not steer the conversation to Jake in any roundabout way, so she finally just blurted, "So how is Jake?" as the waiter cleared their plates and she glanced longingly at a cheeseburger on the table next to theirs.

Rebecca looked at the table, as though fascinated by a bit of salad dressing splattered there. "I don't really know. We"—she hesitated—"we haven't had much time to hang out lately." Marci tried hard not to be happy about this. But not too hard.

One rainy Tuesday afternoon, Jake called and asked whether Marci was free for dinner. She was, or said she was, and then called Suzanne to break off their plans for Tuesday-night margaritas. For the rest of the afternoon, she sat at her desk and tried to visualize her closet, what was in it that was clean and would send the right message. She needed something that was casual but not sloppy, available but not . . . Rebecca.

In the end, none of this hypothetical planning mattered because her boss pulled all the team leads into a late meeting at 4:30, which of course went on forever. She fidgeted and stared at the clock while he droned on, until he finally ended the meeting with a snide, "Apparently, Marci has somewhere more important she needs to be, so we'll close out here." Embarrassed, she slunk out of the conference room under astonished looks from her peers.

Jake's car was in front of her apartment by the time she got home, so the gray skirt and white button-up she'd worn to work would have to do. She couldn't believe how nervous she felt, climbing her stairs. Jake had not given a reason for the dinner date, but it was getting hard to control the hope that they would finally be having the conversation about "us."

"You look nice," he said as she entered the apartment. He and Suzanne were on the couch, watching the nightly news, which Marci found funny because she knew Suzanne would much rather be watching reruns of *Project Runway* at that time of day.

"Thanks. Sorry I'm late; I got called into a meeting."

He stood and grabbed his rain jacket off the back of a barstool, tossing a "see you later" at Suzanne as he did. The bad news was Marci had no time to change clothes; the good news was that whatever his reasons for asking her to dinner, he didn't seem to feel it was appropriate to include Suzanne. *So that was something.*

Marci threw down her work bag as she turned to follow him, when Suzanne appeared next to her as though she'd sprung from behind a bush. "She'll be right behind you, honey," she called into the hallway after Jake.

The woman could have worked for NASCAR. In less than thirty seconds, Suzanne pulled Marci's skirt up by a good three inches and folded the waist over on itself, unbuttoned the top button of the work blouse, revealing more cleavage than Marci was comfortable with, and out of nowhere produced lipstick, blush, and powder. She attacked Marci's cheeks, eyelids, and lips with a quick brush and a critical eye, and then snatched the clip from Marci's hair so that her hair fell to her shoulders.

"But the rain—"

"Go," Suzanne said, ignoring Marci's protests and kissing her on the cheek. "Have fun."

Marci trotted after Jake, tugging at her skirt just a bit. She saw Suzanne's point, of course, but she didn't want to look like a *total* hooker. She held her rain jacket over her head as she ran to his car, where he was holding the passenger door open under an umbrella.

"You really look amazing," he said as he pulled out of the parking space. "This career thing looks good on you."

She could feel herself blushing. "Thanks."

They went to Alfredo's, one of their favorite Italian restaurants. The romantic setting, with low lights and dark corners, didn't seem particularly significant because they had been there often enough with the whole group. Still, her heart pounded as the maître d' showed them to a tiny corner table in the back. She ordered a glass of wine to calm her nerves. Jake apparently had the same idea because he chose a gin and tonic.

Robert was doing well, Jake reported. Recovering faster than most people expected of someone his age. He was driving the nurses and physical therapists crazy, pretending to be asleep when they arrived and correcting their grammar on his little white board. Marci laughed. He had regained some muscle control on the left side and they were optimistic he might walk again. Overall, it seemed very positive.

Jake asked her about work, and she told him the basics about the project she was working on and her upcoming deadline. It felt good to talk with him about it. Things had always seemed more manageable when she talked to Jake about them—he had an unfailing confidence in himself, his friends, and the world. Even when he simply nodded or said "uh-huh" as she told him about it, she felt less nervous about the evaluation that was just around the corner.

When the drinks came, they sipped in silence. Jesus, their go-to topics had not even gotten them through the arrival of dinner. What now? She fidgeted with her wineglass and tried to think what to say next.

Finally, Jake spoke. "I wanted to say thank you for everything you did for my family, for me, in the past few weeks. It's been a rough time; I don't know how we would've made it through without you."

She smiled and looked down. "Of course. It's nothing you wouldn't have done for me."

"I know that," he said, and took her hand. "But that doesn't make it mean any less. No matter what happens between us. Well, just know that I will never forget it."

She wanted to ask, was terrified to ask, and finally decided that she *had* to ask. "No matter what happens?"

Now it was his turn to stare at his glass as though at any moment it would reveal the secrets of the universe. He was still holding her hand, but loosely, lying on the booth seat between them. Even this casual touch electrified her.

"I know we need to talk about us," he said. "Frankly, I've been putting it off, because I didn't know what to say. I'm terrified of losing your friendship, and all this stuff with Dad happened and . . ."

She felt a sudden surge of panic, feeling something familiar about this speech. *I'm terrified of losing your friendship.* Vague memories of breakups and brush-offs past were stirring up in her as he talked, and she felt a compulsion to run out of the room. *Rewind, rewind, rewind,* she thought stupidly, *go back to the part where I had no idea what he was going to say.*

"Jake, we don't have to talk about this now," she said, trying to stop the flow. Any minute, he was going to tell her that it had all been a mistake, he'd seen her true colors, and he could never imagine himself with someone like her. If she could just stop him from saying it, it wouldn't have to be true. "Maybe you need more time to think things through. You really need to focus on your dad right now."

"No, no," he said. "I can't keep putting it off. You deserve to know something. You've been really patient."

This can't be good.

"The main reason I haven't been able to talk to you about us is"—he sighed deeply and continued—"I honestly don't know how I feel right now."

"That's okay," she stammered. "So much has happened—"

"I know I love you," he said, quieting her. He looked directly into her eyes. "I really do. You're my best friend, and if this experience with Dad has taught me anything, it's what a true friend you are. I'm lucky to have you in my life. Dad even pointed that out to me a couple of days ago."

So that was why he'd called out of the blue. Marci thought of Robert and smiled.

She could feel the terrible next word hanging in the air over the table. She said it for him, in the hopes that it might hurt less coming from her own lips. *"But?"*

He nodded. "But I'm so confused right now. I mean, a few weeks ago I thought we were going to be together forever. I had not one single doubt about us, even though I could tell you weren't sure all the time. I just figured I'd been waiting for us to happen for ten years now. I could wait for you to catch up. Stupid, right?"

She shook her head, but he went on. "Of course, during those ten years I knew you were seeing people, just like I was. It's just, whenever I was with some other girl, even for a few months, I guess in my mind I was always comparing her to you. Maybe that's why I could never give my whole heart, even though I didn't understand it at the time. That's why I never really gave anyone a chance, even though I kind of thought I did. Is this making sense?"

She nodded, numb.

"I knew you were dating while you lived in Texas and California and all those places. I remember hearing about some of the guys, and I'd get jealous, but I'd tell myself that they couldn't be that serious. Anyway, we were just friends. When I went to get you in Austin, I knew it was about more than just losing a job. I knew there had to be something more, but I just told myself if it was a big deal, you'd tell me about it. I didn't want to think about it, honestly. See? I've hidden from myself as much as you hid from me. So when that guy showed up on my doorstep, and I saw the way you looked at each other . . ."

"Jake—"

"No, please don't. I know you never wanted to hurt me, but I saw what I saw. There was so much between you; it was all over your faces. So much passion, and your anger. I've never seen you that angry, and I knew there was so much more to that story. I knew then that I was just the rebound guy."

"You're not." Marci choked. *Again, the tears.* She wished she could control her crying, to keep from seeming weak and helpless at the moments she needed most to be strong and convincing.

"And when I figured out he was married," Jake started, and then the waiter arrived with the food.

Marci pretended to look for her dropped napkin on the floor to hide her face. Her worst fears were confirmed. Jake was not just hurt by her feelings for Doug and the fact that she'd hidden the relationship. He was disappointed in her for doing the wrong thing. That hurt more than anything. She'd known her relationship with Doug was wrong all along, but it had never occurred to her that it would cost her the one person she loved and admired most.

She composed herself and tried to focus on appraising her veggie lasagna. When the waiter left, she said quickly, "Please, don't say anything else. I can't do this right now."

He looked mildly surprised, but nodded gravely. They ate in silence and skipped dessert.

In the car on the way back to her apartment, she broke down. "Jake, I know I can't explain it away, what I did. I understand if you don't see a future for us. That's hard for me to hear, but I don't blame you. Not at all." Her voice quavered, but she plowed on, knowing she needed to finish this or she might never have another chance. "But please don't, don't be ashamed of me. I'm ashamed of myself enough already, and I just couldn't stand it if you felt that way, too. It's hard to explain, and I know there's no excuse."

"Ashamed of you?"

"I did know he was married when we got involved, and I hated it every minute, but I don't know. I was so weak, and he was so unhappy in his marriage. He did leave his wife, in the end, or at least he said he did, not that I care now."

"Why would you think I was ashamed of you?"

"You said—"

"Marci," he said, pulling the car over. "I know you, and you're not the kind of person who sleeps with a married man. When I found out, I knew how deeply involved you must've been and why you kept it a secret. It made me so jealous. It still does, right now, just knowing how intense it was." He reached over and brushed a frizzy curl out of her face. "God, sweetheart. I'm the last person who would judge you."

Relief washed over her, and she fell into him. The rain pounded against the windows and the dark deepened outside. When she pulled away from him, he looked sad. "I better get you home," he said, with a glance at the night outside.

He kissed her on the cheek in front of the apartment, and she ran upstairs without looking back into the downpour. Suzanne was hovering just beyond the living room, waiting to see whether Marci was alone before emerging. They collapsed on the couch, and Marci sobbed out the details of the whole evening.

"So I guess it really is over," she summarized when she had hit the highlights.

"Did he ask you for the ring back?"

"No, but he wouldn't. He's not like that. I'll get it to him, I guess."

"You're right, he's not like that, but that is a family heirloom. Maybe he hasn't made up his mind yet."

"I don't know; he sounded pretty sure."

"In any case, I have a bottle of Shiraz already open and Ben and Jerry's that's been melting the perfect amount of time. I'll be right back."

"You're the best," Marci said, squeezing Suzanne's hand gratefully.

Outside, there was a loud screech of tires and the distinctive crunch of metal. It sounded as though it came from the entrance to the complex. They glanced at each other, and Suzanne went to the window to investigate.

"Please tell me it's not Jake," Marci said. Then, as an afterthought, "And that everyone is okay."

"Well, it's not Jake," Suzanne said. "Because he's still right in front of our apartment, pacing back and forth in the rain like an idiot."

"What?" Marci was halfway across the room before her feet hit the floor.

"And I think I can see the accident, too. It's hard to tell, but I think everyone is okay. I mean, since you're so concerned and all," she added as Marci shoved her out of the way.

"What is he doing down there?"

"Getting soaked. And wearing a groove in our front sidewalk."

"Should I go down?"

Suzanne appraised Marci critically and smiled. "Is there anything I could say to stop you?"

Marci raced down the stairs, oblivious of the danger of slipping on the concrete steps. She emerged into the rain, which fell in sheets under the yellow halos of the street lamps. She had not thought to bring her coat or an umbrella. By the time she thought of going back upstairs for one or the other, Jake had spotted her.

"Hey," he said, reddening.

"Hey," she called. "You're soaked."

He walked toward her. "So are you now." He glanced reflexively at her chest, where the rain had saturated her white blouse, revealing a clear view of her bra and cleavage. She made a feeble attempt to cover herself and then gave up.

"What are you doing out here?" she asked.

"I wish I knew. I couldn't make myself leave, Marci. But I couldn't come upstairs, either. I have all these feelings, and I don't trust any of them."

"Oh." What else could she say?

"Tell me one thing," he said, pulling her under the half shelter beneath the eaves, two stories up. "Do you, I mean, could you ever, could you love me the way you loved him?"

"What?"

"I mean, with that kind of fury?" He bent his head, as though it embarrassed him deeply to say this aloud. "The look I saw on your face when he came to the door. I've loved you for years, Marci. I'd give anything to make you look at me that way. I just need to know it's possible."

"Oh, Jake." She looked up at him. Her heart was a puddle between their feet. "It's more than possible. I love you that way already."

He looked up at her, and rain dripped from his messy hair over his eyelids and down his face. His face was searching hers, longing for confirmation that what she was saying might be true. He was irresistible in this state. Marci put both hands on his face and pulled him toward her.

They had kissed many times before this. The drunken kiss all those years ago in a college bar. Quick, affectionate pecks on the cheeks or lips when one or both of them had been dating someone else. The mysterious New Year's Eve, and the exploratory kiss at Nicole's bachelorette party. Most recently, the careful, gentle kisses they had shared as an engaged couple, when there had been a kind of domestic sweetness about it.

But tonight, in the rain outside Suzanne's apartment, something ignited between them that Marci had never experienced before. Of course things had been passionate with Doug; their limited time together and the constant fear of being caught heightened every sensation when they were together. But this was different.

Jake's mouth responded to her own with a warmth and forcefulness she had never experienced from him. It was like water had slowly been brought to a boil around her while she wasn't paying attention. All at once there was freedom and terror, desire and tranquillity, hope and relief. Everything she wanted was here, and nothing could threaten it. Except maybe catching pneumonia.

He pressed her against the wall and they kissed to block out the world and the rainy night around them. They shivered and laughed like teenagers. By the time they dredged upstairs, dripping from every stitch of clothing and inch of skin, Suzanne had gone to bed. She'd left half the bottle of Shiraz on the counter with two glasses and a candle burning for them. Jake poured the wine while Marci pulled every clean towel in the apartment out of the linen closet.

She made a pallet on her bedroom floor for them, and they went together to the bathroom to remove each other's dripping clothes. They laughed at their ridiculousness and then tried to stifle the giggles to keep from waking Suzanne, which only made them laugh more. They ran naked from the hallway bath to her room like streakers.

Marci couldn't remember being happier at any other point in her life. She could scarcely believe that just a couple of hours earlier, she had been afraid of losing Jake forever. Now he was lying naked in front of her on a beach towel on her bedroom floor, tracing the line from her neck down her shoulders to her fingertips and back. Electrified at his touch, she shivered and looked into his eyes, where the laughter had faded completely.

Everything that had happened in the last several weeks—Doug, the hotel, the rings, Jake's dad, the hospital, Rebecca—seemed to intensify the energy between them. As Jake reached to pull her close to him, Marci knew that things had changed forever.

26

She awoke to the usual sound of her alarm, but from far away. Between the tangle of towels entwined with all her limbs and Jake's arms locked tightly around her, it took her a couple of minutes to get to the buzzer. By the time she did, Suzanne was calling at the door. "Wake up, lovebirds! Time to get ready for work!"

Jake groaned on the floor and rolled over, grabbing Marci's ankle and pulling her down as she tried to pass him. "Don't go," he begged. "Call in sick. Let's stay here all day and make love. I think I can promise you at least two more times before lunch."

"You've got to be kidding," she said, and kissed him dismissively before wrestling free. "I think five times in twelve hours is more than either of us can handle. Besides, I can't miss work until after this project gets evaluated."

He let go reluctantly. "Well, at least promise me I can take you to dinner tonight."

"Done," she said, and tiptoed into the hallway toward the shower, wrapped in a loud pink beach towel covered in orange flowers. She threw Jake's still-damp clothes from the night before at him, and he muttered something about hoping he still had some dry boxers in a drawer around here somewhere, assuming Marci hadn't gotten so pissed that she'd thrown them out. When she came back from her shower, he was gone.

She looked for her engagement ring as she got ready for work, thinking it was safe to put it back on after last night, and found that was missing, too. A slight panic set in, even though she felt fairly positive that the ring had been there the day before. She'd looked at it obsessively nearly every day for weeks.

Surely Jake had picked it up, maybe to give it to her again that night? She thought about the alternatives, that she had misplaced it without realizing or that someone had broken into the apartment without leaving any evidence and taken nothing but that single piece of jewelry. This latter seemed particularly unlikely given the extensive and pricey collection Suzanne kept in the next room.

By the time she got to work, the stress of the final preparations for the project had sucked her in completely. She had no time to leave the office for lunch or even return phone calls, much less to ponder the mystery of her missing ring. In any case, her mood was too deliciously good to let worry of any sort bring her down. She was particularly gracious and encouraging with her team and approved everyone's creative suggestions, even the ones that would have made her nervous the day before. This seemed to make the team happy, if a bit confused.

So even though the pressure was on and the pace hectic, everyone's spirits were elevated and cheerful all day. It was as though the whole team had enjoyed a long night of kissing in the rain and great sex, not just Marci. The other teams, feeling the pressure and experiencing lots of infighting and struggling for power, sent resentful glares their way whenever the members met in the art department or the copy room. This only bolstered their mood and solidified their team identity.

By the end of the day, she was exhausted and starving but deliriously happy. She grabbed a granola bar and banana while she changed clothes and waited for Jake. He picked her up at 7:00, kissing her affectionately and being very secretive about his plans. He wore a blazer and tie, though, which made her glad she'd opted for a cocktail dress and put her mind at ease about the missing ring, particularly because she thought she saw him wink at Suzanne on their way out the door. A single red rose waited on the passenger seat for her when she got in the car. At some point in her life, she would've thought this gesture was trite and unnecessary, but tonight it felt sweet and special and wonderful.

They ate at an upscale steakhouse on the edge of Buckhead. Dinner was delicious by candlelight, and Marci found herself struggling to make normal conversation as she waited for something to happen any moment. Jake was wonderful and sweet and the whole evening was romantic, perfect for a real proposal. Looking back, she realized that their first engagement had been based on an evolving, awkward agreement, rather than a question publicly asked and answered. She had never known that she wanted a traditional proposal—that she *needed* it, in fact— until tonight. Now that it was here, or at least, she felt pretty sure this was it, it felt more than right.

As they finished dinner, she inhaled deeply whenever the waitress came to the table, expecting a champagne glass or piece of cake with a ring inside, or maybe a cue for the solo violinist wandering the restaurant to appear to set the scene. Periodically she checked her makeup in a tiny mirror, thinking that all eyes in the restaurant would soon be on her and wanting to look perfect for her moment in the spotlight. But the proposal never came.

Jake paid the check, held the door for her, and kept his arm around her while the valet retrieved his truck. The cool evening was warmed by his touch, and it felt wonderful to be close to him, but she couldn't help feeling disappointed that he hadn't asked. *Had she misunderstood entirely?* Obviously she couldn't ask him about it, but the anticipation and concern were eating her alive. He seemed not to notice and remained smiling and calm. "Dessert?" he asked, lifting her into the truck. She nodded, and he grinned in response.

Wherever they were going, it was somewhere off the beaten track. Jake had exited the interstate in a familiar spot but soon veered into seemingly endless, winding residential roads. Marci didn't mind. He had his hand on her knee, and there was good music on the radio, so she didn't care where they were heading.

It was a complete surprise when Jake pulled the car into a very familiar driveway. Marci had not been at the Stillwells' house in weeks. She looked at Jake for an explanation, but he just smiled and stared straight ahead.

When they stepped out of the car, she saw that there were luminarias flickering along the front sidewalk, lighting their way. Jake took her hand and led her up the path to the front door. Inside were more candles and soft music playing in the great room down the hall. As they entered, she saw Robert, sitting up respectably well in a wheelchair and wearing a suit just a bit too big with the weight he'd lost since the stroke. Kitty was equally well dressed, standing with her hand on her husband's shoulder, and the color had returned to her features.

When Marci's eyes swept the rest of the large room, she gasped. Both her parents, Leah and Dave, Suzanne, and Beth were all there. Her mother held up a cell phone that Marci would soon learn had Nicole and Ravi on the other end. Everyone was smiling. She turned to look at Jake in astonishment, and he sank to one knee as she did. Little murmurs and sighs emanated from the room around them.

"Marcella Beatrice Thompson," Jake said, his voice confident. Marci began to tremble with nerves and excitement. "The first time I asked you this question, I didn't go about it very well. We kind of bucked tradition, didn't we? Well, maybe we learned that there are times when tradition matters. So tonight I'm here with a ring, on one knee, to tell you that I love you, and to ask you in front of our friends and family if you will do me the honor of becoming my wife. Marci, will you marry me?"

For a minute, the words wouldn't come. All she could do was nod and cover her mouth with her hands. Eventually she squeaked "Yes," and the room erupted in applause. Jake stood and took her hands, putting his grandmother's ring back on her finger, where it belonged. She could see that it had been freshly polished and sparkled in the candlelight. Soon they were surrounded by hugs and tears and laughing, and everything finally felt right.

Epilogue

Six Months Later

Marci stared at her reflection in an old wooden mirror, watching the chaos behind her. They were in a small room off the upper chamber of Demosthenian Hall on the North Quad, which smelled like old books and furniture polish. Suzanne flitted around the musty room, pulling things out of boxes and making notations on her clipboard. Her mother was steaming the last wrinkles out of Marci's dress and calling out advice to both Suzanne and Nicole, who wore matching blue dresses.

Nicole's daughter Ayanna, now four months old, also wore a tiny version of the same dress with matching bloomers. The dresses were lovely on the women, but against Ayanna's soft brown baby skin, the effect was gorgeous. The cuteness of this was somewhat diminished by the fact that the baby was uncharacteristically inconsolable. Normally a calm kid, she screamed no matter what Nicole did—sitting, standing, walking, rocking, or singing. Nicole shushed her desperately and kept throwing apologetic looks at Marci. "I think she's teething. She won't be this way during the ceremony. I promise!"

"Don't worry about it," Marci said. "She's fine. Babies cry."

"You have no right to be so calm right now," Suzanne said. "You are setting an unfair standard for brides everywhere."

Truthfully, Marci was amazed at her own sense of tranquility. She knew that she was supposed to be all keyed up about her wedding day, worried about the details, nervous about the rest of her life, and so on. But she just didn't feel any of that. Even knowing that a couple hundred people were filling the University Chapel next door did not weigh on her the way she had imagined it would.

It helped that Suzanne had every last detail handled—from start to finish. This wedding was the first she had agreed to plan in years, and she had gone to great lengths to make sure Marci had a gorgeous event with absolutely nothing to worry about. The Stillwells had contributed, too, by insisting on underwriting the entire cost of the reception at their favorite hotel in downtown Athens.

"Robert's stroke reminded us to celebrate today," Kitty had told Marci with uncharacteristic candor. "Besides, we're pushing all our fuddy-duddy friends on you for this wedding. The least we can do is feed them!"

But Marci suspected that, most of all, her calm came from the rocky road behind her. She had known two loves in the last couple of years and had experienced the worst heartaches of her life with each of them. She knew now how much it meant to choose Jake and how close she had come to losing him forever. Now that they were together, the last six months had been the best of her life. Planning the wedding had been fun, but to her it was only one day of many with the man she had loved for so long and had grown to appreciate so fully.

She had heard from Doug very little since the Hyatt. He had waited a few weeks before calling her, and then had only left messages checking to see how she was doing. She called him back only once, to ask him not to call again. He had respected her wishes for the most part, breaking the silence only to send her a wedding gift.

The return address label read THE STANTONS. *So he is back with Cathy.* Or maybe he'd simply used an old address label. When she opened the box, she found a beautiful and expensive monogrammed desk set with her new initials stamped into the soft leather pieces. It also included customized stationery (also for Marci only) and a Mont Blanc pen just like one she had admired in Doug's office, only in a softer, silvery pink color.

Clearly it was a very personal, pricey gift that had nothing whatsoever to do with her marriage. She was touched that he'd thought so much of her, but angry that he was clearly ignoring the new husband with whom she would soon be sharing her life. Just like Doug, it was generous and selfish all at once. How could she keep it and not think of him every time she went to her desk?

She debated whether to show it to Jake, hide it in a closet somewhere, or even mail it back to Doug with a polite refusal. Ultimately, she stuck with her policy of always being honest with Jake, almost tearful when she showed him the expensive gift and told him why she didn't want to keep it.

Jake pulled her to him and kissed her forehead. "Do what you want, sweetheart. But if I were you, I'd keep it. It's a nice gift from someone who you once cared about; it doesn't change who we are now." She snuggled closer to him, relieved and grateful, more sure than ever that she'd made the right choice.

A few days later, she had opened the new stationery, which really was quite lovely, and written the last communication she would ever send to him:

Dear Doug,

    Thank you for your beautiful wedding gift. It was so nice of you to remember us at this special time in our lives.

    All the best,

    Jake and Marci

Now that the day was here, Marci felt as though all the previous chapters of her life had already drawn to a close. She let her mother, best friend, and sister fuss over her makeup and dress and flowers. As soon as she'd been wrangled into her soft ivory dress, Beth and Leah—wearing dresses identical to those of Nicole and Suzanne—came up the rickety old stairs with their daughters, the flower girls. Jasmine and Caitlin wore ivory dresses with indigo ribbons around their waists and streaming from their hair.

"Aunt Marci!" Jasmine cried excitedly. "We get to ring the chapel bell after the wedding! Both of us get to, but I'm letting Caitlin go first because that's the nice thing to do!"

"Really? That's wonderful!" Marci said. She smiled at Leah, who shook her head in amusement.

"Time to go, ladies!" she heard her father call from below. "Let's have a wedding!"

As Marci navigated down the stairs and into the bright sunshine, she allowed thoughts of Doug to fade into the rustle of the late-summer breeze. The chapel, nearly two hundred years old, loomed in front of her with its Greek columns and antique white exterior. She had walked past it thousands of times during her undergraduate years, sat on its steps to chat with friends or eat lunch, and been inside for a few concerts and other assemblies. The building was as familiar as her dorm hall or the quad itself.

Today, however, she was seeing the old building for the first time. It was acquiring significance in her life that would be recalled every time she looked at a photo album, came to a football game, or told the story of her wedding. Inside, she knew, waited worn red carpets, theater seats, and a rounded stage. Behind the stage would be a famous oil painting of the inside of Saint Peter's Basilica in Rome. There would be candelabras and flowers, and Rev. McClosky waiting with the groomsmen. And standing off to one side, probably fidgeting, would be her old friend and future husband.

The majestic trees of the North Quad swayed, and Marci inhaled deeply. Suzanne squeezed her hand as the bridesmaids lined up. Her father took her arm in his. Marci realized she wanted to leave all of her history, even with Jake, here on the granite steps. She wanted her life to have new significance, too.

As Marci began the walk toward her new life, it was with the fullness of a truly open heart.

Acknowledgments

Anyone who has ever attempted it can tell you: a first novel is a daunting undertaking. I can't say enough about the people who helped me undertake this one, and who transformed *The Marriage Pact* into what it is today.

Many, many thanks to Nicole Sohl of Thomas Dunne, St. Martin's Press, and Macmillan Entertainment for holding my hand through my first foray into traditional publishing, and for being a generally delightful person. Thanks so much to Beth Phelan and Jenny Bent of the Bent Agency for their expert guidance, good humor, and grace. I also owe tremendous gratitude to Lee Morin, Esq., Paula Grothe, and Faith Williams for their professional advice and friendship. Special thanks to the Old 97s, the best band in the world, for letting me use their lyrics without any drama.

Thank you to George Weinstein, Valerie Connors, and the rest of the Atlanta Writers Club for great conferences and unparalleled support for authors. I have laughed and learned more than I can say at the Roswell open critique group. And a special ear-tug to my own erratic and lovable corner of the AWC: Becky Albertalli, Emily Carpenter, and Chris Negron.

This book was initially self-published, a terrifying prospect for a newbie, and I couldn't have done it without the support, feedback, and encouragement of Carla Birnbaum, J. L. Bryan, Sarah Cutler, Jenna Denisar, Kristal Goelz, Marla Kaplan, Anna Turetsky Needle (and the entire Needle clan), Brenda Turetsky, Rob Wack, and the indispensable Ryan Van Meter.

I am so grateful for the support of my dad, Kerry Pullen, who died shortly after I initially published *The Marriage Pact* in 2011. He didn't care for romance novels and refused to read the dirty scenes, but he always encouraged me in creating my own path to success. For giving me a room of my own, and for their unconditional support and endless patience, I want to thank my husband, Sam Turetsky, and our two sons. Living with a writer mom means the laundry is rarely done and the floors are never clean, but you weather it all with grace and giggles.

Last but never least, thanks to all the friends old and new who have read, reviewed, or recommended my writing to others; to those who follow and comment on my blogs, Facebook posts, and tweets. None of this is possible without you.